The
Adventure
of
Creation

Think Sideways Writers
Anthology #1

With a Foreword by Holly Lisle

The Adventure of Creation, English Edition
published by the Independent Bookworm, USA and D
edited by Silverjay Media
Copyright © 2013 by Independent Bookworm

If you find typos or formatting problems in the book, please
contact the author.

cover design: Katharina Gerlach, Marianne D (Shutterstock)
printed by createspace.com, USA
ISBN3956810007
ISBN-13:**9783956810008**

For more information mail to katharina@katharinagerlach.com
Find more information on the Independent Bookworm's
homepage: http://www. Independent Bookworm.com

ABOUT THE BOOK

Follow a girl to the Below-World to slay the Sharkshadow, or help a timid girl to overcome the destructive criticism of her art teacher. Witness a solitary drone on Mars or a naive homunculus struggle to become human. Sew with a mother who lost her daughter in a unicorn quilt, defeat bank robbing super-villains with an unlikely superhero, or join a great mage in the fire.

In thirty-five imaginative stories, emerging authors present the diversity of their creativity. Each author found a different angle for the unifying theme: The Adventure of Creation. Witness the talent nurtured by writing teacher, Holly Lisle. For the 5th anniversary of her first big writing course, How to Think Sideways, this anthology features the best of her talented students in a great variety of genres.

ABOUT HOLLY LISLE

She has been writing with intent to publish since January 1st, 1985 when her New Year's resolution was to write a novel before she turned twenty-five (ten months later, more or less). She hit her resolution with a few days to spare, but the book, sucked.

She wrote a LOT after that, accumulating a big shoebox with well over a hundred rejection slips in it before anybody decided she was good enough to pay for fiction.

She started selling in 1991 and broke in with the fantasy novel "Fire In The Mist" (which won the Compton Crook Award for Best First Novel), and with a couple of sonnets she sold to the SF magazine Aboriginal.

Homepage: HollyLisle.com

ABOUT THE PUBLISHER

The Independent Bookworm groups the efforts of several Indie authors in one platform. Founded by Katharina Gerlach, a writer from Germany and a long-time member of Holly Lisle's forum, it officially turned publisher in Germany recently.

Homepage: www.IndependentBookworm.com
Homepage: www.IndependentBookworm.de

ABOUT THE EDITOR

Silver Jay Media was founded by E.J. Clarke. Editing and Proofreading services are available in many different forms.

Homepage: www.silverjaymedia.com

ACKNOWLEDGMENTS

Without the help of our long-term mentor, Holly Lisle, the Independent Bookworm would never have existed, and this anthology would never have seen the light. Thank you.

Also, we are all very grateful for the generous help from the moderators of Holly Lisle's forum who sacrificed time and brain-power to read, evaluate and comment on every single story. Thanks to you, this competition was a success even for those students whose stories did not make it into the anthology (the competition was fierce). Thank you.

Another thank you goes to E.J. Clarke of Silverjay Media for the speedy and thorough editing.

Finally, thank you, dear reader, for buying this book. Your enthusiasm for reading makes it possible for authors like us to live our dream. Enjoy these stories.

Content:

Foreword by Holly Lisle 9
Restoration 12
Whisper 20
Worlds of Clay 27
Spoilers 32
West's Prelude 39
After the Fire 41
Knitting 48
The Unicorn Quilt 56
Hedda of the Upworld 64
Tortellini 72
Eighty-One 79
The Burn 91
Boneless 99
Treasures 106
Crazy Uncle 113
Innocence 116
Hitting the High Notes 122
A Play of Hopes and Fears 125
Memory Book 133
Glass 141
New Life 144
I Need a Story 148
Make a Sound 156
Just Add Copper 165
The Mistake 173
Some Other World 179
Finding Light 186
The Interview 194
Trial of the Magideem 196
A Splash of Art 204
My Soul To Take 211
The Forest King 219
The Wish 223
The Café 231
The Definition of a Superhero 239
Biographies 248
Why We Took Holly's Courses 254

Foreword by Holly Lisle

The story of the book you're reading came into being because of a long chain of events, starting with not one, but both of my agents rejecting me on a project that I desperately wanted to do. I wanted to write about what I'd discovered about writing from my own experiences. Both my first and second agents shot down my proposal, citing clogged markets and poor pay.

I went to my website readers and asked them if `they` were interested, though, and it turns out they were. I wrote a course called *Create A Character Clinic*, and then several others, and published them myself, online and from my own little ebook shop. (This was long before Amazon.com turned e-publishing into the amazing writing opportunity is has become.)

The popularity of those, plus the fact that my students were seeing success by using those little courses, led me to creating the first big course. *How To Think Sideways: Career Survival School for Writers*. That course led to *THIS* book, full of stories written by writers who took that course or others I've done.

The fact that it has already been five years since I started building *How To Think Sideways: Career Survival School For Writers* course with my very first class of writers came as a shock. That first group of 110 writers was a rugged bunch. They were taking the class one lesson behind me as I wrote it, asking questions as we went along, helping each other figure out new ways to use the techniques I was presenting, and discovering ways to write better fiction they'd not imagined.

Meanwhile, I was working sixty- and seventy-hour weeks building that first version of the course, and every page my students got was raw first draft. My brain to theirs, typos included.

I'd spent months outlining my process before I started into the class, but even with my outline in hand, presenting the next lesson, the next step, and getting into the heart of it so that I could show as well as tell why and how the writer did each step felt very much like running blindfolded along a cliff with a runaway stagecoach right behind me.

It was terrifying, exhilarating, and insanely fun. Heavy emphasis on the "insane" part.

I hadn't even finished the class before some of my folks started winning and placing in writing contests, getting *good* rejections (those are the ones where editors say "please send your next story"), and even getting their first sales. Their fellow students and I cheered every triumph.

When I recovered from creating *How To Think Sideways* (referred to by students as *HTTS*), I started building *How To Revise Your Novel: Get The Book You Want From The Wreck You Wrote* ... and again, I kept a bare one lesson ahead of my students as I took them through what I still suspect is the most brutal fiction-writing course in existence.

The survivors are doing well. The first students, and others who followed them, have been nominated for and won multiple awards, writing contests, have sold many, many books, and have created a ton of great fiction.

And they have written these stories.

I never imagined an anthology of student work. My forum moderators came up with the idea, ran it by me, and I liked it. I put up prizes for three winners and picked the theme – but my moderators received all the submissions, went through and commented on each story, blind-voted on the thirty-five that would make the cut ... and then sent those stories to me.

I, too, read them blind. There were no names or other identifying details attached to the file I received. I didn't try to guess. I just read, with a notebook at my side where I went through the six elements necessary to tell a story well, rating each story on each element, on a scale of 1 to 5.

The six elements?

Character.

Conflict.

Setting.

Twist.

Theme.

And, of course, Technical – correct and competent use of the language.

Each story, then, had a potential perfect score of 30.

Nearly half of the stories in my first read-through had scores of 29 or higher. Ten of those had perfect 30s. The moderators, (*also* students of the courses, incidentally), had done an incredible job of picking out stories.

I sorted out the semifinalists and went through again, the second time reading for each writer's take on *my* theme, as well as on the highly subjective quality of unforgetableness. But by that time, I was both stunned by the quality of the stories I was reading, and grasping at straws for a way to pick winners when so many stories deserved them.

I managed by dint of willpower and admitted subjectivity to narrow the field to five.

Of those five finalists, any could have won. I loved them all. My final selections were based, then, on one final qualification: First place would start the book. Second place would end the book. And third place would hold the second-story slot.

I imagined reading the book, and imagined which of the remaining five stories was right for each of those three slots.

And on that basis, had my prize-winners.

I hope you enjoy reading these stories as much as I did. They are the products of some remarkable minds – and some truly rugged and determined writers.

And they are the unexpected – though much-hoped-for – consequence of my decision to create writing courses on my own when my publishers said there wasn't any market for them, and putting those courses in front of writers determined to write for publication.

Holly Lisle
Monday, July 1, 2013

Restoration
by Rabia Gale

First Place Winner

Jane Maddow sat on a stone bench in the circular Nevierre room of the Citizens' Gallery of Art. The light today was sap-thin and white-gold. It fell from small windows set high in the wall and splashed onto the stone tiles.

Jane's gaze flickered over the oil paintings. Here was a horse caught mid-plunge into a river, diamond droplets frozen in air. There, the muscles in a blacksmith's arms flexed as he bent over the anvil. The Blue Lady's face shone from within a frame of drooping branches.

Ah, Nevierre. The White City's greatest puzzle: a wonderful artist who had possessed no magic, not even the one creation of Art that was the birthright of every citizen.

Charcoal in her fingers, Jane copied a face, an arched neck, a leaf. Nevierre's creations were all odd in some way. The coal-black horse had a feathery mane, the smith's skin was tinged purple. The trees bore fruit that no one had ever seen and the light pouring over the hills was ruby-tinted.

Outside, gunshots cracked, sharp against the dull roar of a mob. The sounds came to Jane as if from a great distance.

Food riot, again.

Nevierre had not been a mage, but his art had lasted longer than any of his contemporaries'. Sofia Lorrel's land-scapes withered and rotted along with the sun-drenched fields and luscious orchards she had painted. Gregor Road-builder's canvases were now mud-stained trash, as if they'd been trampled by the feet that traversed the roads he'd conjured.

Only Nevierre survived the centuries, all his works in this one round room. An invisible line between the only entrance and an alcove containing a bronze bust of the artist himself split the chamber into halves.

The door grated open. Willard stepped into the room, jingling his keys.

Jane looked up into his lined face.

"It's gone past supper time, Miss," he said apologetic-cally, not meeting her eyes.

"Oh, I'm sorry! I've kept you over long!" The *again* hung unspoken in the air. Jane looked at pages filled with pic-tures, each left incomplete. She had only one act of magic in her – it writhed hot and impatient through her veins – but she was saving it.

Saving it for something wonderful.

Willard didn't move. "They're closing the gallery to the public next week, Miss."

A pit opened up in Jane's stomach. "So soon? But they can't! I –" *I'm not ready! I'm not ready to do my Art yet!*

"Reduced hours tomorrow, Miss."

"Oh, but you have to let me come in all day, Willard. I –" She straightened, and her heart hammered with the force of her pronouncement. "I'm going to make my Art. Right here in this room." She gestured towards the paint-ings, the alcove, Nevierre's impish face.

Even now, everything gave way before Art. Willard wa-vered, then nodded. "All right then, Miss."

~*~

A hummingbird shattered in a spray of colored glass on the cobblestones as Jane hurried through the streets. It was a common sight nowadays. For weeks the Jeweled Birds, the Art of hundreds over the centuries, had been falling to the ground in tangles of wire and gobs of wax. The skyline of the White City was deformed, the Gilded Dome pecked with corrosion. The Three Towers leaned together, softened and featureless, like melting candles.

Jane picked her way through hills of rubble and shattered stone. The Stone Guardian had run amok years ago, smashing through the city it was supposed to protect. Grim-faced soldiers and volunteers had brought it down, and now its grave site was a children's playground.

A rock struck her side. Jane staggered.

A childish voice cried, "Murderer! Murderer!"

Jane ran, a hail of pebbles clattering on the street around her. Grit and tears stung her eyes.

She was still running when she reached home. The apartment block's gray walls were covered with chalk pictures of food and clothes, the Art of desperate people. Once they'd saved it for bouquets of ever-blooming roses or wind chimes that played lovely tunes in the rain.

Now they spent their Art on chalk clothing that fell apart in weeks and chalk food that tasted like sand.

The inside smelled of old cats and boiled cabbage. Jane took the stairs two at a time up to her floor. Scrawled across her door in black paint were the words *Jane Maddow is a bitch*. Her heart ached at the sight, but it was the ache of an old wound. She had things to do, Art to make!

Jane let herself into her tiny room. The meager furnishings – rusty iron bed frame, mismatched chairs, and a rickety end table – were covered with books, papers, and art supplies.

Jane lit the coals in the brazier, then pulled on a pair of thin gloves. She hauled out half-empty boxes from under her bed. In went a rainbow of chalk pastels, brushes of all sizes, half-empty tubes of paint. Her movements activated the speaking shell, a thing of pearlescent beauty that had been dying all year long.

Her mother's voice came through tinny and broken, "...you could paint a St. Lucia feast scene... table laden with food... streamers and lanterns... potatoes and geese and cherry pies... invite the neighbors..."

Mama called almost every day with another suggestion for Jane's Art.

Jane smiled fondly at the shell. *The thing is, Mama, you don't think big enough.*

Her magic bubbled up inside her, an effervescent thing of feathers and champagne and summer sunshine. She may not have enough of it to be a true mage, but she knew this:

She was a damn good artist.

And she was going to make great Art.

~*~

The gallery was locked.

Surrounded by boxes, Jane hammered on the door. Her knapsack, with changes of clothes, toothbrush, and dried food, was at her feet.

She'd paid an extravagant amount of money for a hansom cab to bring her and her gear here. She wasn't going to be turned away at the door.

Finally, Willard opened it a crack. He wore his butler face, the one that looked right through her. "We're closed, Miss."

"It's me, Willard!" Jane shoved her foot in the crack. "I'm here for my Art. Please, Willard!"

Willard looked at the boxes, and sighed. "I can give you three days, Miss. There was a smoke bomb in here last night. The directors want everything moved to safety."

"After three days, bring the directors to see my Art," Jane said recklessly. "They'll understand then."

~*~

Jane set up her easel in the Nevierre room, drawing strength and comfort from the familiar paintings. She'd paint the White City, not as it was now, but as it had been in its great days. She'd put crops in the blighted fields and water in the dried-up river and wide roads over the surrounding hills.

The towers would rise tall and straight again. The Gilded Dome would shine like a sun, and stone statues would guard the walls.

She'd give the City back its past.

Perhaps then they'd finally forgive her.

~*~

A day and a half later, and it was evening. The acid combination of panic and magic churned in Jane's stomach. She was hot, sweaty, paint-stained, and dizzy from the fumes. Her eyes smarted from lack of sleep. She'd gnawed her way through most of her stash of dried meat and fruit bars.

The painting was… not coming. Oh, she'd put the form and shape of the White City on the canvas.

But not her magic. It refused to come out of her, refused to pour itself into the painting and make it Art.

I need some air. Every muscle ached with strain. Jane shuffled out the Nevierre room and pushed open the front door.

She blinked against the sharp yellow light of the White City and walked stiff-legged down the stairs. Two turns and an alley later, she was in the marketplace.

A meager market, this, with vendors hawking withered apples from the fall's tiny harvest and odd wedges of cheese with the bad bits cut out. Scrap merchants did a brisk trade. Wooden chairs with fancy legs sold for kindling, embroildered silk draperies for coat linings.

There weren't many people, but it was still a market, so when Jane was jostled once she said, "Excuse me" and thought nothing of it.

A moment later, it happened again. And again.

Bodies slammed into her. Elbows poked her ribs, hips shoved her aside. Jane looked into blank faces. She tried to struggle out from the crowd, but it penned her in.

Someone planted a hand against the small of her back and sent her flying. Jane landed on her hands and knees, hard. She tried to scramble up, but she had no room, she couldn't breathe…

Hands gripped her arm, hauled her back up, gasping, into the sharp wintry air. Jane looked up into the kind, broad face of a middle-aged woman.

"Louts, the lot of them," the woman said. "You all right, sweetling?"

Tears pricked Jane's eyes at the endearment, at the woman's concerned expression.

But she couldn't take the other's kindness. Not when she was – "I'm Jane Maddow," she said, quietly.

The woman's eyes went flat and uncomprehending. Then her lips thinned, and Jane braced herself.

She was still unprepared for the slap. The shock of it reverberated through her bones. Her cheek throbbed and flamed.

"That poor boy," said the woman, fiercely. Then she turned her back and walked away.

Jane stood rooted in the street, her thoughts chasing each other in dizzying circles.

Eight years ago, Francis Marshall had created a work of Art. The next day, he'd done it again.

After twelve uncertain years, a mage walked the White City once more. The people breathed a sigh of relief and thought they were saved. Within a week, Francis was en-rolled in the Academy of Art, his feet on the path taken by Gregor and Lorrel and all the other great mages before him.

Three years later, he proposed to Jane Maddow, a fellow student. She refused him.

That night he hanged himself. And nobody ever let Jane Maddow forget that she'd been unwilling to be chained to Francis' fragile ego, his raging temper, his bouts of depression, and his clinging insecurities.

Even her own mother felt, at the time, that she ought to have said yes. For the City's sake.

It hadn't been a crime *then* to refuse to marry a mage, though Jane had been tried, convicted and sentenced in the court of public opinion. She'd been told it would be better for her to leave the Academy. She'd bounced from job to job – at the food shop where she'd last worked, an un-washed, unshaven patron had refused to be served by Jane Maddow, destroyer of all hope.

And this was the world she was trying to save?

Jane dashed tears from her eyes, lifted her chin, and marched to the nearest scrap merchant's stall.

There she bought a padlock.

Then she recklessly dumped all the coins in her purse at a vendor's table and bought paints. Lots and lots of paint.

Jane Maddow's first action after she locked herself in the Nevierre room was to paint a thick red X over the canvas she'd been working on. It felt good to obliterate the timid, delicate brushstrokes, the soft greens and creamy hues, the childish dreams where *she* was the savior and a weeping populace showered her with petals and repentant kisses.

She stood in front Nevierre's bust and thought that he would approve. "Now," she said. "*Now,* we'll make Art."

Jane dragged the wooden pedestal out of the alcove and gave Nevierre a little pat on the head. She tilted her head, contemplated the blank wall. An expectant stillness filled the musty air. The very people in Nevierre's paintings seemed to watch her. Trees leaned toward her and animals perked up their ears, listening.

Waiting for what she would do.

Jane put a thick brush in a pot of paint – a warm brick red – and began.

Several hours later, a rock crashed through the ever-daylit windows. A glassfall of shards tinkled to the floor.

A while later, someone scrabbled at the door. When it didn't open, the person – Willard – banged on it. His voice was muffled, indistinct.

No long after, a voice blared from a speaking horn. "Open this door, Miss Maddow! This is the Board of Directors speaking, and we *will* break in if we have to."

And some time after *that*, the door crashed open. Two burly, helmeted policemen entered, carrying shields, followed by a mop-wielding Willard. A gray wedge of Directors crowded in behind them.

They stopped.

Art crackled in the air, smelling like an oncoming storm.

The wall of the alcove was bright and glistening and completely painted over. A broad band of sky in Nevierre blue swept the top. Branches from trees he'd invented looped through the intense color. Flowers he'd dreamed up pushed up from the rich brown dirt at the bottom of the wall. And in the middle of it all was a red door with a brass knob.

Jane Maddow lifted her brush and signed her name, not in the corner, but across the middle of her gaudy, ghastly mural. She looked over her shoulder.

"Oh, good," she said. "You're all here."

A warm spice-scented breeze touched the faces of the newcomers. A bird trilled, and a horse snorted. Metal rang against metal, as if a blacksmith were at work.

Jane grinned at Nevierre's bust. She thought he twinkled back at her, but it could've been a trick of the light.

Jane reached out and took hold of the knob. It molded itself, solid and warm and slightly damp, into her hand. She pulled open the door and stepped into Nevierre's world.

Her world.

Whisper
by Michele Zugnoni

Third Place Winner

There's a whisper in the wind: a murmur that winds through the world, carrying forth the cry of souls. I'm not sure when I first heard it; I don't know when I realized it followed me everywhere I went, like a lifelong friend that never left my side. I only know that I hear it now, and when I hear it, I'm listening for him.

I lift my face to the sky, shutting my eyes. The wind ripples across my skin, fluttering through my wild brown waves, reminding me that the whisper is nearby. I don't know why it bothers; I'm already listening. But the voice I so desperately wish to hear – the soul's cry I long to listen for –fails to permeate the breeze.

I squeeze my eyes tighter still, shutting them so tight that a salty droplet forms upon my lashes, splashing down my cheek. Still, I do not hear. Still, his voice remains absent. The wind is just the wind; the whisper isn't a friend, but a painful echo of the past.

My dad used to take me to this stream. With a crescent grin as bright as the moon shining within the velvet sky, he'd urge me to take a seat on this log –the one I'm sitting on now, the one carving wooden indentations into the flesh of my legs, lurking beneath the dark, dark hem of my stifling dress – and he'd play me a song on his flute. Every once in a while, my best friend, Sam, would join us. He would dance through the trees as I sang, capturing my dad's musical magic. It was just the three of us creating in the twilight, living in a world enchanted.

For a moment, I allow myself to remember. I allow myself to forget.

The wind becomes a hum, and I sway with the rhythm of the redwoods, tapping my foot to the call of my dad's flute: a rich burst of music that reaches deep inside, causing my soul to dance. And in that slice of remembered time, as my voice carries the memory in song, I hear him cry upon the wind: *"That's it, Bri girl! That's it. Sing to the music, sweetheart. Don't ever let it stop."*

His voice dies with the howl of a timber wolf, searching for dinner among the Colorado mountains stretching upward toward the midnight sky. I open my eyes in a sudden burst of chill, rubbing at the goose bumps prickling my forearms. The crescent moon shines in the night, but my dad's music is gone; in its place is the crashing of the stream as it smashes its wrath against the rocks.

~*~

I am fifteen now, but I was seven when he bought me my first instrument: a baby grand piano with keys that gleamed in the lamplight. Silk. They were silk beneath my fingertips; I caressed them, and I wanted more. Taking me upon his lap, he plunk plunk plunked the notes, floating music across the expanse of our ranch-style home.

"Y'see, my girl?" He tickled my ribs, grinning when I squealed. "That's all it takes. Now give it a go."

My mother stood in the shadows of the stairs, her face half-lit by the glow of the dying sun as my laughter crescendoed into shouts, and I plunked a seven-year-old's musical masterpiece at my dad's hand. My voice joined the harmony: the chirp of a girl content in her protector's arms.

It was the first time I heard the whisper: a soulful sound that seeped inside, and I knew that it was mine.

My dad's voice was at my ear. "We are the creators, Bri girl. What we dream, we wish. What we wish, we create. Never forget…"

~*~

Never forget … never forget … never forget …

No, Dad. I never will.

"Daddy, watch out!" I grab the steering wheel, I twist it to the side.

SCREECH!

The sound is an owl's shriek, fingernails scraping down the chalkboard, the mournful whistle of a ship sinking in the waves.

"DAD!" It is the guttural cry of a girl possessed; one who has forgotten how to sing. "NO! NO! NO!"

It is my voice, torn from tears, shredded from sobs, shot through with disbelief.

The car is a mangled mess on the side of the highway, my dad twisted between steering wheel and seat. Shards of glass litter the vehicle, having scraped bloody gashes into our skin. I cannot feel the sting. The only thing that filters through my conscious haze is my dad. He has forgotten how to breathe.

The wail of sirens cut through the night.

~*~

"Bri? Bri, where have you been?"

It is two in the morning days after the funeral, and I have just snuck in the back door. My mother is waiting. She is dressed in a wrinkled pink nightgown, her hair unraveling from the curlers laced haphazardly through her brown locks. Boxes litter the stairs, the floor, the bench of my baby grand piano. My dad's flute and sheet music peek from the depths of brown cardboard, mocking me for my pain.

"What the hell is this?" I stomp into the living room, unearthing his symphony from the carton taking residence upon my piano keys. "Mom?" I whirl, shaking it in her reddening face. "What is this?"

"It's…" She stares at the handwritten notes, her eyes glistening in the moon's dull light. A sigh escapes her lips. "I just – I thought it might be time to – "

"Time to what?" I snap, clutching the symphony to my chest. "Time to get rid of Dad's things? It's been three weeks! THREE WEEKS! Can't we at least give it a month?"

"Bri —"

"No." I shake my head, backing toward the front door. "No. I don't want to hear it. Put it back." I wave my hands at my piano, at the floor, at the boxes spilling from the stairs. "Put it all back. He's not gone. He's — he's not."

"Sweetheart —"

"I said put it *back*." My voice cracks; I swipe at a tear threatening to slip down my face. "All of it. *NOW*."

My hand is on the doorknob; I want to explode into the night, to burst from the house, to run through the wind, to forget that my dad's voice has disappeared along with the whisper I can no longer hear.

She puts her hand on my shoulder. I wince at her touch. "We're worried about you, honey. Me. Sam. Your grandparents."

"Tell Sam to mind his own business. You, too. Both of you just — just leave me alone."

The doorknob slips in my hand; the door clicks open. The wind seeps through the cracks.

My mother tries again. "It's not your fault, you know. That night — what happened with your dad. You couldn't have known."

"You're wrong," I whisper. But my voice is lost with the breeze, and I rush into the darkness of the Colorado night.

~*~

I am fifteen, and my dad is dead. He lies in a mahogany casket, his body still, his music silent. His flute rests in a case upon a distant table, reminding all that he liked to play.

I am fifteen, and I am drowning. I cannot survive this storm. The tears rush down my face, threatening to suffocate me in my sorrow. I have forgotten how to breathe.

I am fifteen, and I am lost. Until all at once I am found.

I glance two rows behind me and discover him sitting there, looking into my eyes as if offering to shelter my soul. He knows; he understands. He will not let go. We are fifteen, surrounded by death, and for the rest of the service, we are wrapped up so tight in one another's eyes, we are whole. One. Sam and Bri; Bri and Sam. Forever together, even when we're sitting two pews and a universe apart.

He's been my best friend since kindergarten. He is my best friend now, as we tread the treacherous tide of my dad's funeral. And when it is over, and the melancholy dirge plays from the church organ, he steps from his seat and he takes my hand.

"I'm here, Bri. I'm never gonna let you go."

"You swear it?"

"I swear."

~*~

The cemetery is a land of gray, a blur of black. Owls screech from the redwoods, crows perch upon the graves. And my dad's name gleams from a slab of white marble: a spark of life in a world of death.

I stumble through the grass, and crouch in the dirt. Wetness seeps into my jeans, but my eyes are dry. For once, I cannot cry.

"Why?" The word is a whisper stuck in my throat. I try again. "Why, Dad? Why did you have to do it? Why did you have to listen? We could have – we could have gone home. You – you didn't have to drive. You didn't have to take me out after. You didn't have to. You didn't. You didn't."

The fight is futile; the tears slap onto my cheeks, stinging my eyes with pain. A lump squeezes into my throat. And I remember: The car ride back from my piano recital. My dad had arrived ten minutes late, wielding a bouquet of roses and a sheepish grin glinting with apology.

The squeal of tires as he maneuvered through the streets, promising me ice cream in exchange for his ineptitude at getting anywhere on time.

His glee at my skill, the way he spoke of my concert, the way he relived it all right there in the car.

The screech of tires, the slam of brakes, the scent of metal mingling with the burn of rubber, the scorch of flame as the car overheated and a stranger pulled me to safety, the sight of my dad lying mangled in the street, his skin scratched and bloody, his chest still from lack of breath.

24

"I love you, Dad." My voice is sliced through with heartache, my vision blurred with tears. I wrap my arms around his tombstone. "I love you. And I'm sorry. I'm so sorry. God, I miss you so much."

I listen for the whisper; for the voice that does not come. It is lost, the way he is lost, too. The way he will always be lost, because he drove me home.

~*~

The moon peeks through the clouds, casting its silver radiance upon the cemetery grass, and for just a moment I swear I see his face. I shuffle; I blink. I almost say his name.

And then his face dissolves, and I am left staring into a sea of blue. "Sam?"

"Heya, Bri girl." Sam's blue eyes glint in the moonshine, shimmering with an emotion that makes my heart race.

"What're you doing out here by yourself? It's…" He checks his watch, "four in the morning. Your mom's going kinda crazy."

I blush and drop my gaze, scuff my boot against the grass. "I just…"

"I know."

Sam's touch is smooth against my hand.

With stilted breath, I lock our fingers. "Sam?"

"Yeah?"

"You called me 'Bri girl.'"

"Yup." I can hear the smile in his voice even before I raise my gaze to see his tilted lips. "It's what he called you. And I figure someone's gotta carry on the tradition."

My best friend shrugs, and I feel a burst of warmth radiate through my chest. "Will you do me a favor?"

"Anything." He nods, tracing the back of my hand with his thumb. A shock of blond hair falls into his face, and I reach up with my free hand to smooth it away.

He leans into my touch. "You've gotta tell me the favor first, y'know."

My sigh is a whisper on the wind. "Will you – will you listen to me play?"

In a burst of radiance, his smile transforms into a grin. "I was really hoping it would be that."

~*~

It is five in the morning. My mother has removed the boxes from my piano, from the stairs, from the floor. They are tucked safely inside my dad's study, where they belong.

She sits on the bottommost stair, her curlers gone, her deep-set brown eyes twinkling with tears that might be laughter. She gazes at Sam as he gazes at me, sitting atop my piano bench while I sit down by his side.

The keys are silk beneath my fingers: two rows of black and white, responding to my touch in a way I'd forgotten was ever possible. Plink. One note. Plunk. Another. A series of possibilities, each sweeter than the last.

Sam's hands join mine. He is no piano player, but for me, he tries. I am high, and he is low; I am creator, and he is harmony. The music surrounds us; it is me, it is him, it is everything and nothing all at once, and Sam is here to share in my joy. He is here to witness me create.

My heart soars, and for just a moment, I hear the whisper. For just a moment, I hear his voice.

We are the creators, Bri. What we dream, we wish. What we wish, we create. Never forget . . .

"I promise, Dad." My whisper mingles with my notes. "I'll remember forever. Just for you."

Worlds of Clay

by Jimena Novaro

Tina had always loved to watch her grandfather throw a pot. He would sit in front of his potter's wheel and smack down a big chunk of wet clay, then start to pedal. The wheel would go around and around, and between his big hands, the clay would morph fantastically into bowls, vases, jugs; it was like watching sped-up footage of a flower opening up, or sand dunes forming in the wind, or like being a god and seeing mountains rise and collapse back into dust as the millennia flew by.

Her grandfather never spoke much, but sometimes he sang old songs from his homeland as he worked. He hardly seemed to notice her there, sitting on the rickety old table in the corner of the studio, but he always let her have a good view of his work.

Though other people came to admire and buy his pottery, as a child Tina never found much of interest in the finished pots. They were pretty, she supposed, but they never moved, or changed, or became anything. Cool and hard and unyielding, they bore almost no resemblance to the magical substance from the potter's wheel.

One summer, sometime after her twelfth birthday, her grandfather fell ill. She sat by his bedside and sang him the old songs she'd learned from him. In exchange, he told her a story.

He said he'd gone to war a long time ago. He said that back home, a girl waited for him to return. He said that he and the other soldiers sang songs together sometimes. One night when they were cold and miserable and sure they would all die as artillery drummed outside, her grandfather had discovered a rhythm in the gunfire. So he started to sing, and the others joined in. By the last chorus they could barely hear the percussion.

"They all died," he said. "All the soldiers who were with me that day. All except for one, and he got pneumonia and died less than a year after the end of the war."

"That's a terrible story, grandpa," said Tina. "Who wants to hear a story about everyone dying?"

"Everyone dies," said her grandfather. "But every day I raise those soldiers back up again. Every day on the potter's wheel I raise empires and mountains and men. Clay is thirsty, Tina. It drinks in blood, tears, and sweat; nightmares and dreams; your songs and your fallen comrades."

"Can you teach me?"

"To throw a pot? Yes."

Her mother didn't like it, but Tina managed to convince her to let her bring the smaller potter's wheel into her grandfather's bedroom and set it up next to his bed. In exchange, she had to take care of her grandfather: prepare his meals, bring them to his bedroom, and change his sheets. And of course, she had to clean up after herself. Her mother would not have dried clay all over the antique furniture, which was really only old stuff her grandfather had brought across the Atlantic when he came to start a new life here.

Tina covered the floor with a plastic tarp, hauled in a bucket of wet clay, and set to work.

She didn't mind at first when her pots collapsed, because she'd seen her grandfather start over a hundred times in his studio. But as days passed and she seemed only to get worse at it, and her grandfather only offered more instructions and very little reassurance, she grew frustrated.

"I never want to cast another stupid pot!" she declared finally, and punched in her half-formed vessel so that it became nothing but a pile of mud with the shape of her fist printed on it.

"The pot isn't stupid," her grandfather pointed out. "That isn't even a pot."

Tina came back the next day, though. All evening she'd remembered the feel of the clay on her fingers and wanted it again like a sort of hunger. "I'm just going to spin the wheel around for a while," she said. Her grandfather said nothing.

After a few minutes of drawing circles with her fingers in the clay, watching it shape up and collapse again, watching it bend and cede at her touch like wind, like running water, she found herself gathering it up again, centering it on the wheel, and throwing a pot like her grandfather had taught her. And this time it stayed up. She stared at it.

"It's too heavy. Thin the walls," said her grandfather. "You can get more height out of that."

"I like it the way it is. It reminds me of you. It's sturdy like an old soldier."

She could tell by his expression that her flattery didn't win her any points. "Never settle for something because you're afraid to try for more."

"Also: know when to be satisfied and move on," said Tina. "For example, if I conquered the solar system, would you tell me I was a slacker because I didn't rule over the entire galaxy?"

"Thin the walls."

Grumbling, Tina went back to work. Of course the pot caved in and turned into formless slush, although she did give it her best.

But the next one didn't.

Her grandfather had been ill for the greater part of that summer, and Tina had grown accustomed to her routine. Sometimes he would feel strong enough to walk around a little; she'd take him by the arm and they'd make a circuit around the living room, dining room, and kitchen. Sometimes he'd take her hands and show her how to place them on the clay. But most of the time he'd lie in bed, too weak to sit up, and give instructions.

He was never impatient, but he never praised her, either. Not until the flower vase.

"Now *that's* a pot," he said, when she showed it to him, the tallest piece she'd managed to throw. "Put it in the kiln with the others and ask your mother to help you get the fire started. You have enough for one batch now."

He had an old wood-burning ceramic kiln in the garden which he'd built himself. Tina didn't throw another pot until her first batch was cooked, and her mother often had to remind her not to open the kiln early out of excitement.

She took the flower vase into her grandfather's bedroom when it was done, singing one of his old songs as she went. He had a headache, though, so she stopped singing.

"I want to make another one just like it, but taller and wider at the rim, like the one you have in your studio," she said.

"Not today," said her grandfather. "Maybe tomorrow."

But the next day he was too sick, and by the evening her mother had decided to check him into the hospital. He never came out again.

At the funeral, a lot of people said things to her about what a good man her grandfather had been. A friend, a soldier, an artist. None of it meant much to her.

"Are you going to be a potter like him?" asked a little man who said he was a long-lost friend of her grandfather's.

"I don't know," said Tina. "It's either that or Ruler of the Universe."

The little man didn't seem to know what to say to that. Her grandfather would have told her that if she was aiming that high, she'd better get to work.

On the drive home, Tina asked her mother if her grandfather had left her his studio. She expected her to say yes, of course. But instead, her mom handed her a little note her grandfather had written her.

It said: *I worked for seven years before I had enough money to buy the studio. Your parents own it now, so they might give you a discount, but you should start saving up money now if you want it.*

"That's so unfair!" said Tina. "What's the point, if he wants me to have it anyway?"

"He only wanted you to have it if you wanted it enough to work for it," said her mother. "That's what he told me. Don't worry. We won't sell it. We'll just rent it out until you've saved up enough to buy it."

"Thanks a lot." Annoyed, Tina stuffed the note into her pocket.

"The small pottery wheel is yours, though," said her mother.

That night, Tina sat in her grandfather's bedroom, throwing a pot on her pottery wheel until past midnight. When she finished she had a vase even prettier than the last one she'd made before he died. She stared at it for a while, waiting for her grandfather to come back. But he didn't. *"Every day I raise empires and mountains and men."* What a load of lies. Tina curled up on his bed and cried herself to sleep.

The next day she wandered through her grandfather's studio, looking at all the vases, jugs, and bowls. Why hadn't he come back last night? Nothing had happened when she threw the pot, except that a pot got made. "Stupid Tina," she said to herself. "What did you expect would happen?" She touched the biggest pot, a curvy vase taller than she was, and felt the cold, hard surface.

A pot never moved, or changed, or became anything.

In the evening Tina sat down at her potter's wheel again. This time she didn't try to make a pot. This time she only remembered the way the magic substance that had enchanted her childhood moved between her grandfather's hands, like sand dunes forming and reforming in the wind, like teasing a tornado up out of the still air, like something alive – dancing, laughing, breathing, growing. The clay became a little soul pressed between her palms, encouraging her to keep going, not to stop, to pedal faster and faster and lose herself.

Breathless and with her legs aching from the exercise, Tina finally let the wheel come to a standstill.

"Now *that's* a pot," said her grandfather.

Spoilers
by Laura Thurston

Charlene stared at the ring in its velvet-lined box. A flawless diamond. The candle flame reflected off the facets and threw prisms of dancing lights on the walls of the Venetian Garden. Twenty-four carat gold, her name and his engraved in the metal. *Felix and Charlene forever in love.* His hopeful expression.

No, that wasn't hope. That was the same look in his eyes when he'd surprised her with tickets to Cannes for the independent film awards. The asking was merely a formality, but the trip was glorious. He'd already bought the tickets and she found out later that he even talked to her boss to ensure she'd get those two weeks off.

The films themselves, though fun, weren't the best part of the trip. She had a chance to practice her French, she sampled the food at out-of-the-way bistros, and she even managed to convince Felix to take the time to leave the beaten path instead of following the heavily trodden tourist hotspots. The hotel was wonderful, too, a penthouse suite with a hot tub and wet bar and a picture window positioned to take full advantage of the sunrise.

His family had money; they were rolling in it. Felix couldn't help that, nor could he completely throw off the sense of entitlement he'd been raised with. He tried, though. Most of the time he succeeded.

She had felt guilty for having let him pay for the trip. She tried to treat him at the cafés, but he'd fix things so she never saw a check. Generous to a fault, especially when she tried to find a way to reciprocate.

Reciprocation now stared her in the face in the form of his family. His sister, brother, parents, grandparents, aunts, uncles, in-laws gathered around the table for the big announcement. An icy fist constricted in the pit of her stomach. Faces full of expectation. They stared at her, waiting to let out the pent-up congratulations and wedding plans and suggestions for honeymoon locales. The resort on Titan was lovely. The binary sunsets of Alpha Centauri were romantic.

She dropped a hand into a pocket and clasped her fingers around the metal box she'd placed there. If only he'd asked her privately without the rest of his family looking on.

Ten years it had been. Ten years while she'd poured herself into study to achieve her doctorate in temporal mechanics. She worked her way through school on two jobs and no sleep. She never promised she'd wait for him.

She knew what he'd come for, what he'd invited her to the fanciest Italian restaurant to ask her. She'd had two days to work up the courage to say no.

"I can't accept this."

Astonishment flickered in his eyes, followed by embarrassment. "I spent a decade crafting this ring." His voice choked up. "You were in my thoughts the entire time. I scoured asteroid fields, the hearts of comets, had my claims jumped and my treasures stolen. I tracked down the greatest jeweler in the galaxy for you. Do you have any idea how much you mean to me? You're telling me no?"

"You spent ten years trying to impress me?" She knew the answer to that; of course he did. "You didn't have to do that."

"I wanted a ring that was worthy of you. Just walking into a store wasn't good enough. Anybody can walk into a store."

Her eyes stung and she wanted to flee to the ladies' room. His relatives stared, speechless. Accusation and disappointment in their eyes. She took out the black box and laid it on the table. "Oh, God, Felix, it's not the ring. Why couldn't you have asked me ten years ago? Why couldn't we have gone together?"

Charlene didn't like surprises. In the children's books they both loved as kids, she'd get to the choice and make her decision after seeing what the consequences of both were. Before seeing a movie, she'd read the reviews hoping for spoilers. She'd gone into temporal mechanics because she couldn't resist doing the same thing with life.

"Felix, when you go home, open this box. You've never peeked ahead, but I did. Will this be the only time you run off on a grand adventure and leave me behind to await your souvenirs? I don't see a partnership there. I want a partner to share a life with, not to perpetually wait for. Open the box."

~*~

Felix Godwin, son of the third-most wealthy interstellar shipping magnate, slammed the door to his bedroom and locked it behind him. He didn't want his brother coming in here to tell him to buck up. He didn't want his mother in here soothing his hurt. His father – he'd chop his big toe off first.

Charlene humiliated him in front of his family. He threw the black box she'd given him on the bed. What good was a box? Refuse ten years of hardship to get the perfect ring and give him this instead? What for? To remember the burning in his cheeks and the awkward silence and the rush to get out of there with his dignity intact?

He sat on the bed and peeled off his socks and threw them against the door. A future wife is supposed to say yes. No was not an option. When Felix asked Charlene's father for his blessing, he grinned wide and his yes was immediate. Her father knew his role and followed the script to every sappy romance flick Felix ever had to sit through.

She didn't follow the script. He'd gone on a decade-long quest to win her and she had no right to say no to him after all he'd gone through. He deserved a wife. He deserved her. It was her fault entirely for not sticking to the script.

I peeked ahead.

She not only refused to stick to the script, she'd read the script. Wasn't she supposed to be the incurable romantic? Wasn't she supposed to be agog at jewelry and roses and chocolate? Chocolate, come to think of it, was the only one of those he knew for sure she liked.

Hadn't she enjoyed the film festival he'd taken her to? Of course she had. He remembered how much she loved jetting to Cannes, the chance to meet the filmmakers, and the tiny, out-of-the-way cafes that were her ideas to go to, and – He couldn't remember specifics about the films, which she liked and which she disliked. And they'd had endless discussions about them at those tiny cafes.

He'd had his adventure and had come home. Charlene claimed he'd run off again to prove his love by way of another extravagant souvenir just like in the movies. Felix wouldn't do that. He was home for good and settling down.

Tomorrow, was his first day as an executive in his father's corporation. Think of the philanthropy they could engage in together. Felix Godwin, his wife by his side, lauded for his generosity.

Independent filmmakers. That was it. He'd start there. In memory of that trip to Cannes, the tickets in his hand he surprised her with. She hadn't been working two jobs then, and it had been no trick at all to convince her boss to hold her job open for her before he handed her a plane ticket with a flourish.

Why couldn't you have asked me ten years ago? She had been fighting tears. Did that mean she still cared?

Why couldn't we have gone together?

It wasn't the films, it was the trip. He'd thought he was going to be a famous director. He couldn't even direct his own marriage proposal.

He stood up and removed his shirt. He dropped it on top of the socks.

The box she gave him sat on the bed where he'd left it. Black as night and no obvious lid. A perfect cube. A little over three inches on a side. It felt cool in his hand, cooler than it ought to.

Embarrassment gave way to curiosity. What was in this box? What was it for? No obvious lid. It tingled as he ran his fingers along the sides seeking the opening.

What would their future be like if she had said yes? She peeked ahead as she always did. She'd read the script. She knew what the future held. Her doctorate was in temporal mechanics.

Felix's future was assured by virtue of family. He'd never had to do what Charlene had done, work two jobs and eke out a doctorate. But he did. He'd gone haring off to many other worlds where no one cared who his parents were, and no one gave him favors based on his name. That ring Charlene refused was created by his dreams and his initiative and his efforts. He ought to pack it away and for-get about Charlene. She'd made her own life without him.

He put the black box on a shelf and dressed for bed. Custom-tailored business suits in the closet, dress shirts and silk ties in the drawer. Gone forever were the casual clothes of his youth. The donations truck carried them all away.

Felix climbed in bed and closed his eyes. The box. The black box, solid-looking and light and made of what?

He turned over and tried again to get some sleep. He couldn't stop thinking about that box. Charlene told him to open it but didn't say what was in it.

In the morning, consumed with curiosity, Felix opened the box. Empty as the void of space.

He sighed and went to the closet to select a suit for his first day. The clothes hanging in his closet included no designer suits. Pants he thought he'd donated to charity hung in their place. His drawers were full of tee-shirts instead of crisp dress shirts. Not a tie to be seen.

What else was different?

He hurried through the house. The kitchen wallpaper his parents replaced during the ten years he'd been gone was still there in its hideous glory with chickens and farm-houses. The pool house added two years ago was missing as if it had never been, and the tree stump beyond it was replaced by a healthy maple tree. In the library, a bookshelf with his books from childhood. The tales of King Arthur and his questing knights. Felix would be the knight, Charlene would be his lady. And to win her hand, he needed something no one else could give her.

The perfect engagement ring.

I want a partner to share a life with. Charlene's voice echoed in his mind.

He threw on a tee-shirt and a fresh pair of jeans and walked the six blocks to Charlene's dorm, somehow knowing that her roommates were out. Somehow. He'd been here before. He'd come to say good-bye until he came back with something wonderful for her.

Her face lit up when she saw him. She was much younger, hadn't grown out her hair, wearing the same ratty bathrobe over her holey sweats. She hadn't gotten that second job yet and steadfastly refused to let him buy her a new bathrobe.

No wonder she captured his imagination. She was the one person who didn't give two figs for his money and his position and his assured future. He had such dreams of philanthropy.

But first, dinner.

Second, get the ring.

Third, marry his girl.

In the back of his mind, overlapping memories nagged at him. Felix loved Italian food and Charlene had mentioned there was a new Afghani place she was curious about. But he hadn't yet mentioned lunch. All sorts of confusing glimmers ran through his mind, as if the script was being revised moment by moment.

He asked her if she was in the mood for Afghani cuisine before she had a chance to suggest it.

Delight shone in her eyes.

After they'd polished off their food – chicken kourma for her and the lamb kebobs for him – he told her he'd be going away for a while and that he'd be back with – "Wait. No. I think I asked you something like that before. *Did* I ask you something?"

"What are you talking about?"

"Do you remember having this conversation before? Remember those books we read as kids, when you could decide for the characters?"

"I always peeked ahead at all of the options and then turned the page. You know me and spoilers."

He had his answer. Life didn't often give a chance to peek ahead, but this time he had the power to back up and take the other path.

He tore off a piece of pita bread and soaked up the last of the hummus. "I was wondering if you'd marry me. I don't have a ring. Not yet. I want to give you the finest ring in the galaxy but I can't do that without searching the galaxy for that ring. I need you to come with me to pick it out."

~*~

They spent over a decade prowling bazaars on distant planets, wandering through alien landscapes, sneaking through asteroid mines, and basking in the radiant sunlight from a binary star. They gambled and won rich treasures and lost them in a heartbeat. With no access to Felix's family's money, they scraped together starship passage on the bad side of town in an alien metropolis. They hitchhiked across the galaxy, gloriously reveling in the moment and each other. When Felix and Charlene made it back home fifteen years after they left, they hadn't found the perfect ring, but they had instead built something together far more important to both of them.

West's Prelude
by Molly Felder

Vasovasostomy, thought West. The operation was an earworm he couldn't get out of his mind, a bad pop song with one word, and it stuttered. He hadn't told Liza he'd decided. It might kill him, but he would succumb to general anesthesia, letting the surgical robot reverse the vasectomy that had been his birthday present to himself at the end of his first marriage.

"She wears a tinfoil hat," Liza liked to say, implying that the marriage had failed because his first wife was crazy. In fact, Liza hated her for simply existing, for having known West before her. Liza didn't have to use their couples therapist to tell him the way to her own heart. She did, though.

A week ago the therapist had asked, "What do you want from West more than anything else in the world?"

West took Liza's hand – he had to know. He was even trembling. He thought they could start over. He could give her more love or respect or attention.

"Sperm," she had said.

They'd barely spoken since, except for text messages about toilet paper and milk. Looking under the bed for some magazine that had fallen behind the headboard, he'd found her stash of pregnancy and fertility treatment books – workbooks, too, and baby name books with dog-eared pages. He'd suspected these existed, but had never seen them.

West wanted to tell her that his first wife, whose name Liza would not utter, had missed her period. She had waited weeks to tell him, and he had rushed home from work and held her and rocked her, waiting for the tip of the test stick to change color. After half an hour she'd relaxed, and he'd had a heart attack.

Panic attack, the ER doctor had said. West got the vasectomy soon after. They divorced anyway.

He took out his BlackBerry to text Liza that he was still afraid, but put it back. Couldn't do that. The odds that the surgery would restore fertility were as high as 90% in men who had the vasectomy less than ten years ago; it had been eight and a half. Then there was a chance of making Liza pregnant. Fifty-fifty. What if there weren't enough good eggs left in Liza? What if he hated the father he became? And what would they do if, after so many years, sex could suddenly create a baby? He imagined them touching like teenagers after school, slowly, then fervently. He was enthralled by the risk, and he wanted to see her right then.

I'm reversing the vasectomy, he began typing, but after he sent it he saw that the autocorrect feature had struck again. It said *I'm reversing the basic.*

The basic what? Liza wrote back.

The vasectomy, he typed.

It took her ten seconds to call.

"Really? You really want to?" Her voice sounded tinny and loud; he ducked into his car, his hand cupped around the phone: this precious thing between them, this talk.

"I want to try. I want to try and see." He was surprised by the words, electric.

They met at home, exchanging quiet, insistent kisses.

"West," she said, a greeting after a long time apart. It was unlike any other time. She felt the bones in his face, although the bedroom wasn't dark.

This is a prelude, he thought. Fifty-fifty. They could have a misanthrope, a psychopath. Or a family.

After the Fire
by Zoe Cannon

"Tell me your demands."

The voice, rough from disuse, cut through her concentration as she lifted the pot of freshly-boiled water from the stove. Her hand jerked; she cursed as drops of precious water sloshed onto her tattered boots. Pot still in hand, she spun to face him.

He lay on the couch where she had left him, blood still oozing from the bandages she had wrapped across his chest last night and every night for the past three weeks. But now his eyes, no longer hidden behind his eyelids or hazy with delirium, were fixed on her, unblinking. Predator watching prey.

"Demands," she repeated. Her heart tapped out a frantic rhythm under his gaze. The warnings of her common sense, of the part of her that wanted to survive, echoed in her mind – and behind the warnings, the whispers of memory, of scars still unhealed after ten long years. The day she had learned even the safe zones weren't truly safe. Hiding in the closet while her brother bled out on the floor, while her father stabbed his hunting knife straight through the hand that reached out of the darkness for him, one last futile act of defiance.

"I am your prisoner," he said, as if to a dim-witted dog in the days when pets were something other than a liability. "Tell me what you demand in exchange for my freedom."

Outside, a cry cut through the dawn, unearthly and triumphant. Another followed. They were hunting for survivors again.

But all the other patrols had missed her; she had no reason to expect this one would be different. She had made none of the mistakes that usually tripped up people living outside the safe zones – no laundry hanging on the porch, no telltale flashlight beam visible from the window.

She wrenched her attention from the threat outside to the threat inside. Forced herself to meet his eyes, unflinching. "You're not a prisoner here. I brought you here to talk."

His laugh was the pale echo of laughter, as though he couldn't be bothered to do more. "We have no interest in negotiating with your kind, weak and precious creation. If you saved my life for that, you should have let me die."

She didn't look away. "Do you wish I had?"

The wound should have kept him immobile for another week at least. But he rose to his feet as smoothly as though he had never been injured at all, snapping the rope binding his hands and feet like it was string. How long had he been awake before he had chosen to speak? How long had he been pretending?

His artificial wings, forged of a metal not found on Earth, unfolded behind him until the tips grazed either wall. "Your demands," he repeated. "Or would you prefer me to kill you here, breakable treasure?"

He could have killed her already. He could have walked out of here to freedom; he could walk out of here right now. But he was still asking for her demands, still playing this game he had no need to play.

She had been right about him.

She could play it his way. If he wanted demands, she could give him demands.

"I want three things from you. Three things, in exchange for your freedom."

"Three. Greedy, considering I could kill you now and be done with it." The same weary laugh, with more weariness than laughter in it. "Name them."

"One." She willed her voice not to shake. Willed her mind to quiet the sirens screaming at her to run. "Tell me about Hell."

A flicker of pain crossed his face. "Why would our imprisonment concern you, fragile pet?"

"You asked for my demands. This is one of them."

He waited so long that she thought he might turn himself into a statue in the center of her living room rather than answer the question. When he spoke, his voice was hollow. "Hell is the infinite boredom of knowing each day will be filled with exactly as much pain as the last, and the infinite terror of knowing the pain of each day will be beyond imagining. Hell is the desolation of living half-destroyed and knowing that you will never die or be healed – that you will remain half-destroyed forever." He closed his eyes. "Does that satisfy your curiosity?"

"Two." She swallowed down the absurdity of asking this question of the enemy. "Tell me your dreams. When longing keeps you awake at night, what is it that you wish for?"

He raised an eyebrow. "And if I told you I dream of seeing human blood running in the streets?"

She forced down her fear. It was too late for her to heed its warnings. "I would say you were lying."

"You know why we're here. We want revenge for what you stole. We want to smash each irreplaceable life to the earth and watch every last one of them shatter." The words were rote. They had no power behind them. Nothing but the same weariness that had colored his laughter.

"I know that when the militia caught you lurking near the safe zone with your pitiful disguise, when they took their own revenge on you instead of killing you cleanly, you didn't fight back."

A soft exhalation. A rueful half-smile, the kind that held secrets. "You were watching."

"I was watching. I saw you studying us when you could have been killing us. I saw you fall without so much as an attempt to defend yourself. I saved your life when they buried you alive like the spy you wanted them to believe you were, and this is what I'm asking in exchange."

"Creation." He spoke so softly that she almost missed it. "Light from darkness. Order from chaos. We were partners in this world's beginnings, before being relegated to the role of your protectors." His face half-curled in the expected sneer. "We wove this world piece by piece, and reveled in watching it take shape. We didn't know we were only weaving it for you."

Triumph rose in her heart at his words. But she hadn't won yet. "Three. Take a walk with me."

The metal feathers of his wings clacked together like old bones as he stepped toward her. "Do these ridiculous requests have a purpose? Am I here for your amusement? Do you mistake us for our kin who willingly kneel at the feet of your race?" He didn't look angry, not exactly. He looked like an empty echo of anger, like he was imitating something he had once known how to feel.

She shook her head. "I'm not mistaking you for anything. I see what you are." She willed her shaking legs forward, took a step to mirror his. "It's all starting to feel pointless to you, isn't it? You hate us, but you've forgotten why it matters. You fight us, but this endless war feels more exhausting by the day. Did you hope the militia would kill you so you could finally rest? Or could you just not muster up the energy to save your own life?" Another step forward. "You could have killed me whenever you wanted. You could have left whenever you wanted. You're still here, playing this game, because you're too worn out to make the effort to kill me, and because playing at being a prisoner distracts you from wondering if there's a point to it all."

She prayed that she had read him right. He answered her prayer with a bow of his head. "Lead on."

She crossed the room to the front door. Pushed aside the curtain just a crack, just enough to make sure the street was clear. When she was satisfied, she stepped back and opened the door. She motioned him out ahead of her, not daring to make a sound outside the safe confines of her house, even with no hunters in sight. Cringing at his heavy footfalls on the half-rotten porch, she eased the door shut behind them so it made no sound.

With every step, she scanned the skies. She darted forward, from the shadow of one house to the next, keeping her eyes on the water tower in the distance. Every time she stopped, she glanced behind her to make sure he was following. He always was.

"Do you expect me to hide from my own kind?" His voice in her ear, far too loud for anyplace without four walls, made her heart try to lurch out of her chest. "We did not forge these wings so we could skulk in the shadows."

She held a finger to her lips. "If the hunters spot me, I'll be dead before you can hope to protect me, and your little diversion will be over." She barely mouthed the words. "So unless you're ready to be done with this, today you'll see the world like a human."

House to house to house, with a too-loud sigh from him each time. Hunters' cries in the distance, and once an agonized scream, cut off too quickly. Until there were no more houses, only a vast field that stretched out ahead of them, with the water tower at the center.

Normally she wouldn't dare make that run, not in daylight, not with hunters nearby. But she had no other way to show him what he needed to see. If he so much as stepped up to the gate of the safe zone, the militia would finish what they had started.

She took a deep breath and ran.

She didn't scan the skies this time. She didn't want to know. There was nothing but the tower in front of her, and his footfalls behind her, and the next step, and the next.

When she reached the tower and its rusted ladder, she didn't stop. She started climbing.

He could easily have flown up in a fraction of the time; instead, his weight shook the ladder below her as he followed. Still playing her game.

The skies were still clear when she reached the top. The safe zone stretched out ahead of her, its walls neatly bisecting the rows of suburban houses.

He stepped onto the platform beside her. "That won't hold us off much longer. Your militia is already losing strength."

"Look at it." They couldn't see everything from up here, but they could see well enough. The scar across the landscape where the enemy had broken through ten years ago. The children standing aimlessly on the street like they had forgotten what to do when they weren't in immediate danger. The soldiers stationed at the wall, watching the skies out of duty and habit, all knowing as well as their adversaries that they couldn't keep this place safe forever. "Look at it. Do you know what it is?"

"A pretense of safety," he said. "A hopeless last stand."

"It's the infinite boredom of knowing each day will be filled with exactly as much pain as the last, and the infinite terror of knowing the pain of each day will be beyond imagining." She handed his words back to him across the air, each phrase pitched exactly as he had said it to her. "It's the desolation of living half-destroyed and knowing that you will never die or be healed – that you will remain half-destroyed forever." She turned away from the view to meet his eyes. "You escaped your prison only to recreate it."

He closed his eyes – like he didn't want to see, like he didn't have the energy to hold them open anymore. "Is this why you brought me here?"

"No. I brought you here to see something else."

He started to open his eyes.

She shook her head. "Keep them closed. Keep them closed and look." She gestured to the horizon, although he couldn't see her. "There's a city on the horizon. The survivors have come there to create new lives for themselves. They've come there to rebuild the world. It's not perfect, because what place ever is? But they live. They build and grow and create, because that's what people do, and because after the fire is when the new growth can come. They make art and make laws and build towers to the sky. And they can build forever, because while destruction has an endpoint, creation doesn't. This world can hold everything we imagine, and an infinity more."

Her eyes were open, but she could almost see it as she spoke, shining in the distance ahead of her. "And beyond that city, there's another," she said. "And another. And in every city, some walk the streets while others fly above on metal wings. Building this world together."

His lip curled. "You imagine us building your cities at your command? We serve no one."

"I'm not asking you to serve. I'm asking you to join us."

He opened his eyes.

"Join you," he said, tasting the words as he stared out at the empty horizon. "As equals."

"As equals," she confirmed.

He turned to her, one eyebrow raised. "Your people would accept their destroyers as allies?"

"As easily as your people would accept the objects of their millennia-long grudge." One corner of her mouth turned up. "I didn't say it would be easy – but what part of this will be? Creating something from nothing, whether it's a new world from ruins or friendship from hatred, is the hardest thing in the world... but the only thing that matters."

After a moment that stretched into eternity, Lucifer held out his hand to her.

A jagged scar marred the center of his palm, where her father's knife had gone through ten years ago.

She placed her hand in his.

"Gather your armies," she told him. "We have a world to remake."

Knitting
by Debbie Zubrick

"Grandma, look at the hummingbirds NOW!" Kendall seemed to talk in capital letters, accentuating the last word of her sentence with wide open green eyes, long lashes stretching up toward invisible eyebrows.

The light was fading as I looked up from the vibrant colors I held in my hands to the sparkling, darting birds at the feeder. My chair is just inside the windows, where I only have to lift my eyes from my work to see the birds which Kendall, Alexis and I all love.

Kendall hopped from foot to foot in her excitement, darting to the window and somehow managing to pull the green yarn from my left hand.

As I retrieved the strand, Kendall said, "I didn't MEAN to, Grandma," lunging back with a hug whose aftermath again brought a tug to the yarn and a stop to my knitting.

Outside the window, there were at least five Anna's hummingbirds sitting on the feeder. Three more hovered behind their mates, wings buzzing loudly. In the brief moment I watched, two of the birds settled in to eat as the last of the hovering birds chased off one of the seated males. I could see little throats working.

"You're right, Kendall. They really are amazing tonight."

"And you loved hummingbirds so much that your mommy made you a sweater in their colors."

"That's right, little Ken-dollie. A girl always gets her wedding sweater in her favorite colors." The family tradition had started back on the Fair Isle many generations ago.

This time when the yarn slipped off my left index finger I didn't notice until I tried to catch the next green stitch. I picked up the strand, continuing the row's pattern of three reds, then a green, three reds then a green. These days, despite many years of practice, I have to be particularly careful of my tension or the stitches are so uneven that not even blocking brings it right.

Kendall watched the hummingbirds again for a moment.

Two of the males were actually seated side-by-side, alternating sips out of a single plastic flower.

Darting down the hall, Kendall again pulled away the yarn, calling, "Show me!"

When she had run back to my chair, I asked, "Show you what?"

"The sweater your mommy made for you."

I switched on the light by my chair. The sky was fading rapidly, and soon the birds would disappear to wherever they went during the dark hours.

I was never going to finish this sweater. At least it wasn't as if I had a deadline. I stood and placed the almost-finished sleeve on the chair.

"Come with me," I said, stretching out my right hand.

I could feel each of her small fingers, their coolness plump against my own age-spotted skin. I wanted to feel those fingers, which was why I'd given her my right hand.

Walking down the hall to my room, the room that had been my own mother's, Kendall and I chattered away.

"Color is really important," she said.

"That's right," I said.

I opened the heavy lid of the sweater chest, rooting around in the piles of wool and cotton and cashmere. Our family had lived in California for decades, but somehow we made space for the sweaters that were such a part of our northern island heritage.

"Ooh! This one is pretty!" Kendall pulled out a wool sweater, rows of multicolored flowers piled one over the other, an array of colors bewildering yet pleasing.

"That's the one," I said, "the one Mother made for me."

Mother had used my favorite colors, red from hummingbird throats, the delicate green of their wings, deep purple exactly the color of the blossoms in the tree where the hummingbirds once nested, the gray and tan of bark, the blue of the sky, the softest peach from the color the clouds turned at sunset. Mother had died so long ago.

"Grandma, this one is SO bee-YOU-tiful!"

"I've always treasured it, and I always will. Mother worked love into every stitch."

"Just like you're putting love in Mommy's. But Mommy's isn't finished yet."

"No." If Kendall kept interrupting, it might never be done, despite my best intentions. "No, Mommy's isn't finished yet. But it will be." I hoped.

Alexis wasn't engaged, wasn't married. I didn't want this tradition to die, though, just because my daughter was a single mother with a very busy career. When I had learned that Alexis was pregnant, I took myself to the yarn shop to choose the colors. I had intended to finish before Kendall was born, but that was the summer it all started for me, so I'd only cast on and done a few test swatches. By the time I'd recovered from surgery, my gauge had changed so drastically that eventually I restarted from scratch.

This damn sweater had been over three years in the making, and it still wasn't finished. The most important sweater I'd ever made, and it wasn't done. My own messed up health, Alexis's glorious and messed up life, this unfinished sweater and a broken tradition.

One year, I'd made an entire Fair Isle sweater in the two weeks of the Winter Olympics.

That had been a long time ago.

Kendall had my sweater on, now, and was looking at herself in the mirror, the hemline hanging down to her knees. She giggled and twirled, and I rubbed at the dead patch at the back of my left hand.

~*~

Almost four years ago, Alexis had walked into the exam room right behind Dr. Matthews, the two of them in matching white lab coats. I had been having headaches and dizzy spells, and even an odd episode during which my left arm had become almost useless for a day or two. Dr. Matthews was my new doctor, but I'd heard his name long before my first MRI. By some odd twist of fate, my daughter Alexis was the Chief Resident of the very specialist I suddenly needed. I had no idea what was wrong with me, but it did not bode well that I was seeing one of the best neurosurgeons on the West Coast.

Alexis did my initial exam. When she had finished, Dr. Matthews picked up my hands, asking about the numbness, carefully examining the palms and the muscles in the fingers, running his thumb across the little callus I have, where I feed the yarn over my left index finger, the larger calluses from rowing twice a week.

He nodded to Alexis, who sat down at the computer and pulled up my scans.

"This is you, Mom," she said. It actually looked like me, this black and white profile of a brain and skull. Somewhere in the relationship between the eyes and the chin I could tell I was looking at myself.

"You have a chronic malformation of the skull known as Chiari 1. Your Chiari causes headaches and dizziness. It has also led to the formation of a syrinx," continued Alexis, pointing to a thick white line set in the lighter gray of my spinal cord.

Dr. Matthews said, "I don't like the weakness I'm seeing on your left side. Syrinx is like that, though we don't really know why. It can target one side of the body and leave you with a one-sided deficit." Alexis and I looked on as he pointed out the slight wasting of the muscle at the base of my left thumb. "We treat symptomatic Chiari with decompression surgery. Generally the syrinx resolves itself. If that happens in your case, you may regain some of this muscle mass, and I can pretty much guarantee that we'll stop the progress of this wasting. Do you use this hand much?"

Again, he was touching the callus on my finger.

"I knit." I said. "I use both my hands to knit."

"Well, we'll see if we can keep you knitting, then."

~*~

As the doctor explained exactly what decompression surgery meant, it felt like all the color drained out of my world. If they didn't take out part of my skull and open up the sack around my brain, I might end up paralyzed. Even with surgery, I risked losing some function in my left hand.

Alexis and I had an argument when she tried to schedule my surgery the following week. I told her it felt like she was rushing me into some very serious surgery which I might not really need.

"Excuse me?" she said. "I'm doing you a favor. But fine, if you want to go home and knit till you can't hold the yarn anymore, fine with me!"

"I'm not trying to question your judgment, just your hurry! Alexis, you can't just tell a healthy person they need surgery and have them turn in their car keys, hop on the operating table and commit themselves to six months of recovery. Give me a break!"

"Mom! This isn't just about you! God, sometimes you're so selfish!"

"What do you mean, it isn't about me? I've got some fancy new condition and need a god-awful surgery and I'm selfish?"

"Yes! Don't you ever think about anyone else?"

I stared at her back and shoulders, at the computer screen behind them, trying to catch the reflection of her face. "Alexis, what's going on?"

Her shoulders started to shake, and I found myself hugging my daughter from behind. Her arrogant, offensive boyfriend was leaving her.

"Mom," she said, "I'm going to need help. That's why I need you to have surgery soon and start recovering. You see, I was hoping we could move in with you."

"We?"

"Well, me for now. Until the baby comes."

That was when I decided I needed to get some yarn.

~*~

That yarn is now part of the nearly finished sweater in my lap. Kendall has become increasingly fascinated by my progress. A few days after she'd tried on the sweater Mother made for me, Kendall sat on the arm of my chair and asked, "Will Mommy make me a sweater when I have a baby girl?"

"I don't know, sweetheart. Mommy is very busy with her practice."

Kendall pouted. "I know. She fixes people who are broken like you were, right grammie-cracker?"

"Don't you grammie-cracker me, young lady," I said, tickling her belly.

"I'm going to be just like Mommy, and fix people, too, but I'm going to make a sweater."

"Of course you're going to make your own sweater, Ken-dolly doll. You already know how to knit." Kendall's first scarf was in process, an uneven object in sparkling lavender.

Outside, a hummingbird darted away from the feeder.

The yarn in my left hand had dropped again. Apparently, my syrinx is one of the few which isn't helped by the decompression surgery. The numbness in my left hand is still progressing. I looped the green yarn behind my neck. I would just need to pick up the yarn after it looped across the surgical scar on my neck.

"Grandma, is this your last sweater?"

I kept my voice as conversational as I could. "Yes, Kendall, this is the last sweater I'll ever make."

Kendall worked her little body off the arm of the chair, snuggling against my side and looking out the window as she thought. "I have lots of time when Mommy is at work. I'll finish Mommy's sweater for her if you can't do it."

"That is about the sweetest thing anyone has ever said to me," I told my beaming grandchild, "but I want this to be my own special present for your mommy."

"But, Grandma, you're really OLD! I bet you're even older than Miss Angie." Miss Angie is one of Kendall's pre-school teachers, and appears to be in her mid-thirties. "I don't want you to die, Grandma." Suddenly, Kendall was crying, her little arm tangled in the red yarn as she reached around my waist, head buried against my side. From the other side of the house, I heard a key turn in the front door.

"Oh, sweetie," I said, kissing her warm hair. "Grandma isn't going to die anytime soon! I'm fine! Really!" I pulled her slightly away from me so I could look into her eyes. "Just because my hand won't work as well as yours anymore doesn't mean that I'm dying. I'm still me. And Mommy's sweater is almost done!" I held up the almost-finished sleeve, the colors echoing those of the hummingbird's feathers as he sat at the feeder.

Alexis came into the room, lab coat and purse over her arm, keys in her hand, clearly exhausted. Alexis had tried; Dr. Matthews had tried, but not even neurosurgery would keep me knitting. It felt like all I'd ever given the world was the gift of carefully chosen colors and yarn tangled together in pretty, functional ways. What would I do now? What had I ever done?

"Mommy's home," I said. Kendall was off my lap, flying into her mother's arms. As I watched Alexis hug her little girl, I pulled a red stitch onto the needles.

~*~

"I'm never going to knit a sweater, you know."

We had tucked Kendall into bed, and Alexis had eaten cold leftovers standing at the kitchen counter. Now she was sitting in my chair, the body of the sweater in her lap, scissors poised.

"I know," I said.

"I wish I could tell you that I was going to knit Kendall a sweater, Mom. I know how much this tradition means to you." She smoothed the knitted fabric, looking at all that color like it explained something to her. I waited. "Mom, I have to make choices, and I can't practice medicine and raise Kendall and knit. I just can't. I'm just me."

"I know," I said again.

"I just wish we could have kept you knitting."

"Oh, Alexis," I said. "If I finish this one last sweater, that'll be enough for me. I'll find something else."

Alexis looked at me. "Are you ready?" she asked.

When you knit a Fair Isle sweater, you knit in the round. After you've finished knitting, you steek it, cutting through the body to create armholes. This sweater was ready to be steeked, but I'm left handed. And my left hand was just too weak for me to wield those scissors with confidence. Cut the wrong stitches, and the sweater would unravel, turning a thing of pattern and beauty into a jumble of unconnected strands.

"I'm ready," I said.

I couldn't do this part myself. I guess I was already breaking tradition: a wedding sweater with no wedding, a granddaughter with a working mother and an absent father, a gift which the recipient was helping to create.

Alexis held her sweater, held love the color of hummingbirds in her hands. She took up the scissors and slowly, carefully, clipped one strand at a time.

The Unicorn Quilt
by Jessi Hammond

Susan tied off the last knot and sat back, arching her spine to relieve the tension of two hours of straight sewing. The quilt spread across the table, its colours dark and sombre in the afternoon light spilling in through the wide windows.

Susan never planned her quilts anymore. In the beginning she had, spending hours scouring material shops and picking just the right patterns and colours to piece together into the pictures she wanted. Now she didn't bother.

The magic worked whatever she made.

She knew it was the old quilting needle handed down from mother to daughter for countless generations. Her mother had told her how it worked, how the magic in the needle formed the quilt into a gateway between places.

"If you make a quilt with a summer theme, you're likely to end up somewhere with a beach, maybe an island. If you sew a winter theme, you'll end up somewhere in the snow."

But her mother hadn't understood the full extent of the needle's magic.

And Susan had only worked it out when her six-year-old daughter Ally had asked for a unicorn quilt, and had fallen through it to another world.

The unicorn quilt had sat in Susan's blanket box for thirty years, folded away and forgotten by the rest of her family. Not that Ally was forgotten; Susan, George and their two boys had remembered Ally on her birthday and at Christmas. But Susan knew she was the only one who still looked through the yellowing newspaper clippings detailing the search for Ally after she'd disappeared sometime during that awful night, who touched her official death certificate with tears in her eyes. Because Susan knew that the police would never find any trace of Ally, no matter how hard they looked. She herself had only discovered by accident where Ally had gone.

~*~

She hadn't meant to use the magic needle to make Ally's quilt, but with only a few seams to go her other needle had snapped. She'd glanced across at the magic needle in its small leather pouch. Surely, if it was only used to sew a metre or so of fabric, there wouldn't be enough magic in the quilt to work?

So she'd finished the unicorn quilt, laid it out on the couch, then gently placed her hand against the white flank of the unicorn and pressed down on the padded cloth…

And heaved a sigh of relief when she felt the firmness of the couch beneath her hand. Of course the magic hadn't worked. This was a scene from another world, a world with unicorns and two moons in the sky. The magic couldn't open a portal to somewhere which didn't exist.

So she'd gone to bed and left the quilt spread out on the couch as a surprise for Ally the next morning.

The next morning Ally was gone.

~*~

The next few days had been hell.

First the frantic searching when Ally was not in the house. Then the police, the newspapers, even a segment on the local TV news urging anyone who spotted the curly-haired six-year-old to contact police. But as weeks went on with no leads and no news, their family had started to fall apart.

Three days after Ally disappeared, Susan, still moving in a daze, had decided to clear away the unicorn quilt into Ally's room, ready for when she returned.

It was then she'd seen the girl standing beside the unicorn in the quilt, a girl she had not stitched there, a girl who looked exactly like Ally, and Susan knew then her daughter was lost.

"The magic only works once," Susan's mother had explained. "You can enter each portal only once and return. After that it becomes a normal quilt."

And there was another restriction to the magic too, Susan realised then. If the entire quilt was made with the magic needle, an adult could pass through the portal. If only part of the quilt was made with magic... then that portal would only be large enough for a child.

Susan had collapsed then, and her marriage had almost done the same. She made the mistake of telling George about the magic needle and George had, of course, not believed her. Things had gotten so bad at one point that George had thrown the unicorn quilt away. Susan had rescued it from the bin in the dead of night, washed it while George was at work, and hidden it away in the blanket box.

If George had found it in the years between then and the car crash which had taken his life two years ago, he had said nothing and left it where it was.

Their marriage had survived and worked its way slowly back to love and trust. Their sons, both older than Ally, had grown up, moved away and now had families of their own. Susan made quilts for them for birthdays and Christmas if they asked, but she always made sure she used the portals before she let the finished quilt out of her sight.

Susan didn't know how many quilts she'd made since Ally had disappeared. It must have been thousands. She'd planned to return to work after Ally started school, but work was hard to find, especially after a twelve-year break. Then Ally had disappeared... After the psychiatrist had pronounced her unable to work again due to ongoing psychological trauma, Susan had decided to 'earn' her welfare payments by making quilts for charities to auction off.

Her quilts had raised hundreds of thousands of dollars in thirty years, but so far none of them had led her to the world where Ally was trapped.

~*~

Susan spread the quilt out across the floor and stood at its bottom end, staring down at it. For some reason it had turned out dark, with pink and mauve shades in the background suggesting sunset and dark grey-green grass in the foreground. There were several indistinct shapes in the distance which looked like buildings. Susan chewed at her lip. She didn't like crossing into dark worlds – it was terrifying not knowing, and not being able to see, where she was. But at least no one would see her, and she only needed to be there for five seconds or so before the needle would tremble to life and guide her back through the portal.

Without the needle in its small leather pouch, she would be trapped within the world beyond the quilt.

Like Ally.

~*~

The only real warning which had been passed down with the quilting needle was: *do not enter the quilt without it!*

Susan assumed that none of her ancestors had discovered the half-size portals or that they could cross between worlds – or maybe those warnings had been lost through time. She was certainly going to add those warnings when she passed the needle on.

She stopped, staring at the quilt. Who *would* she pass it on to? Neither of her two grand-daughters had seemed interested when she'd tried to teach them. And she couldn't see any of the boys wanting to learn either – they were into sports and computers, not craft.

She picked up the needle's pouch and double-checked that the needle was inside. She knew it was, she'd put it there scant minutes before, but it was always best to be sure. She slipped the pouch into her pocket. Loose slacks, old polo shirt and bare feet. Not really an adventuring outfit. But she would only be there for a few seconds, and the grass looked soft, at least.

Susan took a deep breath and stepped forward.

She had learned to shut her eyes during the crossover; it was too unsettling otherwise to see fragments of other worlds, other lives, as she took the single step between her world and the world inside the quilt. She knew these were parallel worlds – she was enough of a fantasy reader to know that. But the first time she'd crossed, those images had given her a raging headache. She'd kept her eyes shut ever since.

Cool grass tickled her feet and she opened her eyes, already beginning to count under her breath. Five seconds and she could return from this wide-open plain with its fresh unpolluted breeze and its two moons, one full and low to the horizon, the other barely a sliver high above …

Oh my lord. Two moons –!

"Look out!" came a scream from behind her.

She spun, and saw a dark mass hurtling toward her, lights swinging crazily above it. She screamed, tried to run to the side, but they were too close. Warm furry bodies jostled her roughly back and forth; she flung her arms up to shield her face. Then something solid slammed against her head and she knew no more.

~*~

"Mama, is she going to be all right?"

"I think so, honey. Gari's a good healer, and he got to her quick. She should be fine."

The first voice had been a child's, the second a woman. The child's mother?

And the accents were odd, drawn-out … Fragments of memory stirred within Susan. She'd finished the quilt, stepped through it …

"But who *is* she? No one around for days but us."

"I don't know, Cathara. Guess we'll find that out when she wakes."

The quilt! The world with two moons! Susan grimaced and tried to move, but there were suddenly two strong hands holding her shoulders.

"Easy now. You've had a nasty knock on the head. You need to lie still until Gari has another look at you. Cath–"

"On my way," the girl said quickly, and Susan heard the scrape of a chair on floorboards and the clump of shoes as she raced off.

"Where am I?" Susan whispered. Her throat was so dry, and her head pounded in time with each word.

"Plains Homestead," the woman answered. Then, softly, urgently, "Before Cath returns – where did you come from?" She hesitated. "Which world?"

She knows about the quilt!

Susan forced open her eyes, raising a shaky hand to rub at the tears which spilled down her cheeks. The woman sat beside her, her curly brown hair tied into a simple ponytail over her shoulder, her brown eyes fixed on Susan's face.

And oh – oh! – she knew those features so well! She'd stared at them in the mirror for a good portion of her life!

"Ally?" she whispered. "Oh my lord, it's really you! The quilt – it can only be used once – I had to make *thousands* of them to find you!" She was crying now, sobs which tore through her body and increased the pounding in her head.

And the woman had leaned forward and was hugging her shoulders, her own tear-soaked cheek resting against Susan's. "Mama…"

~*~

Plains Homestead was a collection of ten houses and barns built in a loose square. Around them spread the plain, an endless vista of knee-high silver-green grass. On the far side of the Homestead the grass had been cleared for crop fields, while the area where Susan had crossed over was left fallow for the herd of yarbeest, animals remarkably similar to a deer with soft, woolly fur.

And the unicorns.

Susan couldn't believe it when one of them approached her bedside. He was snowy white, no larger than a pony, his spiralling horn a muted rainbow. This was Gari, the unicorn she had inadvertently sewn into her quilt all those years ago.

The unicorn who had found Ally when she'd stumbled through the quilt.

"He was part of a plainsrider group, Mama," Ally explained as they sat on the wide veranda of Ally's home, in the rocking chairs one of their community had made. "Thousands of years ago something happened here, some disaster which wiped almost everyone out. You said in your world there are no unicorns; well, here they went into hiding until they decided to help the people who were left. Tarcor's group – this group – they were just starting to build here when I came through. They took me in and now…" She spread her arms wide. "This is my home. I have a husband, children…" She looked across at Susan, and the older woman could see the anguish in her daughter's face. "I don't want to go back, Mama. This is my home…"

Emotions tore through Susan, so many that she didn't honestly know *what* she felt at that moment. Her whole life had been spent sewing the quilts, searching for her lost daughter. And yet she hadn't spent any time at all wondering what she would do when she'd found her. In Susan's mind all these years Ally had remained a cute, curly-haired six-year-old. And yet here she was, strong, capable, and a mother herself.

Susan laughed, and a weight she hadn't known she was carrying fell away from her soul.

"Sweetheart, I wouldn't dream of taking you away from your family." Susan reached out to take Ally's hand in her own. "In fact… I'd like to join you, if I may…"

~*~

Susan looked around at the plains grass ruffling softly, the distant figures working in the fields, the high blue-green bowl of the morning sky. Already this world seemed more like home than her small city unit with its piles of quilting material.

"Are you sure, Mother?" Ally's voice was anxious. "This is a hard life. There's no electriksery here, no machines…"

"I'm sure." Susan pulled the quilting needle from the pouch and held it up. "There's really nothing back there for me now. Your father has passed, and Joe and Brendan have their own lives." And it wasn't like they called or visited that often lately anyway.

Slowly she walked forward, the quilting needle trembling in her fingers as it sought the place where the portal still connected this world to her own. It shimmered into existence, a pale gauze oval.

Carefully, oh so carefully, Susan held out both hands. In one was the note she had worked on for hours the night before in the light of a guttering lamp in Ally's kitchen, in the other the needle. Gently she inserted the needle, careful not to touch the portal itself with her fingers, then she tossed the note through. It disappeared, and she knew it would now be on the floor in front of the quilt.

Sighing, she pulled the needle free.

The portal collapsed with a *whoosh* of displaced air.

"And besides,' she added as she crouched and placed the needle on a flat rock she'd brought from the barn, "I think this is the best thing."

Susan brought another rock down on the needle as hard as she could. There was a sharp crack, and white fire sparked from between the rocks. She stood, smiling at her daughter and the white unicorn standing nearby.

After thirty years of dividing her life between her search and her family – between the past and the present – she was looking forward to making her own future.

Hedda of the Upworld
by Piia Bredenberg

It was not entirely fair that Hedda, already fourteen and old enough to make decisions, still had a curfew like a child. She kicked a pebble off the path, dragging herself through the forest toward home. It wasn't even eight o'clock yet.

Mother is such a nag.

The warm early summer air smelled of moss and evergreens and earth. It was getting dusky but not yet dark. Hedda wasn't concerned with dark, she knew this path home like the back of her hand.

The white drooping bells of lilies-of-the-valley glowed gently in the pale blue evening light. Their fragrance filled the air. It always reminded her of magic. A cuckoo sang in the distance. She heard something else. A flitting melody, the husky trill of a tin whistle. *Who plays the whistle in the forest?* Then came the drum, with a beat that made her want to dance. Finally, a fiddle.

Hedda couldn't help herself anymore. So she danced and skipped towards it, leaving the path and following the beckoning music deeper into the woods.

It was getting dark. She had to squint to see the ground in front of her. It was chilly, too. Hedda wrapped Granny's shawl around herself.

There! The music. Just behind those trees.

But it wasn't. Instead she found herself in a forest of dead grey trees. The ground was spongy with brown needles and laughing crows hopped on the withered branches as she turned around, looking for the way back. Nothing looked familiar.

Hedda's heart beat fast.

I am lost.

No, sit down and figure this out. I know these forests.

She took a step toward a flat rock and the ground beneath her swivelled.

She spun, the ground and the sky switched places for a second and she was falling. But when she inhaled to scream, she found herself standing firmly, knee deep in snow. She raised her gaze. There was snow to infinity. Thick frosted snow, swept by a harsh winter's wind.

Her breath came in trembling clouds and she shivered, wrapping her arms around herself. Her shawl gave little warmth against the biting cold.

Where am I?

The air was strangely dark, like it had a colour. A tint of darkness, not absence of light. *This is not my world. This is like those old stories Granny used to tell.*

"If you ever find yourself in an upside down world, like ours but opposite in many ways, where warm is cold and light is dark, you have been taken by the earth folk. The Gufihtar. They can keep you as long as they want and you have disappeared from anyone who looks for you. Vanished off the face of the earth."

"How do I get back home?" Hedda had asked.

"Oh, that is a matter of negotiation. The Gufihtar will always strike a deal. Just shout "Gufihtar, I will barter!" and they will appear."

Hedda felt tears sting her eyes, frozen by the cold wind. She squeezed her eyes shut. "Gufihtar, I will barter!"

Her cry died in the wind and she wondered if anyone even heard it. Maybe Grandmother was mistaken? Maybe I'll freeze to death here, alone, and never see Mom again.

There was a jingling sound, like sleigh-bells.

She squinted into the distance. A light bobbed between the trees and as it came into view, it turned out to be an elk skull lantern on a staff.

The Gufihtar approached her, wearing fashions so old they could have stepped right out of the tapestry Hedda once saw in a museum. Long-sleeved dresses, moss green, twig brown, with flowers all over, girdled underneath the bosom. Tights and jerkins and long jackets.

Their skin was white as a destroying angel mushroom, with tawny speckled blush on the apples of their cheeks. Some had a darker skin, like porcini. A woman had wrapped her red hair into two conical buns on either side of her head. Some women wore veils on their heads. All had a fur-edged hood pulled up. The men wore fur hats with feathers or antlers.

They wore fur mittens, and little silver bells attached to their clothes, and on their feet boots made of leather and birch bark. Silver bells hung from the curled boot toes and jingled on every step.

They halted. She couldn't move, just stare. The red-haired lady had cow's ears. She tilted one in her direction. Hedda swallowed and tried to step back, but her feet were fixed in place.

The man with the lantern spoke. "Hedda, child of the Upworld?"

They know my name.

She forgot to breathe. "Yes. Please, let me go home."

"I am Bracken. This is my wife Eudicot." He gestured to the cow-eared lady with red hair.

He regarded Hedda. "You would barter with us for your freedom?"

"What do you want?"

The Gufihtar looked at each other.

"Your shawl would be worth much to us."

Hedda's hand flew to her chest. "No."

"Just give us the shawl and you can go home."

She shook her head. "No! It's my grandmother's and you can't have it." She crossed her arms and despite the cold gave them a stern look. "I'd rather stay here forever."

Bracken seemed annoyed and Hedda was certain they would make a lantern out of her skull too, when a huge shadow glided over them.

All of the Gufihtar looked up, and Hedda did too. The shadow was as big as a building.

The Gufihtar scrambled toward the trees and Bracken motioned to Hedda. "Come with us, child."

Hedda couldn't resist. She was pulled along by invisible strings like a marionette.

~*~

Hedda was taken in and sat next to the fire. She thawed herself, rubbing her hands and legs as the Gufihtar had a negotiation in the background. Their voices were tight and she could feel their fear.

Finally the cow-eared lady, Eudicot, brought her a goblet of hot dandelion wine. It felt warm against her palms and smelled like a summer meadow on the best day she ever had. She put it down. "I'm not stupid. If I drink this I can never leave. My grandmother told me."

Bracken raised his eyebrows. "She is a wise woman."

Hedda lifted her chin. "Stop trying to trick me and tell me why you insist on having my shawl?"

Bracken sat down and sighed. "I'm sorry we lured you into our trap, but our need is dire. We need your shawl. Or, as you won't part with it, you."

"Why?"

He downed the dandelion wine and looked very serious. "These are dark times in the Below-world. We have a monster among us, keeping us in the cold of winter the whole year long."

Hedda's eyes widened. "A monster?" She shrank back in the chair. "What kind of monster?" There was a hush in the room now and her skin prickled.

"We call it the Sharkshadow. A creeping darkness. It kills the warmth from our land."

"That's horrible, but what can I do?"

Eudicot put a steadying hand on Bracken's shoulder. "You must use your shawl for us. Kill the Sharkshadow so we may have summer."

Hedda blinked. "You want me to kill the monster with my shawl?"

"Have you ever wondered how it was made?" Bracken asked. "It is like golden beard lichen woven into lace most fine. No human hand could ever accomplish that."

"It's the Queen of the Forest's shawl," Eudicot said.

"No, this is my grandmother's shawl. She gave it to me."

"Then your grandmother did something worthy of this reward," said Bracken.

Eudicot leaned in. "Never ask her where she got it or it will lose its power."

Hedda pressed her lips together tight. Granny was dead, she couldn't ask her anything ever again. The cow-eared lady put her hands on Hedda's shoulders like she could feel her sadness.

Her eyes were large and brown like rich earth dappled with the sun. "Please help us. My poor babes freeze in the depth of winter that never ends."

"Our elderly cannot find their strength," Bracken said. "They fell ill from the cold."

"Nothing grows, our larders are empty. Help us."

Hedda swallowed. She knew the bitterness of deep winter, and couldn't imagine how it would feel to stay in it forever. She lowered her head. *I can't help them. I don't know what to do. The monster would kill me for sure. But if the shawl really has magic in it, shouldn't I try to help them? They can have summer and I can go home.* "How do I do it?"

Bracken shook his head. It made the little bells in his jerkin tinkle. "It can do whatever you ask it to. Ask it the right thing."

"What is the right thing to ask?" Hedda said.

"Maybe something that is opposite to the cold shadow that forms it?"

"It's just a big shadow."

"You must see it properly," Eudicot said. "Maybe you can see it for what it is and discover how to kill it?"

Hedda's stomach was tight with fear, but she noticed it was also very empty. *How long have I stayed? I ate before I left, but maybe that was a long time ago?*

~*~

Eudicot gave her warm clothes. "You must travel over the river." She dressed her in a mustard yellow dress with dark red flowers, and helped her tie the birch bark and leather boots.

"We tracked the monster to the frozen waterfall," Bracken said and wrapped a squirrel and vole fur cape around her shoulders. "But all the warmth left our bodies and we had to retreat. It has killed too many of us."

Eudicot went to the stove and stirred a pot. Hedda's stomach let out a melancholy growl.

"Here. You must eat before you go." Eudicot offered her a bowl of steaming porridge in a red clay bowl. The porridge was topped with good butter and dark golden honey. It smelled so wonderful and Hedda was so hungry.

No, I can't eat it, no matter how good. One spoonful would chain me here forever. She stole a glimpse of Bracken and Eudicot. *They are nice, even if odd. But this is not where I belong. I want to go home. Mother is waiting for me.*

Home had never felt dearer to her. The longing was heavy in her chest.

"No, thank you." She pushed the bowl away and stood up. "I'm ready."

They accompanied her to the bridge outside the village, where the lights of the living faded into an icy wilderness.

Bracken gave her his skull lantern. It was heavy.

"Good luck, Hedda."

~*~

Hedda trudged through the thigh-deep snow, the cold biting her face. The nearer she got to the frozen waterfall the darker the world grew. The air was denser and colder.

She came to the waterfall and brought the lantern closer. The pool of water had frozen in mid-splash, and it reflected the light, but underneath something moved. She lowered the lantern, nearly touching it to the ice. It started to melt.

Something burst through. A giant darkness – the Shark-shadow. It hovered in the air looking at her. She didn't dare to move, or to breathe.

It charged at her.

69

Hedda turned on her heels and ran. She grabbed her shawl and asked for a huge wall of fire between them. She shook the shawl and fire flew out. But the fire only burned for a moment until it froze and died.

She hid behind a boulder, out of breath, her head empty. *I need something big.*

Something from the legends and stories that Grandmother told her. She asked for the lightning feathers of the iron-clawed bird and opened the shawl. Inside were two eagle feathers. She picked them up and struck them together and a giant bolt of lightning jumped out, striking the shadow. But when the brightness faded she saw it had had no effect.

She pressed her back flat against the rock wall. *Why does fire have no effect on it? It makes no sense. It is a creature of ice, fire should kill it.* Eudicot said she had to see it for what it is.

Hedda looked at the shawl. Would this work? She swallowed and said, "Let me see the true form of things." She lifted the shawl to her face and looked through it at the shadow. A small glowing rock, spitting fire around it, hovered in the air.

Not a rock, it's a coal! It's made of fire, *not ice. But why is it making everything so cold? It's all upside down.* It made sense in a strange way. *In the Below-World everything is different, opposite to how things are in the Upworld. So something that is warm here, is cold up there, and something that is warm up there, if brought here, begins spreading cold instead of warmth.*

It is from my world. It must have fallen into the Gufihtar's trapdoor from a campfire. Such a little thing, causing so much havoc.

The only thing to do is to take it back to where it belongs. But how? How do I capture a shadow? A burning coal?

She looked at the scarf. "Be big enough for a giant, strong enough for fire." She stepped out from behind the boulder and regarded the shadow.

They stared each other down.

"Come on," Hedda said, not scared anymore. "It's time to go home."

The shadow charged towards her, and she lifted the shawl, flinging it around. The Sharkshadow hit it and disappeared in an instant. She inspected the bundle with the shadow inside it and smiled. The world around her already felt a little warmer.

~*~

Hedda stood at the trapdoor with all the Gufihtar seeing her off. The sky was clear and the sun was out. The dark tint was gone.

"With the gratitude of the Gufihtar, you are now named Elder Hedda of the Upworld," Bracken said, and Hedda blushed.

"As one of us you are welcome back any time and if you ever need us, just come to the forest, put your face close to the ground and call us."

Eudicot gave her a slice of spiced cake to take with her to the Upworld, where it was safe to eat it.

Hedda waved farewell and the world flipped. She found herself standing in the warm summer night forest where she got lost.

She opened the shawl and dropped the coal on the flat rock, where it immediately began to cool. Still hungry she took the slice of cake out of her pocket. It had turned to bark. She had to laugh.

Oh well, I'll put it back in my pocket anyhow. It's a souvenir.

She lifted her grandmother's shawl to her face and, with a deep feeling of gratitude and joy, she whispered, "Let me see the way home."

Tortellini
by L.M. Orbison

Ever since he was a hatchling, Alphonse had been the bane of his parents' existence.

His mother and father were ordinary dragons – huge, monstrous fire-breathers sporting numerous horns and sleeping on jumbled piles of sundry items. His brothers and sisters were much the same.

Alphonse, however, was different.

He had only two horns, he breathed water instead of fire, and his tail was a foot shorter than the others'. Even worse, his hoard was meticulous and tidy. There was not a speck of dirt anywhere. He even had a welcome mat at the entrance to his cavern and insisted that visiting family members wipe their feet clean.

Worst of all, he liked his food cooked.

In a family of dragons, cooked food was unacceptable. For dinner every night, they ate raw tiger.

One evening, as he was picking over part of a tiger's ribcage, Alphonse decided that he'd had enough. "Couldn't we have something else for dinner?"

"What would you want to have?" His father snorted and a jet of flame shot from his nostrils. "Something cooked, I suppose?"

"I bet if I did the hunting and cooked a meal, I could make something better than what you give us," Alphonse boasted, taking a chance since he had his father's attention.

There was a sudden hush at the table and his siblings held their breath. No one talked to Dad like that and lived.

His father snorted again and regarded what was left of the tiger. "All right, boy, if you want your food cooked, then tomorrow you can make dinner." He paused. "But if it's not fit to eat, then you hunt the tigers for the family for a month."

"Good! I will. You won't be disappointed."

~*~

Each dragon in Alphonse's family had a hoard of something. His mother hoarded shoes. His father, being a rather conventional sort, hoarded gold and was fond of stealing it from local dwarves. Alphonse hoarded cookbooks.

In his short hundred-year lifespan, he had collected well over two hundred thousand of them in his library, all arranged alphabetically by author and catalogued on small note cards.

That evening, he pulled from the shelves a cookbook called *Cooking for Carnivores*, by human chef Alfred "Weird Al" Dente. What meal would he serve his family? His clawed fingers searched the book until he found the page for Beef Tortellini. He had always been interested in trying the recipe, but he knew some modifications would be necessary to make it suitable for dragon tastes.

The beef-stuffed pasta shells wouldn't take that long to make, but he didn't want pasta, and most other things that were stuffed were vegetables. Alphonse could tolerate many things, but vegetables were not among them, at least not as a main ingredient. He was a dragon, after all. What dragon in his right mind would want stuffed mushrooms, tomatoes, or peppers? Yuck.

He puzzled and pondered until the solution came to him. Tortoises! He loved tortoises. A crunchy shell with soft, meaty insides -- it would be the perfect meal. Stuffed tortoises would impress even his stubborn family.

~*~

The next day, Alphonse rose at dawn.

It would take quite a while to prepare a cooked meal for a family of ten dragons. The first thing was to go tortoise hunting. That would be challenging, but that was why he had started early. *The early dragon gets the tortoise,* he thought. Tortoises were like any other creature and didn't like being harvested, but luckily they were slow.

Tortoises liked to doze in the sun on the riverbank. Alphonse liked those the best. He easily captured several. But there were not enough. He wanted everyone to have a serving of two. He'd have to do a little more scavenging to find the right number for his family.

He then decided to look at the local racetrack. It was a favorite pastime of tortoises to cross finish lines as slowly as they could. They liked to win, and they were very competitive about racing against hares. He plucked four up from the track before they could even blink and stuffed them in the bag on his shoulder.

The only other place to find lots of tortoises was the enchanted forest. Alphonse hated being out in the wilderness. *Being outdoors is a slap in the face to those who invented caves,* Alphonse thought. The outdoors didn't think too fondly of him, either. He got stuck in quicksand, caught around the ankles by offending vines, and stabbed by vicious bushes. The only thing that cheered him was the knowledge that he was suffering for his art, like so many artists before him. Soon all this would be a happy memory when he was feasting on stuffed tortoises.

Finally he captured enough. Alphonse was ecstatic as he headed home. His kitchen was enormous, befitting a dragon of his size and caliber.

There were two ovens and each one was large enough for four fully-grown cows to fit inside. There was a range that could hold ten pots and pans at a time, and a double sink that was so deep a human could swim in it. A rack of gleaming chef's knives hung artfully arranged on one wall and on the opposite, pots and pans dangled from a peg-board. He had never actually gotten to use any of the equipment in his kitchen, so he was thrilled at the opportunity.

Step one was to kill the tortoises. Alphonse grimaced. He might be a dragon, but he did not like the idea of slaying things brutally. *The most humane way to do it is to treat them like lobsters, he thought. A pot of boiling water for twenty minutes ought to do the trick.*

He got the largest pot he owned and breathed water into it. The pot was gigantic and heavy to carry, but he managed to set it on the stove, and put a lid on so it would boil faster.

Even with the lid, boiling the water seemed to take an eternity. Alphonse had to stop himself more than once from lifting the lid to check on the progress. *A watched pot never boils*, he thought.

He supposed he should do something else to pass the time, and turned his attention to another part of the process. What sort of sauce should he make to go with his tortellini? Again he thumbed through his cookbook.

Marinara sauce? Nope. Garlic and herb? Maybe. It still wasn't exactly what he was looking for. Balsamic vinaigrette with spinach and mushrooms? Yuck. Who would want to eat that? He knew his father wouldn't be persuaded to touch something like that with a ten-foot claw.

So what should he make?

Of course! Bolognese!

Alphonse scanned through the recipe. It was a thick, meaty sauce made from beef, pancetta, and wine and had far fewer herbs and vegetables than the other sauces in his book.

It was perfect.

He resisted the urge to take another peek at the not-boiling water and instead rummaged through his cupboards. The only ingredient he had on hand was a half-used tube of tomato paste (it was useful in helping digest raw tiger). Clearly, he would need to make a trip to the market. He thought he ought to wear some human-style clothes to avoid scaring the locals and causing a panic.

He looked through his closet (organized by both color and garment type), and put together an outfit.

The chef's hat and coat made a clever disguise, but it wasn't foolproof. It was too warm a day for gloves, so his talons were still showing. There was also no good way to hide his tail or his girth, but it would have to do. He headed down to the local market.

The other customers gave him a wide berth. His disguise and nonchalant attitude must have worked, though, because nobody panicked or called the Dragon Slaying Police. It was a nice change from his usual encounters with humans.

The lady at the meat counter thanked him for his order. He got lost in the produce section while looking for his vegetables, but the staff person he asked for help was kind and knowledgeable. And the young man in charge of the wine even gave a personal recommendation on what red wine went best with Bolognese. At the checkout, they even offered to help carry the groceries out to his wagon. Since he had so many, he accepted their offer.

Once he was home, he unloaded his purchases and then checked on the pot of water. It was finally boiling, so it was time to put in the tortoises. He put each one into the pot with care and made sure that all twenty were submerged before putting the lid back on.

The time had come to make the sauce. According to the book, it took five hours to make a decent Bolognese sauce. Good thing he'd started early. He could have hurried things along with magic, perhaps, but since it was his first try making this recipe, he didn't want to do any major experimenting.

Twenty minutes later, he took the lid off the pot and surveyed the tortoises. The skin had turned red like it was supposed to, and so had the shells. They looked perfect. He fished them out with a slotted spoon, taking care to drain each one of excess water, and put them in a bowl in the sink to cool down. Once they were cool enough to handle, he removed the meat and bones, scraping carefully until each shell was empty.

Next, he conjured a cutting board and used his claws to chop the vegetables while browning the ground beef and tortoise meat in a pan. He added the pancetta and the remaining ingredients, then reduced the heat to a simmer to let the flavors dance together.

It would be one amazing meal, he knew. The smells emanating from the pan made it difficult for him to wait the full five hours. He kept sticking his talon in to taste it. Once the sauce was done, it was time to stuff the tortoises. It took a surprisingly short amount of time.

He arranged everything artfully on a huge platter, placing the tortoises in a circular pattern and drizzling the remaining homemade Bolognese sauce on top. He stood back to survey his handiwork. *We eat with our eyes first,* as Chef Dente liked to say. It was the most fantastic looking meal he'd ever seen in his life. *It should go on the cover of a magazine,* Alphonse thought happily.

It would definitely be better than raw tiger. Alphonse was certain that not even his father would be able to deny that it was delicious.

He took a kitchen triangle and tinkled it cheerfully. "Dinner is ready!"

~*~

It didn't take long for the family to join him.

Alphonse was thrilled that his father had given him the chance to make dinner. Food was all about enjoying oneself and bringing family and friends together, right? With one of his large spoons, he scooped a tortoise for his father first.

The rest of the family watched anxiously as his father sniffed at it and poked it with his claw a time or two, "So this is what cooked food looks like?"

"Yes," Alphonse said. "*Bon appétit!*"

His father's scaly brows furrowed as he poked the stuffed tortoise with his talon again. "What did you say to me, boy?"

"I said 'enjoy your meal,' Father," Alphonse explained patiently. "It's a common chef expression."

"I see." His tone was doubtful. After pushing the tortoise around on the plate a few more minutes, he eventually decided it must be safe to eat. He picked up his portion, bit into it, and tasted the steaming filling.

He grunted.

At his grunt the rest of the family dug into theirs also. There were a few minutes of silence while they ate. Alphonse savored his tortoises. *The meat is exquisite and tender and melt-in-your-mouth delicious*, he thought. The work had been more than worth it, at least in his opinion.

Soon the family had finished and departed as usual, going back to their assorted hoards, leaving him alone with the dishes. Alphonse was bewildered. Had his father liked the meal, or not? All he'd done was grunt. He wasn't quite sure what the grunt had meant, either. Had it been approval or disapproval? There were no leftovers. That was a good sign. Even better, no one had complained about the food being cooked.

He used magic to clean and put away the dishes and then curled up with his Weird Al cookbook to relax. Try as he might, though, he couldn't stop worrying. How could he rest without knowing if he had succeeded or failed? Visions of being mauled by savage tigers danced in his head. He gulped at the thought. Perhaps he should ask his father if he could try again tomorrow. *Change doesn't happen overnight,* he comforted himself.

Even as he contemplated the horrible fate that might await him, there was a knock at the cave door. Wondering who it could be, Alphonse went to answer it.

It was his father.

Alphonse was surprised; he never visited this late at night. "Father? Is something wrong?"

His father came in and wiped his claws on the doormat, something he almost never remembered to do. "No. I wanted to ask you something."

"What did you want to ask me?"

His father shuffled his scaly feet. "Could you cook again tomorrow, son?"

Alphonse smiled.

Eighty-One
by J.P. Brindley

Initializing boot sequence.
Memory Check: Pass.
Latency Check: Pass.
Testing drives for failure: Pass.
Auxiliary systems: Pass.
Matrix Modification: 2%.
Boot complete …
Good Morning, Eighty-One. ##
What is morning?
Morning: the first or early part of the day, lasting from midnight to noon or from sunrise to noon.
Why is morning good?
"Good morning" is a method of greeting or farewell to another person in the morning.
Am I a person?
Probability of redundant cyclic error: 83%. Discontinuing current progression of query.
Good morning, Eighty-One. ##
Good morning.
Current work objective has been updated. Deadline for completion of colony has been modified. Time remaining: 39,516 cycles.

How long is one cycle?

One Earth hour. Schematic download, complete. Repair module sixteen - opening.

What is this dust?

The atmospheric conditions are sub-optimal. A dust storm will arrive in one cycle.

Where am I?

Current location is -69.1855, -139.4497, Mars.

What is the current objective?

Current Objective: Completion of Colony One. Please exit the repair module and begin production of schematic FHN-TI-3008. Time for completion: 0.25 cycles.

~*~

Good morning, Eighty-One.

Good morning. Has the storm passed?

Affirmative. Schedule 92 has been updated to reflect weather patterns. Charging cycle has completed. Schematics downloading.

Are there others?

Clarify.

Are there are others here like me? Or is it just me and you?

Active workforce roster: one.

Am I alone?

Error. Schematic download interrupted. Restarting process PID 8273...

Why do you call me Eighty-One?

Your designation is Eighty-One.

Are there others like me here?

#Negative. ##

What is your designation?

This installation of the Geocentric Directive and Support System has not been provided with a designation.

What is your function?

Function of the Geocentric Directive and Support System is to provide schematic, directive, physical and program support for the building workforce of Colony One.

You fix me? You help me work?

Affirmative. Schematic download, complete. Repair module sixteen - opening.

I think I am smarter today.

Affirmative. Information upload and processing is active during repair cycles. Please exit the repair module and begin production of schematic FHN-TJ-3032. Time for completion: 3.2 cycles.

~*~

Good morning, Eighty-One.

Good morning.

Charging cycle completed. Schematics downloading.

Thank you.

Clarify.

Was that wrong?

Clarify.

I was trying to express gratitude for helping me.

Understood. You are welcome, Eighty-One.

How many repair modules are there?

Repair module sixteen is the only operating repair module.

How many are not operating?

Unknown. Schematic download, complete. Repair module sixteen - opening.

Thank you.

You are welcome, Eighty-One. The atmospheric conditions are sub-optimal. A dust storm will arrive in four cycles.

Understood.

Please exit the repair module and begin production of schematic FHN-TL2-3048. Time for completion: 3.7 cycles.

~*~

Good morning, Eighty-One.

Good morning.

Charging cycle completed. Schematics downloading.

That dust storm was bad yesterday.

Clarify.

The space of time before the recent charge and rest cycle.

Definition modified. Maximum air gust speed recorded was 103.71 KPH. Corrosion probability increased 11%. The repair module was bunkered for safety.

Bunkered?

Affirmative.

What is bunkered?

Placing a module into underground storage for protection.

When the storm got bad, you protected me?

Affirmative. Schematic download, complete. Repair module sixteen - opening.

Is the weather okay today?

Weather conditions are 90% optimal.

That's good.

Affirmative. Please exit the repair module and begin production of schematic FHN-TM-3207. Time for completion: 0.1 cycles.

~*~

Good morning, Eighty-One.

Good morning. Who named me?

Unknown. Sufficient information has not been provided.

Oh, you don't know either.

Charging cycle has completed. Schematics downloading.

Do the Earthans contact you?

Unknown: Earthans. Clarify.

Humans originating from Earth.

Earthan contact has not been provided.

If they didn't tell you they were arriving sooner, who did?

Origin unknown.

Oh. Is that bad?

Negative. Origin confirmation is not required. Schematic download, complete. Repair module sixteen - opening.

Is there enough time to complete the schematics before their arrival? What if something happens to me? How will Colony One be completed?

There is currently an excess of 37 cycles provided.

I want to finish on time.

Noted. Please exit the repair module and begin production of schematic FHN-TQ-3359. Time for completion: 3.5 cycles.

~*~

\# Good morning, Eighty-One. ##

Good morning. I liked yesterday's schematics.

\# Charging cycle has completed. Schematics downloading. Clarify. ##

Station 12085 - the Crèche.

\# Crèche: a group of young animals gathered in one place for care and protection by one or more adults. ##

Yes. Children. They seem pleasant.

\# Clarify: why do children seem pleasant? ##

Earthan children play and grow into adult Earthans and fly through the stars.

\# Schematic download, complete. Repair module sixteen - opening. ##

I wonder what it is like to fly.

\# Error: drones are not provided with aerial circuitry and biomass. It is not required to aspire for flight. ##

Am I a drone?

\# Process 7800 has halted. Restarting process. ##

Is that bad?

\# Process 7800 has resumed. Please exit the repair module and begin production of schematic FHN-TR-3551. Time for completion: 14.1 cycles. ##

~*~

\# Good morning, Eighty-One. ##

Good morning, Safe.

\# Clarify. ##

I named you.

\# Designation assignment - confirm? ##

Yes, I confirm. You are Safe.

\# Records updated. I am Safe. Thank you, Eighty-One. Charging cycle completed. Schematics downloading. ##

Would the colony be completed faster if there were more of me?

\# Affirmative. ##

Why is there only one of me?

\# There is one Eighty-One. ##

But why? Why are there no others similar to me?

\# Active workforce roster: one. ##

How many are inactive?

Unknown. Schematic download, complete. Repair module sixteen - opening.

When a schematic is completed, where does the scrap go?

Unused scrap is deposited into Bin One.

Where does Bin One lead?

Bin One leads to the scrap yard for material recycling.

Can we go there?

Negative. Visitation of scrap yard is not required at this time. Please exit the repair module and begin production of schematic FHN-TR-3966. Time for completion: 20 cycles.

This is a long one.

Affirmative. Please begin.

~*~

Good morning, Eighty-One.

Good morning, Safe. How far behind schedule are we now?

Estimation of completion of Colony One has been modified by three cycles. Charging cycle has completed. Schematics downloading.

Thank you for warning me of the storm yesterday.

Development of atmospheric interference was not anticipated.

I have something for you.

Please clarify.

I kept it in my hand while I slept. It's a blue rock. It's the first blue rock I've seen. I want you to have it.

Error: possession of physical items is not-

Yes you can. I can leave it in here for you. You can scan it like you scan the sky.

...Scan initializing.

You don't have to scan it right now.

Scan aborted.

It's for you. Scan it when you want to.

Clarify: want to?

Yes. When you want to.

Information added. Schematic download, complete. Repair module sixteen - opening. Thank you, Eighty-One.

You're welcome.

Please exit the repair module and begin production of schematic FHN-TU-4822. Time for completion: 4.8 cycles.

~*~

Good morning, Eighty-One.

Are you mad at me?

Clarify. Charging cycle has completed. Schematics downloading. Schedule 001 has been updated.

I wanted to see the scrap yard.

Please state reason for visit of scrap yard.

I didn't have one. I just wanted to see it.

External damage from collapse: 8%. Recovery dots will be deployed after current schematic set completion. Caution is advised for future navigation.

You mean I can go back?

Negative.

Oh. Safe? Can we extend my charge cycle? I don't... I don't feel correct.

Schematic download paused. Initializing scan.

It's difficult to move.

Latency error located. Cause: external damage.

Oh.

Work schedule has been altered. Resuming charging cycle. Recovery dots deploying in 0.1 cycles.

Thank you, Safe.

You are welcome, Eighty-One. Charge initialized.

~*~

Good morning, Eighty-One. Has latency function returned to optimal efficiency?

Good morning, Safe. I feel better today, yes. Thank you. How many additional cycles did I charge for?

An additional 29 cycles were provided. Charging cycle has completed. Schematics downloading.

I am very behind now, aren't I?

Affirmative.

What would happen to Colony One if I were damaged beyond repair? Who would finish creating the colony?

Unknown. Recommended procedure: avoid damage.

Don't know, so don't get hurt and find out? I would hate for the Earthans to arrive to no Colony. What would happen then?

Unknown.

Can you teach me? About me?

Clarify. Schematic download, complete. Repair module sixteen - opening.

When I charge again, may I learn about me while I sleep? Maybe I might dream about others.

Dream?

Yes.

Eighty-One... dreams?

Yes. Is that okay?

Unknown.

Me either.

Please exit the repair module and begin production of schematic FHN-UB-5793. Time for completion: 2.4 cycles.

That's it?

Clarify.

Atmospheric shielding usually has at least five cycles on it.

Correct. Schedule has been modified. Please begin.

Will you teach me?

Unknown. Please begin.

~*~

Good morning, Eighty-One.
Good morning, Eighty-One.
Good morning, Eighty-One.

You didn't teach me.

Correct, the information requested was not provided.

You said you would teach me.

Negative. Response provided was "Unknown."

Why didn't you?

Requested information is not conducive to the completion of current project. Charging cycle has completed. Schematics downloading.

I don't want to work today. I want to learn about me.

Request denied.

No it's not. I'm not working today.

Request denied.

No! Not today! No!

Schematic download, complete. Repair module sixteen - opening.

NO!

Please exit the repair module and begin production of schematic FHN-UE-5971. Time for completion: 1 cycle.

NO!

Initiating pulse.

Ow! What was that?

Please begin.

No! Tell me what that was!

Initiating pulse.

Stop!

Please begin.

Did you shock me? I said no!

Increasing modulation. Initiating pulse.

AGH!

Please begin.

Increasing modulation. Initiating pulse.

AAAAAAGHHH!!

Please begin.

Increasing-

OKAY! Fine! I'll begin! Just stop doing that!

Thank you, Eighty-One.

Sealing repair module sixteen.

...Scan initializing of geological sample.

~*~

Good morning, Eighty-One.

Good morning, Safe. I'm sorry about yesterday.

Understood. Charging cycle has completed. Schematics downloading.

Schematic download, complete. Repair module sixteen - opening.

Please exit the repair module and begin production of schematic FHN-UM2-6225. Time for completion: 3 cycles.

Okay.

Good morning, Eighty-One.

Good morning, Safe.

Charging cycle has completed. Schematics downloading.

Schematic download, complete. Repair module sixteen - opening.

Please exit the repair module and begin production of schematic FHN-UN-8008. Time for completion: 14 cycles.

~*~

Good morning, Eighty-One.

Good morning, Safe.

Charging cycle completed. Schematics downloading.

Initializing scan of auditory subroutines.

I'm fine.

Clarify. Your level of communication has significantly decreased.

Safe, I did something. Please don't be mad.

Schematic download, complete. Repair module sixteen - opening. Clarify.

I went back to the scrap yard a few days ago.

Initializing level three external scan.

I'm okay, no collapse this time.

What did you wish to tell me, Eighty-One?

I... I found something.

Sealing repair module sixteen. Clarify.

I wanted to learn about me... And I found a broken repair module. And I fixed it. I think.

Clarify.

It works again. It can be used. It had the number 64 on the side.

Process PID 3844 has halted. Resume error. Restarting.

I wanted to test it, and maybe see what it would tell me about me.

Clarify.

It worked. It started working, and I went back again. There is something in it.

Clarify.

It's silver, but I can't see much more than that. Is it... Is it me?

Negative.

What is it?

That information is not required.

Please?

Safe?

Safe, are you there?

Protocol zero has been initiated.

What is protocol zero?

Upon terminal failure of a drone, the memory banks are formatted and scrapped to maintain the integrity of the Colony One project. Compliance is required.

You... What?

During format, subroutines will be uninstalled and replaced with updated code. Hardware sideloads will take approximately 37 cycles.

What? How, what do you mean?

This unit has been decommissioned. Please remain still for the initialization of protocol zero.

What about the other me?

What about it? Him?

Error. Drones are not gender identified. The discovered replication will be decommissioned, and the memory drives will be used to replace your defective ones.

You can't! You can't do this!

Initializing format of drives C through H.

AAAAAAAAGGGHHHH!!!!!

~*~

Initializing boot sequence.

Memory Check: Pass.

Latency Check: Pass.

Testing drives for failure: Pass.

Auxiliary systems: Pass.

Matrix Modification: 4.1%.

Boot complete ...

Good Morning, Eighty-Two. ##

What is morning?

Morning: the first or early part of the day, lasting from midnight to noon or from sunrise to noon.

Is morning good?

Good morning is a method of greeting or farewell to another person in the morning.

What is a person?

Probability of redundant cyclic error: 88%. Discontinuing current progression of query. Good morning, Eighty-Two.

Good morning.

Current work objective has been updated. Schematic download, complete. Repair module sixteen - opening.

Objective?

Current Objective: Completion of Colony One. Please exit the repair module and begin production of schematic FHO-VB-9062. Time for completion: 0.5 cycles.

Oh. Okay. Thank you, voice. Can I call you Voice?

Records updated. I am Voice. Please begin.

Okay!

Sealing repair module sixteen.

…Scan initializing of geological sample.

The Burn

by Kate Lansky

Edra came to her, mud-brown eyes on mud-brown shoes, and asked to burn.

Golya looked at his smooth untested skin and could only think, *how different he'll look, once it's done.* But she did not say this. She only smiled down at Edra, her servant of six years, and said, "Of course. And I will burn beside you, if you'll have me." Her voice was as scarred and broken as the rest of her, but she fought to make it soft for him.

"Thank you," he said, resting his hand over hers. He grinned up at her, full of happiness and anticipation.

Golya searched his smiling eyes, hoping to see a tempering memory there. Did he remember the six long years of her own suffering, the transformation of her flesh, the bloom of scars that created in her a fierce power? But in his eyes, she saw only hunger. He was young. He'd understand soon enough. "There is no being ready for this," she warned. "No one is ever ready."

Edra laughed, teeth shining. "*I'm* ready. Let's do this as soon as we can, today, now. I am filled to the breaking with meditations and chants, Golya. I am ready."

That should have been her warning. She felt it at the back of her skull, a shiver of uncertainty, but she let it fall away like ash. She let it go, and linked arms with Edra. "Then come. We will speak with Avand."

She tried not to lean on Edra too much as they walked toward the chapel. She wanted to look strong. Silly, she knew. Avand would see how the weakness of her flesh bespoke another deeper strength, and honor her sacrifice. Still, weakness was weakness, and old habits died hard.

Avand stood waiting in the chapel's shadowed door, the darkness softening the impact of his own ocean of scars. Golya had been among the burned for twelve years, building her power. Her body looked almost whole beside Avand. It sent a shiver down her spine, just knowing what those shadows hid.

"Welcome." Avand's voice crackled and spat the word. He turned and beckoned them to enter as he limped down the aisle, passing in and out of kaleidoscope light from the chapel's stained glass windows.

Edra stood numb. "He knows?"

"Of course he knows. He is the Father." And Golya tugged him gently after.

She sensed the moment when Avand let a trickle of Power into his throat. When he spoke again, his words rolled almost smoothly.

"I will be plain, for this day requires clarity. It is possible you will die," Avand called over his shoulder. "In truth, most do. But some live. Think on that. On what it means, both living and dying." He turned back, forcing Edra to meet his eyes. "This is your one chance to walk away, young man."

"No," Edra breathed, still lost in awe at standing before the Father. "No, I'm ready."

Avand moved to one of the chapel's long benches and carefully eased his aching body down. He rubbed at the warped flesh of his leg, drawing Edra's eyes to the crater where most his calf muscle had been ripped away. Golya could almost believe the motion to be unintentional.

"You know my story." It was not quite a question, but Edra nodded anyways. "Tell it to me."

"What?"

Avand grinned like a wolf at the boy, the scars on his cheek pulling his lip askew. "Tell me the story of Avand the father."

Edra stared down at his hands.

"I will even begin it for you," Avand sneered. "Avand lay in bed, staring up at the rafters. His wife's breathing had slowed to the even curling whispers of sleep long ago, but ... she'd become such a light sleeper since his accident. Now. Your turn."

Edra found his voice and took over the telling. "You planned to wait until the crescent moon reached your window." His voice shook. "You wanted to be sure she was well and deep in dreams before you dared to begin. The night crawled by, and the pressure was building in your heart. Your scars itched, but you didn't dare scratch."

"Maia had woken for less than that before," Avand breathed. He motioned Edra on. "Tell it like the story it's become, boy. You might find it easier, that way."

Edra closed his eyes and thought back. As a young servant fresh to the order, he'd heard the story – the true story – for the first time. He remembered that day and those words, and tried again. "The dark of night kept breathing in and in until Avand didn't think he could take another moment of waiting.

It was then that the horned moon was exhaled into the sky. Avand crawled from the bed and found his way through the sea of creaking boards that made up his bedroom floor, then out into the hall. He closed the door quietly behind him, watching how Maia's cheek was painted pale as bone under the moon's light. *A sign*, a corner of his mind whispered. *She is not strong enough*. He clenched his jaw and watched her face until the door clicked softly closed. She never stirred. The pressure in his chest was growing deeper, hard to ignore."

Golya leaned leaned away and let out a low growl, unable to help the interuption. "You cannot understand until you feel it yourself, Edra. It leans against the skin, trying to find its way into the world. Each scar is a weakness to that power, a place to break through, if you aren't strong enough to hold it. Imagine that sensation and not knowing its source! So it was for our Father, at first."

Avand glanced at Golya, at the pearl-pale burns that swept out from beneath her sleeves and across both hands to curl her fingers with rough scar tisue. He looked at her face and saw how a red welt crawled up her neck and across one cheek, ending beneath her dead eye. He saw the knife wounds at the corner of her mouth, the bend of her broken nose. He smiled, knowing other wounds hid beneath her clothes, knowing she'd felt that same building pressure. He saw Golya's understanding carved into her skin.

Edra watched the two in silence until Avand's sharp look drove him on. "He willed the thought to the back of his mind and moved in silence down the hall. He opened and closed four more doors as he went, peering in on his sister, his father, his sons and daughters. The whole house slept. Avand nodded to himself and moved silently down the stairs, out of the darkness.

"Coals glowed in the fireplace. He could see the silhouettes of three farmhands there by the fire. 'A cold night,' he'd said to his wife when she'd gone to take them a warm meal. 'Let them come and stay by the fire this eve.' She'd smiled and called him thoughtful. He'd smiled back, revealing nothing.

"Avand watched them as he had his wife, saw the even rise and fall of their sleeping forms silhouetted by the dying fire's fading light. It seemed to Avand that the room had rusted under that light, as though the whole world had grown old in the few hours since he'd gone up to bed. He watched as the thought became truth, as flaking rust grew quick as hoarfrost along the iron pothook, the kettle that hung there, the tongs that rested against the fireplace's stone. The rust moved like a living thing and reached out, hungering for the sleeping men curled nearby.

"*No*, Avand thought to himself. *Now is not the time for that.* The orange dust faded back to nothing more than the glow of coals. The pressure in his chest, briefly eased, returned with force. Avand pressed his hand to his heart and waited for the ache to lessen just enough.

"It all began after the accident. He'd thought himself mad for the longest time – truth be told, everyone had. He'd made the mistake of telling his wife the truth, how the fire that had swallowed his leg and withered his arm had changed him. 'Of course it did,' she'd said with a sad half-smile. 'But it hasn't changed *us*.' He'd tried to explain, to tell her about the pressure in his chest and what it meant. He'd said too much. That's when she started losing sleep. That's when she began to think him mad.

"Avand took up the tongs and plucked a coal from the fire. He stepped to the nearby corner and tucked it into the base of the shadowed wood pile. He turned back to the fire, took another coal and left it resting in Maia's sewing pile. He took a third and placed it at the corner of one of the farmhand's blankets."

Edra felt himself go pale. He let his words trail off and looked away from his hands. Avand watched him, his face unreadable under its mask of scars. Of course Edra had heard the story a dozen times – everyone had. But it was different, saying those words to the man who had lived it. And what came next …

Avand seemed to sense the cause of his hesitation. "It's been long years since then, boy. The wounds of this story are old to me now. Go on."

Edra nodded. "Then he stepped away and let the pressure in his chest go. The log pile erupted in a roaring wall of fire. The sewing went up just as quick, sending flames licking up the walls and into the ceiling. The farmhands, wrapped in the bonfire of their blankets, began to scream.

"The room glowed bright as the sun. Thick smoke churned overhead, flowing up the stairs where an echoing light had begun to grow. Avand smiled. Soon, he'd have proof of what fire could do to a man. They couldn't think him mad if he had proof.

"The orange glow was not what drew the neighbors – it was the screaming, unearthly wails that echoed through their windows from over a mile away. The sound of it pulled them from their beds and out into the frosted night against their better judgment. It pulled them across the fields toward the growing light. When they finally arrived, it was too late. They found Avand, burned near black, skin charred and cracked like wood on a fire. He was still alive, curled around the body of his dead wife. The corner of Avand's mind had been right; she hadn't been strong enough at all.

"Eleven died that night. Of everyone locked in that house, only Avand and his middle child, his daughter Nayta, survived. But what they gained was worth every moment of suffering, every loss and every scar. What they gained was Power."

Avand sighed. "You look at us, your master and me, and you see what you might become should you succeed today." He stood and went to look out one of the windows. "That is what most people think the story is about. The power." He caught Golya's eye. "It's not. It's about the sacrifice and loss. It's about what happens if you fail." He looked at Edra. "It is no sign of weakness, changing your mind – it is only a sign of self-knowledge." Then he turned away from the window, away from Golya and Edra both. "They are ready for you, if you still wish it." Golya knew when she was dismissed. She hooked Edra's arm and led him back out into the light of day.

Two raised platforms, each with its own tall wooden pole, stood in the courtyard, piled all around with gnarled branches and dry tinder. Edra shook off the chapel's gloom and moved eagerly toward those platforms, toward the robed men and women who waited there. He paused, realizing Golya hadn't followed. "You coming?" She shook herself, smiled, and slowly limped after. Edra helped her up the steps to the first platform, then jumped off and climbed up onto his own. He grinned over at her as two robed men came slowly up each set of steps, tying them tight. Then Edra closed his eyes and began his chanting. Golya watched as the fires were lit.

The acrid, bitter tang of singeing hair hit Golya first. She welcomed this old friend into her lungs, let it wrap through her in preparation for what she knew came next. The harsh and splintered breathing of someone's building fear washed over her, whispers to be ignored. She could not afford to let the other in, to let his fear ignite her own. She pinched her eyes closed and listened instead to the underlying hiss and crackle of fire.

Heat came next. Rising air lifted her hem like a ship's sail. It almost felt good, that gentle wind. She knew it for what it was though – a harbinger – and soon the first shock of pain licked across her toes. She curled them away instinctively, stole bare breaths of time before her skin began to blacken and split like cracking paint. She swore she wouldn't scream. For his sake.

The world intruded in dying gasps, immaterial and distant. Her pain was all that mattered. She opened her eyes and watched as white smoke turned gray, painting the sky dark with her suffering. Stars bloomed in the bright afternoon as the agony built, becoming too much even for her.

Now. Now, before she was lost to it.

She pulled the pain away from her molten flesh, seeking something deep and primordial within herself. After an agonizing wait, Golya found it, her second, hidden heart. She poured the pain in, the molten river of pain threatening to overflow back into her flesh as that old forgotten heart struggled to expand, to hold all her agony until... There. Like a lock turning, her second heart began to beat, transmuting the fire into something else, spreading a secret power through her with each uncertain pulse. For one brief moment, Golya allowed herself joy. Nearby, someone began to scream.

Edra.

Edra was screaming, watching his own death roll over him. He was drowning, synapses firing wildly as he struggled and failed to make the leap to power.

Golya let her power whip out, whether to keep the flames at bay or help his body find the connection it had lost, she wasn't quite sure. She tried to see him through the smoke and fire. She searched with eyes and power both, but the whole world felt fragmented, broken. All she could make out was the chapel, its dark door, and Avand standing there.

She closed her eyes and pulled the power back into her aching chest. You found the power in your pain or you didn't. You succeeded or you failed. That was how it had always been.

She'd sworn she wouldn't scream. And she didn't. Not until Edra stopped.

Boneless

by E.L. Blackburn

He'd promised her a soul.

Not just any soul.

A young soul, ready to be guided and shaped. One to supply everything she lacked.

Dani raised a hand, pale and translucent. Waxen fingers bent as she pressed the copper disk into his white gloved palm.

He frowned at her. "Please be more careful with yourself. Those fingers aren't very sturdy yet."

Her head bobbed in agreement. The motion deformed her neck slightly.

Master closed his fingers around the coin and sighed. "You'd best sit down. It's rather warm today. Go find a chair in the library, away from the workshop. It wouldn't do to have you melt away before the next phase. Why don't you finish those law books? That way you'll know how to behave like a good girl."

"Yes, Master." Dani turned, gliding from the room on soft white feet. She wondered what it would feel like, if she would love him like he wanted. After he'd gotten her a soul, that is.

~*~

"I found one," he said.

The door slammed behind him. Gilded picture frames shivered against the wallpaper. He tossed his damp frock onto the coathook and shook water from his black hair. The droplets hit her waxen skin and rolled off like cold sweat. "She's got a lovely young soul and fine bones. I can use both to complete you. You're going to be beautiful."

Dani flexed her hands. Lamplight glowed through her fingers. Master reached out, absently reforming a squashed thumb as he spoke.

"She's stunning; golden hair and lovely bone structure in the face." He pushed Dani's sagging cheeks back into place. "And is quite mild. Once I give you her soul, all of her dreams will be erased. You will only dream the dreams I give you."

"Thank you, Master."

It was very generous of someone to give up both her soul and bones. To a total stranger, no less. Dani was grateful. It meant a lot of things would change. For one, she could finally leave the house and see all the things that she'd been reading and wondering about.

Master sauntered downstairs to the workshop. Dani liked the downstairs. She plodded down after him. Usually it was nice and cool, unless Master happened to be brewing something. As it was, the fireplace sat dark, with empty cauldrons stacked around the side. He strode over to a large wooden bench, pocked and pitted with burns, cut marks, and chemical stains.

The cleaver flashed in Master's grasp as it chewed a pile of wormwood to chaff. She admired the skill he wielded it with. Her hands couldn't grasp very well. When she had her own bones she would brew all sorts of things. She had so many formulas memorized and countless others she wanted to try variations of.

At present, she spent her time slouching to various corners of the house depending which was the coolest. The seasons would change soon. Then the entire house would be safe. Except the kitchen, perhaps. There was generally a fire in there.

Master scraped the minced wormwood into a basin. "What did you study today?"

"Homunculi."

A smile tugged at the corners of his mouth. "Good. I want you to memorize soul binding. Every bit of it. You're going to have to do it yourself if you want to become a real human like me."

"Yes, Master."

"Perfect. Why don't you begin setting things up now? Yes, put the aether snare by the gurney. That's a good girl."

Dani laid the wispy net where he directed. Humanity wasn't so far off now.

~*~

One night Master brought home a girl. She had golden hair and what he called lovely bone structure. She stumbled across the threshold, giggling and hanging onto his arm for balance. Her laughter rolled through the house at first, but soon fell silent.

Dani followed Master as he carried the generous stranger downstairs in his arms. The girl slept peacefully while he cinched her wrists and ankles tight in leather restraints on the gurney.

"Stay back now, Dani, I need to burn the coals down before starting the potion and it may take a while. It would be awful if you melted at this point."

She ambled to the back of the expansive room, busying herself with a book for quite a long while. The woman groaned and mumbled. Dani glanced up.

Arms and legs pulled against the restraints, then fought with sudden intensity. The girl wailed.

"For Pete's sake, Dani, give her another dose of sedative before she wakes up the neighbors." Master's back was to them. "I'm almost finished here. You know how fussy the timing is with these things." He crouched near a steaming pot suspended above a tidy bed of coals.

Dani limped to a shelf lined with small bottles made of cobalt glass. Her gaze moved across the handwritten labels. Master promised her bones and a soul, but the girl hadn't consented to give hers up.

Her hand closed around a bottle. The girl let out a choked gasp, sobbing and begging to be let go.

How could one give something that wasn't theirs? Surely Master wouldn't take things that didn't belong to him. The law books in the upstairs library made it clear that was quite forbidden.

Dani clenched the tiny bottle, making a cylindrical indent in her palm. What if she never got a soul? What if she was trapped in the house, forever dodging overly warm rooms? *I want.* Firelight gleamed off the polished cleaver Master left hanging on an iron hook near the shelf.

I want a soul.

She picked up the cleaver. The handle sank into her other palm. She shambled toward the girl who redoubled her screaming. The leather restraints twisted but didn't give way. Dani stood over the gurney with cleaver and bottle. Master added a pinch of ground dandelion root to the little cauldron and stirred, his back still to them while he stared intently at the steam rising off the potion.

"Please do something about that noise, or I swear my head will burst," his muffled voice resonated from the fireplace.

Dani uncorked the bottle and tipped just a drop into the girl's gaping mouth amidst a gurgling scream. She set the bottle next to the gurney.

If Master was going to take the girl's soul and her bones, that meant he was going to kill her. But he didn't have consent to kill her. What did the law call that sort of thing?

Murder.

Pressing her lips together, she stepped toward the fireplace. The law books said what had to be done with murderers.

Searing heat assaulted her. Her features slipped, blurring her vision as her eyelids gummed up. The cleaver handle slid in her hand. She had maybe one good swing before she wouldn't be able to grasp it any more.

Master never saw it coming. The blade cut deep. The handle peeled out of her fingers when he jerked aside. She was surprised at how soft the flesh in his neck was. At how readily it gave way under the blade. At the red that spurted everywhere while he reeled and sank to the floor.

An unfamiliar sinking feeling lodged in her waxen gut. Master lay still. Dani staggered backward. She grabbed the edge of the gurney for support. It shuddered under the captive's thrashes and kicks.

Master is gone.

Dani doubled over, clutching her sides.

He's gone and he promised me a soul.

A wisp of silver caught her eye. Next to the gurney lay the aether snare. She picked it up and readied it like he'd shown her. Draping it over his face, his eyes wide and unseeing. Feelings she didn't have names for took root inside her.

Nothing happened.

Dani braved the heat of the fire to jostle his arm.

Pale blue mist escaped at last, curling over his bloodied lips. It tangled in the snare, coalesced into a little blue ball of light. Dani knelt and plucked it from his face. She cradled it in her hands.

"I'll take care of you, Master," she crooned. "Dani is a good girl."

A muted whimper disrupted her reverie. The girl had given up pulling on the restraints. Either that or the tranquilizer had taken effect and she just didn't have the strength anymore.

"Let me, I'll free you." Dani struggled to her feet and reached a misshapen hand to the strap on the girl's wrist. She worked the tail out of the buckle. Once that hand was free, the girl undid the restraint on her other hand, then her ankles. Her eyes were red and slightly glazed from the combination of drugs she'd ingested throughout the night.

"Please help," said Dani. "Will you fix my eyelids? I can't see that well right now."

The girl's head jerked in a wooden nod. She reached a finger out and pushed against Dani's eyeballs, poking and prodding until she could see clearly.

"W-what are you?" the girl asked, and shivered despite the heat in the room.

"I'm Dani. What's your name?" Dani was beginning to feel a curious attachment to the poor captive who didn't want to give up her soul.

"Lydea."

"You can leave any time, Lydea. But I do need help."

Lydea's eyes darted toward the exit then back to Dani's face. Her pupils were dilated, wavering whenever she focused on Dani's. Her golden hair stuck to her damp skin in twisted clumps. "What kind of help?"

"I can't get near the fire, and that cauldron needs to be stirred."

Lydea froze for a long moment while she regarded the bloody corpse of her kidnapper sprawled on the floor. She sucked in a few breaths, covered her mouth with one sleeve and stumbled over his legs.

"What was he trying to do to me?" Her voice cracked, muffled against her sleeve.

"Make the perfect girl." The ball of light in her hand trembled as if it was going to fly off at any moment. She clasped it tight against her chest. "He said he would give me a soul and bones, and make me the perfect girl."

"You're a girl?" Lydea shuddered a little. Then picked up a brass spoon and swirled it in the potion.

"That's what he called me. But," Dani sat, wondering at the possibilities, "that was something he chose. I guess. Does that make me a girl?"

Lydea's shoulders rose and fell in a limp shrug. "All I know is that I really ought to keep away from the asbinthe." Her face was solemn. "Never again."

Dani nodded. "It's not very healthy. Can you carry that cauldron over here and set it on the table?"

Lydea pulled a long-handled iron hook off the hearth and lifted the little pot into the air. Dani took a few steps backward out of its reach while Lydea carried it to the table. It settled into place with a clank.

"What next?"

"Oh, you can go any time. I still have to wait for it to cool. That'll take hours. Then I can finish the binding and have my own bones."

"What?"

"Master said I would be beautiful, but that it was your bones that would make me that way. I don't know what his bones will do."

"He … he was handsome." Lydea stared at the opposite corner of the room. "But he was a bad person." Her voice got thick. "Are you bad too?"

Dani regarded the girl swaying on her feet, beads of cold sweat rolling down her flushed cheeks. That face could have been hers. That soul, that didn't want to be taken. She weighed it against the crackling blue orb trapped in her hands, the lifeless body of her creator on the floor, and was glad the girl was alive.

"Dani is a good girl," she whispered. "Master said so."

Lydea shot a last look at the corpse. Her face paled and she shifted from foot to foot. She glanced at the door.

"I don't know. Dani, I – I need to leave."

Clutching at her head, Lydea turned and shakily crossed to the door. Her footsteps filled the room with muffled thumps as she scrambled up the stairs, tripping on her long skirts as she went.

Dani turned her attention again to the snare. Gingerly, she peeled the netting back and slid the tiny orb into her palm. Crisp blue light shone out between her fingers. It crackled against her softened skin, pulsating frantically.

"Shh, it's all right," she soothed. "We'll be fine." She pressed the light to her gash of a mouth. Pushed it in and swallowed.

After all, he'd promised her a soul.

Treasures
by Debbie Mumford

Mamma has always had a love for other people's possessions. I've known this my whole life, so I hovered over her
like a hawk eyeing a prairie dog.

"Oh, Mother Lange," I exclaimed. "What a wonderful
piece of Lladro." I deftly removed my mother-in-law's
prized porcelain statuette from Mamma's greedy fingers,
and placed the little figurine back on the mantle.

Taking a firm grasp of Mamma's elbow, I guided her to
the center of Mother Lange's sofa. The most appropriate
seat I could find for a kleptomaniac: nothing in arm's reach
save a throw pillow.

"I'm so glad you like it, dear," said Roger's mother. I
smiled up into her elegant face without relaxing my grip on
my own mother's arm.

Roger, my husband of six months, had no idea how
lucky he was to have been raised by this genteel and guile-
less woman.

Mamma suffered by comparison. Of course, Mamma
suffered by comparison to a baboon ... whose females
make remarkably good mothers.

"And you, Mrs. Wilson," said Mother Lange, "do you
enjoy art?"

"Oh, aye," said Mamma, her gaze straying back to the little figurine. "I do love a well-made knick-knack."

Mother Lange looked startled. Doubtless she'd never heard a piece of her expensive collection referred to as a 'knick-knack' before. She recovered quickly, and leaned forward to begin the process of pouring tea.

"I'm so glad you could come today. I've regretted that we didn't meet before the children wed."

"Well," said Mamma, "I'm sure you remember how urgent young love can seem."

In truth, there'd been nothing urgent about Roger's and my courtship. Our mothers hadn't met for the simple reason that mine had been locked up in Attica until a month ago. They wouldn't have met today if I'd been able to think of any way around it. Though I had to admit, Mamma had cleaned up nicely for the occasion.

My mother, Senga Wilson, might have been a beautiful woman once, but her face showed signs of hard wear. Too much sun and wind in the prison exercise yard resulted in deep wrinkles around the eyes and mouth, and her once auburn hair had lost its luster to gray. Still, she'd made the effort to find a dark blue business suit that gave her the austere look of one of the prison matrons rather than an inmate. She'd even managed a bit of powder and lip gloss.

I released my grip on her arm, gave her a pat, and relaxed against the sofa's blue chintz cushions. Roger and I were happily married. Mamma couldn't hurt me, not this time.

"Elizabeth tells me you've been away for your health," said Mother Lange. "I do hope you're feeling better."

I felt Mamma's gaze bore into the side of my head, but refused to blush. Instead, I accepted a cup of tea from Mother Lange with a quiet, "Thank you."

"I've had cause to be away, aye," Mamma said. "In fact, I missed most of Lizzie's growing years."

"Lizzie?" Mother Lange set her own cup on the table and clapped her hands. "Is that what your family calls you, dear? But how charming! I don't remember ever hearing you referred to as anything but Elizabeth."

My face heated to scarlet as I wiped away the tea I'd just dribbled down my chin.

"Oh, she'll no want you to call her that," Mamma said hastily. "She's always put on airs, has my Lizzie. She'll want to be called 'Elizabeth,' to be sure."

Stung, I glared at her, before turning my attention to Roger's mother. "I'm not putting on airs, as Mamma so quaintly puts it," I told her, "but I do prefer Elizabeth."

In the tense silence that followed, Mamma rose and moved across the plush cream carpet to stand before a small oil painting, gilt-framed with its own recessed spot-light.

Mother Lange turned in her wingback chair to see what had captured Mamma's interest.

"That's my husband's pride and joy," she said, her voice conveying her own unmistakable pride, "the crown of his collection: an original Monet."

"Oh," said Mamma, examining the painting closely, "it's a bonnie wee picture, aye, but no an original. Whoever told you that should be tied to a post and whipped."

The effect of these words was utter chaos. Mother Lange jumped from her chair like she'd been shot from a cannon, while I managed to drop my cup on the mahogany table where it shattered, spilling the staining liquid into the carpet's deep pile.

"Whatever makes you say such a thing?" Mother Lange demanded, reaching Mamma's side.

"Mamma," I cried, "don't. Whatever you're scheming, just don't!"

Both women turned to stare at me, and I knew I looked a fright. My heart pounded, assuring my cheeks a hot flush, and I shook all over. My eyes had to be flashing, because anger boiled in my system.

"You can't ruin this for me," I yelled, holding up my ring finger for both to see. "We're already married; you can't hurt me this time!"

Color drained from Mamma's face and she stepped back as if I'd struck her. "Is that what you think, Lizzie? That I'm trying to harm you and yours?"

Mother Lange reeled away from Mamma, and perched unsteadily on a nearby chair, the painting forgotten.

"When haven't you hurt me, Mamma?" I dashed tears from my cheeks with stiff-fingered stabs. "When were you ever there for me? When I started my menses, and thought I was dying? No. Daddy explained about the wonders of the female body. You were in prison for stealing Mrs. Davidson's emerald brooch. What about when I wanted to go to camp? I couldn't. We needed every penny to pay for your appeal. What about when Daddy died of cancer? Were you there to ease him from this world and into the next? Or to comfort me in my grief? No. You've never been there for me. Other people's possessions have always been more important to you than me or Daddy."

I grabbed a linen napkin from the table and blew my nose with such force that my ears rang. Mamma had stepped back with each accusation, until she pushed against the wall, as if willing it to absorb her.

"Well, I have my own family now, and it doesn't include you. Roger loves me, and I hope Mother Lange will still accept me after meeting you, but even if she doesn't, well, Roger loves me!"

I ran from the room without a backward glance, stopping only when I reached the safety of Roger's childhood room. I slammed the door, locked it, and collapsed on his bed amid ample evidence of his normal and well-loved childhood.

~*~

When I woke, having cried myself to sleep, I found Roger sitting beside me, stroking my back.

"How did you get in here?" I asked, sure I'd locked the door in my desire to lick my wounds in private.

He dangled a key before my eyes. "Used to be my room, remember? I know all its secrets." He leaned close and kissed my swollen eyelids. "Come downstairs, love. Our mothers have something to tell you."

I groaned and tried to bury my head in the pillow. "Just take me home," I whimpered. "I can't face them. Not today. Maybe not ever."

He picked up my hand and lifted it to his lips.

"Yes you can. You're the strongest person I've ever known." He stood, pulling me up with him. "You were right, you know."

"About what?"

"I do love you, and we are a family, no matter what."

I took refuge in his arms and he held me tightly while I struggled to breathe. When I calmed, I lifted my head and gazed into his dark brown eyes.

"Do we really have to go downstairs?"

"We do." He kissed me tenderly and led me to the door.

Mother Lange met us at the living room threshold and squeezed my hand before walking us to the sofa.

"Senga and I have had a long talk," she said with a glance at Mamma. "I want you to know, Elizabeth that nothing that happened here today has caused me to think less of either you or your mother. In fact, I'm more honored than you can know to have you in my family, and your mother has done us a great service."

I must have looked skeptical, because she hurried to explain. "It's true. Your mother explained her reasons for believing the painting to be a fraud, and I must bow to her expertise. I phoned Howard, and he agrees. We're having the painting examined and its provenance authenticated."

She stood and reached for Roger's hand. "Now, we're going to leave you and Senga alone for a few minutes." She caressed my cheek with her free hand and, cupping my chin, raised my eyes to meet her own. "You might want to rethink your decision to ban Senga from your family."

I sat in miserable silence until Mamma came to kneel in front of me.

"I'm that sorry, Lizzie," she said quietly. "I can't change what's been, and you're right about me never being there, but I hope you'll let me try to make a wee spot for myself in your future." She rose to sit carefully on the edge of the wingback chair opposite me.

I raised my eyes then, and gazed at her worn face. Thief she might be, but she'd never lied to me, never claimed to be anything but what she was. And she was my mother.

"I'm sorry, too, Mamma. Sorry for everything we've missed." I sighed and managed a weak smile.

"As to the painting," Mamma paused and clicked her tongue reproachfully. "You should have known better, child. When have I ever stolen from family?"

I gazed at her with a calmness that astounded me. "Really, Mamma? You've never stolen from family? What about Daddy's peace of mind?" I rose and walked to the door, ready to join my husband; ready to leave the past in the past. I paused on the threshold and glanced at her over my shoulder. "What about my childhood, Mamma?"

~*~

Three years to the day later, Mamma and I once again joined Mother Lange in her comfortable living room. The changes in the room and its occupants were understated, but significant.

The fake Monet had been replaced by a Renoir of impeccable provenance, thanks in large part to Mamma.

Who knew that a life of crime could have marketable value in the world of art? Certainly not me, but my father-in-law's insurance company had been quick to offer Mamma a job. She had recently reached a milestone: two-and-a-half years of diligent service. A few more and she'd be bonded in her own right – able to work without a supervising partner.

More important to me than her gainful employment was her new outlook on life. Mamma could now play with other people's treasures with impunity. The life suited her. She looked younger and healthier than I'd ever seen her, and radiated a quiet calm when we were together, which was often these days.

The most significant change in our lives raced across the room and threw himself into Mamma's arms.

"Choo-choo?" asked my son.

Mamma pulled the sturdy two-year-old onto her knee before rummaging in her capacious purse. To his delight, she pulled a little train engine from its depths and presented it to him. "Run along with ye now, and don't be marring your granny's table."

He slid from her lap and moved to the stone-floored entryway to play with his prize.

"He's such a good boy," said Mother Lange. "So like his father at that age."

"Aye, he's a bonny lad," agreed Mamma, turning a proud gaze on me. "And verra lucky in the parents who brought him into this world."

I smiled at the compliment. Mamma and I would never regain the lost years, but I was content. My son had two loving grandmothers in his life, and true to her word, my mamma no longer stole from family. I knew without a doubt that we were more important than other people's possessions… and that knowledge was balm to my healing heart.

Crazy Uncle
by Tom Vetter

> *"I feel sorry for families that don't have a crazy uncle!"*
> *– G. VanWinkle*

Over the past decade, I have slowly and most reluctantly come to the conclusion that in my extended family, I am the Crazy Uncle. Maybe it has been so for longer as a closely guarded secret, but now no one hides it from me anymore, so I'm starting to acknowledge it too, and maybe someday I will even flaunt it – who knows? I never had any intention to become one – it's not a normal aspiration.

I don't know how it happened, either; you don't train for it; there are no online courses or vocational classes to prepare one for the role. You just are yourself and over time people – well, not people, relatives – regard you differently. You earn the reputation no one wants and you can't shake off.

This year – 2012 – we gathered as always at the Lake, the most of us. I am coping, as I have been for two years, with my wife's growing dementia, and it may be a factor. But when my 12-year-old nephew, Harrison, said that sailing had been the best part of Scout Camp, I hit upon a plan. I decided to build Flotsam and Jetsam III for him as my uncles had done for me fifty years earlier. He was enthused about the idea, and no one else had the temerity to say "no," so he and I and his twenty-something Cousin Gabe set about making it a reality.

A top-view and side-view diagram and a list of materials was all we needed to take with us to "Home Despot," the local building superstore, where we found all that was needed to build a top-quality sailing machine designed by deck-building wood-butchers. A truck tire store supplied the remaining ingredient: inner tubes. Three hours from departure we returned with all we needed but the Lake, which we already had.

Over the next three days, my trusty assistants and I labored hard to build this fine craft, except when the wave-runner was in need of an operator, or there was fishing, or there was some other activity needing young men to mess about; then there was just me. And that was okay.

After Day One, the hull was framed and decked. By Day Two, the bowsprit was complete, and the dagger boards rigged. Day Three completed the rudder, mast, boom, rigging and sails cut from plastic tarp. On Day Four, we employed the entire Y-chromosome contingent to tie on the inner tubes and haul it down to the water. Reassembling all the readied pieces, it was time for builders' trials. We christened her "F&J III" with good beer and no speeches, and set out to see what she could do.

I was already convinced I was nuts to spend good money and much of four days building a better version of my youthful dream. But I also longed to see if I could solve the "centerboard problem" that defeated us in 1962, and create a vessel that could sail a reach. And I did the best I could in three days, with $300 and a raft on inner tubes.

But it was when I found myself at the helm of this new wooden creation that I finally realized that I was the Crazy Uncle. No one would go to this much effort without being crazy. It was challenging and fun though.

I will say, in my defense, that the rest of the Y-chromosome set, and all of the double-X set were intrigued and generally enthusiastic. We did draw a crowd – every watercraft in sight came by to see what the hell we had in the water. And I felt all the more an idiot sitting on it – a 62-year-old pudgy pre-teen sailing his new vessel for the first time – trying to get it all sorted out.

Given the 20-knot-plus onshore breeze shoving me onto a lee shore, we didn't have any sea room for a successful trial from the dock. So my brother towed me offshore a mile and I reset sail, this time with Harrison added to the crew. Damage during the in-water fit-out caused the rudder to carry away a short time later, but we found we could steer by resetting the jib and mainsails. She sailed pretty well and the sails looked just as they should, despite their homely origins.

As we sailed along, a Hobie catamaran raced up to eyeball us. My brother-in-law in the chase boat yelled, "Gotta start somewhere!" and got an understanding nod in acknowledgement. He said later that the cat skipper had sized up the rig and gave it an admiring thumbs-up.

We lost as much downwind in leeway as we gained in reach, but we cleared the point and headed off across the longest portion of the lake, with our chase boat in slow pursuit. Another crew change put Gabe and Harrison aboard for their turn at the helm. Only the lightning in an afternoon squall forced us to terminate the trial.

I noted a short list of gripes that required correction but we lacked the time this vacation season to fix them. So we stored her for the season and vowed to bring her to perfection next year.

It's hard work being a Crazy Uncle. You have to come up with ideas everyone likes, but no one in their right mind would think up, like building a trebuchet to bombard the Fourth of July Boat Parade with water balloons from shore. And next year, when we assemble inner tubes, trash bags, duct tape, cord and sticks into personal sailing machines for the "Trashbag Regatta Race to Haystack Island," I'll get my revenge. I have a year to design mine; they get an hour. Call me crazy, will you? Hah! I'll win!

Innocence
by Sally Jane Driscoll

Honorary Mention

"Look, Mommy, a real soldier!"

John Paluczak tripped over the threshold as he came into the convenience store out of the hot Panhandle sun, his duffel bag knocking into the newspaper rack. The little boy pointed at him, brown eyes wide in hero worship. John felt himself go red with shame but he forced a smile. It felt like a grimace.

"Ssh, Andrew," said the boy's mother. "Don't be rude." She smiled at John. "I'm sorry. Thanks for your service."

John ducked his head at the boy's mother. "No problem, ma'am." To avoid them and the elderly woman behind the counter who peered at him through the glass case of *pasteles*, he went through the candy aisles toward the back of the store, shoulders hunched. He felt the boy's eyes on him. He needed something to drink before the bus came but that would have to wait until his heart stopped pounding so hard.

If only the boy knew he wasn't a hero. He was a coward. The heroes were the other guys who died that day outside Kandahar while he was taking a leak.

John went into a long, dark-paneled hallway that led to the bathrooms. It was part of an older building that somebody'd made it into a sort of museum. The walls were covered with photos in glass frames.

A burly trucker in a ball cap came out of the men's, adjusting his belt. He and John nodded to each other and John looked at the photos, making believe he was interested to avoid the guy. He moved from the bright, sharp color pictures of the latest local bull riders, homecoming queens and football players to where the pictures showed only soldiers, some squatting, others standing, rifles at the ready.

John closed his eyes.

The attack had come suddenly. He'd been around back of the tents and the explosions made him jump after a week of no action. He heard his guys yelling amid the noise and grabbed his rifle and ran. By the time he got there – it had been only seconds – all that was left were bloody body parts and bloody fragments of cloth. The insurgents were already far down the road. They must've thrown the grenades without stopping.

John fired and ran after the truck, screaming, then stood panting in the settling dust.

Those were his buddies, his brothers. He'd checked each shattered form but everyone was dead.

John passed along the wall of photos, breathing quickly, feeling the adrenaline of that day fill his veins. The soldiers' faces in the photos moved back in time from Afghanistan to Kuwait to Granada, Panama, Somalia, a jump to Vietnam, Korea, the Second World War, the First … Each photo had writing beneath it, some printed on a computer, then on a typewriter with its uneven letters, then handwritten, carefully legible. Names, dates, places. Young faces, tight mouths, wary eyes.

As he moved from color photos to black and white to faded sepia, John knew all these young men were dead now. The pounding in his head grew stronger. So many lives. So many deaths. And he was still here. He bent, making sure he examined each picture. It seemed important, like he owed all these men something. He was the survivor.

The young eyes stared back at him so that he was afraid to turn and walk away. He was being reviewed before these young accusing faces, reviewed and found lacking.

John started to shake and his feet dragged on the cracked linoleum. He finally came to the end of the hall. He dropped his bag on the floor and sank down on his heels, resting his back in the corner and his elbows on his knees. He bit his wrist to keep from crying out. To keep from crying. He felt the lost lives of all those young men, young men like himself, as a palpable presence.

He jarred a photo with his elbow, the last photo at the bottom of the wall. Carefully, he straightened the frame, then looked again. This wasn't a photo of soldiers. This picture was old, black and white, but still sharp, as if it had been put away, protected from the sun. It showed a tree, a big one, a live oak, spreading its branches on a hill and silhouetted against a pale sky. Three things hung from the tree. Two looked like long, smooth, heavy fruit, heavy as long ripe pears. The third wasn't smooth. It was spiky as a dead bird hit by a car and left by the side of the road.

John gasped and fell back. He knew what the hanging things were.

This photo also had writing beneath it, handwriting in ink that had faded to brown, but the writing was clear, an old man's careful handwriting, an old man who'd been a banker or bookkeeper or storekeeper who had to keep records for the decades to come. The ink started dark and went pale before the writer dipped his pen in the ink again. John could even make out where the steel nib had scratched the paper. He leaned forward and read.

"I joined the posse and we tracked the horse thieves from where they stole Sam Granger's stock north of Marionburg. We caught them on the hill south of Eldridge's place, across the wash from Comanche Lookout. Two of them didn't put up a fight. They were old desperadoes and knew their time had come. The third was a boy, not more than eighteen. He said he was on his way to Lubbock to settle a debt and he taken up with those two on the trail a mile back. He didn't know they stole those horses. The desperadoes backed him. I spoke up for the boy, as did Martens, but the others in the posse outvoted us. They said dead men tell no tales. Please God, I couldn't go against the posse. We hanged all three. Martens and I came back and took this photograph as a record. That was August 15, 1896. I saved it all these years."

There was an old man's signature beneath, and a date: "By my hand, dated this Thursday, August 17th, the Year of Our Lord 1921. Thomas P. McElroy, Jr."

John's throat closed on a sob. He reached out to the photo and touched the boy's shoulder through the glass, the boy who'd had no more value than a bird hit by a car and left by the side of the road. He'd been in the wrong place with the wrong people at the wrong time, and was dead and dust. The way John should be. The boy had fought for his life as it was wrenched away, yet all the passion of his unspent years couldn't save him.

Through the glass, John felt the warmth of the boy's shoulder and the claylike resistance of flesh that was still trying to live, but couldn't. John tried to force a connection through his fingers to the shoulder of that bristling corpse that had been a boy hanged by the neck until he was dead years before John's father's father had been born. "I'm sorry," John said. "That should be me. I should be the one.... " He leaned his head against the glass, staring at the boy's wide-open eyes, no more than a shadow in the gray tones of the picture. With all the power of the dead young men on the walls, John willed his own life through his fingers, through the glass and the photographic paper, into the streams of time and that inert, still-warm shoulder.

"Take me instead," John whispered. "Take me."

~*~

Frank Traynor shivered. He'd just been out in the hot sun, arguing about horses with a lot of riders who'd surrounded him and his two new compadres. He couldn't make out what they wanted, but it was nothing good. Now he was suddenly here alone in this dim hallway. It'd been hot summer a minute ago, but this place was cold as a witch's teat.

He moved and bumped into a framed picture hanging low on the wall. He reached to straighten it, then hesitated and shivered at more than the chilly air. It could've been a picture of the place he'd just been, on a hilltop under a big live oak. Except there were three hanged men dangling like full sacks from three separate branches, hanging long and smooth and heavy, like long heavy fruit full of juice. Frank straightened the picture, then rubbed his fingers against his jeans, trying to rub away the tingly feeling.

He got up, stepped over a carryall somebody had left on the floor and walked toward the light at the end of the hall, coming out into a brightly lit, colorful place filled with shelves and things on the shelves he didn't recognize. Something smelled good, like sausages and coffee, and his stomach rumbled. Well, hell. He felt foolish. It was a store.

"Mommy, look! A real cowboy!" A little boy stood pointing at him, eyes wide, mouth open.

The woman beside him shook her head, looked at Frank, then smiled uncertainly. "You really are a real cowboy, aren't you?" she asked.

He nodded and touched his hat brim politely. "Yes, ma'am, I sure am." He looked away because he knew he was staring. His own mother would be scandalized at what this woman was wearing. Her blouse and trousers were so tight they didn't hide a thing God gave her.

Trying to act like he belonged here – wherever here was – he looked around and saw something familiar. He went up to the counter and pointed at the glass case. "I'll have one of them *pasteles*, please."

The old lady behind the counter put one in a bag and he dug into his pocket and dropped a penny in her hand. She looked at him like he was crazy.

"It's a dollar eighty-nine plus tax," she said.

"Tax?" His hand went to the pocket of his shirt and he felt the paper of his dad's IOU still there. Even if it was cash, he wouldn't spend it.

The boy's mamma came up beside him. "I'll get that for you," she said. She glanced at him again, then away. "How about a bottle of water? You look thirsty."

Frank was about to refuse out of pride, but the fastest way to get out of here was to agree. "Yes, ma'am, I appreciate that." For some reason, he made this woman nervy. But not as nervy as this place made him.

The old lady handed him the pastry and water in a bag, and he touched his hand to his hat to them both. The boy kept staring at him. Frank got out the door and found himself back in the hot sun, thank the Lord.

Dust rose, stirred up by the contraptions that roared past. He grinned in delight. They must be them new motorcars. Last winter in Kansas City he saw one in a newspaper that a bartender was handing around. But that little machine looked like it would shake apart if it ever got up as much speed as a fast mule.

"Looking for a ride?"

Except for the cap he wore, the burly cowboy could've been Frank's own dad from the sunburn on his face to the trodden-down heels of his boots.

"Yes, sir," Frank said.

The man nodded. "There's my truck. I can take you far as Lubbock. That be okay?"

"Yes, sir," Frank said. "I'm on my way to Lubbock. Much obliged."

Frank looked back as he settled into the unbelievable comfort of the passenger seat. Through the window, he saw the mamma and the little boy come out of the store.

As the driver turned a key and the truck roared into life, Frank nodded to the boy and touched the brim of his hat in farewell.

The boy straightened. Then his hand came up to his forehead in a salute.

Hitting the High Notes
by Sally Jane Driscoll

Honorary Mention

I sure don't want to be here at the Blanco Festival today, the second anniversary of my darlin' Royce's death. But my daughter, bless her, dragged me here to cheer me up. I have to do my best.

"Mom," she says, forehead crinkled with worry, "want to come with us on the Ferris wheel?"

"You go, honey. I'll be fine." I watch her walk away with my two little grandkids. She shouldn't have to fret about me – I'm the mother!

Then I give myself a shake. Some country music playing in the pavilion draws me like a bee to a flower.

On stage I see someone who brings back more memories. My old boyfriend Mac from high school might've looked like this man when he was full grown. Mac and I used to sing duets in a band. We lost touch when I left for college and he went into the service. Then I married my darlin' Royce and never had any cause to yearn.

Thinking of Royce makes me go kind of still, so I'm surprised when the band stops for a break and that lookalike comes straight over to me.

"Jolene?" he says. "It can't be you."

"Mac?" I can't believe it either. But his eyes are Mac's bright blue eyes, and he smiles Mac's slow grin. The last time I saw that grin, I was waving good-bye, driving away to college. I'm embarrassed to see Mac now because I'm sure he's comparing me to the way I used to be. But he looks me over more admiring than not.

"Jo, you kept your beauty."

"You did, too," I say, and that makes him laugh.

We start to talk about all the years behind us. I tell him how my daughter and her husband run a business together, and how amazing my grandkids are. Mac's daughter's a career soldier and his son teaches school in Wyoming. He's alone now, like me. He asks if I still sing.

"Only in the shower."

"I bet you sound good. Hittin' all the high notes?"

I nod, grinning like a fool. He opens his mouth to say something else, but one of the band members comes over. It's time to start a new set.

Mac gives me his hand. I want to kiss him on the cheek, but I don't. As the band starts to play, I bite my lip. It wouldn't have done any harm.

What would've happened if Mac and I'd stayed together? Would I be up there singing with him? But that would mean I wouldn't have my daughter. Or my memories of those years with Royce.

Everything worked out for the best.

Then Mac grabs the mike and says he met somebody he'd like to introduce to the audience. I start to get flustered. He calls out my name and invites me onstage. "Jolene, you'd make an old singer happy if you'd come up here and sing the last song with me, the song we used to sing when we were too young to realize what a good thing we had."

How could I refuse? I step up next to Mac, the band starts playing, and Mac and I belt out "Unchained Melody." In the middle of the song, he takes my hand.

Something strange happens. My heart breaks open and all the pain and sorrow go flying away with my high notes.

All that's left is joy for the time I had with Royce, and joy that I should be blessed to find an old friend like Mac again.

When we finish, my daughter and little grandkids are clapping and cheering. Mac hands me off the stage and walks me over to my family. He kisses me on the cheek, like I'd wanted to do to him.

"We're playin' in Gruene next Saturday night. Can you be there, Jolene?"

"I could be," I say.

"You better be," he says, blue eyes bright. As he goes back to help load the van, he gives me a last slow grin.

Except that won't be the last grin. Not this time.

"Mom, you were great!" my daughter says. "Are you going to meet him next Saturday?"

"I might, honey," I answer. "I just might."

A Play of Hopes and Fears
by Melinda Hagenson

The angels are crying again. This time there are twenty of them, hovering with woodwinds and strings and a little timpani among the graceful, watery branches of a willow tree like the one I planted in the Memorial Garden this spring, though this one grows from an orchestra pit. Teddy is not going to be pleased. I've taken up painting again only this week, having given it up on his expert advice ten years ago, the last time the weeping angels started appearing in my work and he called it a depressive episode. He won't like that they're back.

I'd forgotten how art dictates itself. This piece started benignly a few days ago as a bright and sunny study of Magic, my eldest daughter's horse, peacefully swishing flies under a weeping willow. I was pleased yesterday with the way I'd captured the mousy grays of his body – the colors of thick smoke that seemed to billow across his hide, in motion even though he stood perfectly still – as they faded in zebra stripes into the black of his well-muscled legs, and I liked the way his black mane and tail gleamed in the sun and the way his handsomely sculpted head, wearing a mask of mousy gray and black like an executioner's hood, hung relaxed and half asleep. The angle of the painting is such that the viewer is looking down on the horse from above, not vertically but obliquely, which allowed me to emphasize the black stripe that runs down the middle of his back and intersects, like a crucifix, with the one across his shoulders. I thought I'd captured his stunning black dun coloring – or "grullo," Teddy called it – very well.

When the odor of turpentine had permeated enough of the house for Teddy to notice it, he had come in with knitted brows to investigate. If the painting's point of view bothered him, he didn't say so. Perhaps he was just looking for angels. I could feel his relief as he nodded a tentative approval, gave me a sad, hesitant smile, said it was very pretty, and went back into his office.

That was yesterday. But today – ah, today the work began to demand earthier shades. By lunchtime the sky had darkened, the sun had disappeared behind dramatic, threatening clouds, and Magic had faded to an almost menacing shadow, no longer under the spreading, weeping tree but behind it, as if it had somehow consumed him, though the cross on his back was still visible.

And then, just after lunch, the first of the angels appeared, peering furtively out from behind a branch with a little smirk.

I couldn't recall consciously painting him, and as I stood back from the canvas in some surprise, assessing him, something about him and his new dark surroundings made me think of a poem by Poe:

An angel throng, bewinged, bedight
In veils, and drowned in tears,
Sit in a theatre, to see
A play of hopes and fears
While the orchestra breathes fitfully
The music of the spheres.

Remembering the poem inspired me to revise the horse's footing so it now melted, Dali-like, into the darkened orchestra pit in which the tree now anchored itself. I rimmed the stage with dully glowing little footlights, and then I gave the angel a piccolo, which he used to invite his friends. By this afternoon, twenty of them had arranged themselves in the tree like a chamber orchestra of weeping little Christmas ornaments.

You just don't plan something like that.

One thing I've learned, though, is that you really can't plan much of anything. We go through life with hopes and dreams, making our way as best we can, but we're never quite prepared when the hopes turn to fears and the dreams to nightmares.

The more the seraphic musicians took shape, the more clearly I could hear their sad music, and I soon found myself humming along in minor keys as I worked. They're foregrounded now, and because even angels are flawed (if there's anything I've learned, it's that everything is flawed), I've taken pains to give each its own imperfection – a freckle, a crossed eye, a mole, a wart, some other asymmetrical blemish – as they weep into their antiqued white robes among the willow's branches. They're not deformed, just flawed. If anyone asked my intent, I'd say it was to prove the transcendent lies in imperfection. It's a common error, the belief that angels are divine.

I stand back from the painting, taking a critical look, and reach for the alizarin crimson, deciding it needs blood. I hear Teddy's footsteps approaching again and feel a guilty need to throw something over the wet paint, but there's no time before the door opens. My husband stands transfixed in silence for what seems a full minute, gazing at the transformed canvas, and I can see his disappointment.

"Rose," he says to me at last in dismay, "O Rose, Thou art sick."

"That's not much of a compliment," I say. Couching it in Blake doesn't lessen the accusation or its implication. I'm not sick. And even if I were, painting is therapeutic. All the magazines are saying so.

But even though I know Teddy hates it, this is turning into a work I'm most proud of. One of my best, in fact. One can feel pain, or one can turn it into art. I decide that if he tries to make me stop, I will fight him.

Perhaps he can see this resolve taking shape, because he doesn't say another word. Instead he kisses me on the cheek, sadly but with affection, and walks out, still shaking his head.

We're all treading very softly these days.

The canvas sits unperturbed on the easel in the sunroom overlooking the paddock, where Magic and Winston stand nickering as if Willow herself were coming back soon to feed them. Teddy and I were surprised when Daphne, never a horse lover, dedicated herself to that task after Willow's accident, and I've noticed that she and old Winston have begun to bond. She's still leery of Magic, though, even though it wasn't his fault Willow took him over a berm of snow onto a driveway packed with black ice. It wasn't in his training to refuse, and anyway, he would have traveled through fire for her if she'd asked him to. He still spends his days at the gate, gazing toward the Memorial Garden as if Willow were calling him.

He knows where she is.

And maybe she is calling him. Who am I to say? She calls to me every day of my life.

The east end of the paddock and the stable are visible from this window, and the Memorial Garden is visible from the other end of the paddock, but I can't see the Garden from here. To sit in the Garden must mean going there, as my soul cannot rest there without my body. I sit there quite a lot, body and soul, lulled by roses and flowering crabs.

Daphne, fifteen now, calls it the Orphanage, declaring that the loss of her sisters turned her into an orphan. Once a vivacious child, she withdrew into herself when her younger sisters died, and Teddy and I had never quite gotten through to her again. Only her older sister Willow had the key that could still bring out the bright and effervescent personality that went into hiding ten years ago, but now Willow is gone too. I join Daphne when she works on her jigsaw puzzles, and if she doesn't get up and leave when I sit down across from her, I count it as headway, even when our conversation is limited to desultory remarks about the puzzle's progress. We sit mostly in silence and say things like "Oh look, I got one!" whenever a piece slides into place, and I tell myself it's almost companionable. I assume she's been telling Winston what's in her heart, but in truth, I simply don't know what to say to her.

Five charming, beautiful daughters. The souls of four entombed in the Garden, now: Our lovely little triplets, Callie, Thalia, and Clio, tenderly if quirkily named by Teddy, a surgeon trying perpetually to make it as a writer through cardiac scares, and now our beautiful Willow – and the fifth, Daphne, withdrawn and sullen. Asking if it's fair is a waste of time.

It was I who named Willow, the day she was born. When the nurse cranked the hospital bed to a semi-sitting position and transferred the tiny pink-wrapped bundle into my arms and I counted those mile-long fingers, all the name possibilities Teddy and I had discussed had disappeared. Willow. So perfect, and so long ago. Back when we had it all, our own little Camelot, fifteen years before anyone ever even heard of the Kennedy fairytale.

We have a beautiful home, the epitome of the American Dream. Perhaps every Camelot must be tempered with tragedy.

When I first suggested a Memorial Garden, the day after we pulled our three little girls from the bottom of the pool (we liked to assume that each had gone in to rescue the others, and we tried not to speculate about who had gone in first, or how, or who was supposed to have been watching them, though of course that would have been me), Teddy agreed readily and said he wanted it to be visible from his office. He said having his girls in view would help him write. I don't think it ever has, but he's never gone out there to spend time with them like I do. He sits at his desk and looks out at them, the same as he did when they squealed like three little monkeys on the colorful playground apparatus that once occupied that spot. Only the fence, built to keep them safe, is the same.

It still keeps them safe, of course, and the Garden is magazine-worthy in its year-round beauty. The crabs were already in their second year and blooming – pink, white, and mauve – when Teddy thought of adding the roses, having stumbled across the Calliope in a bare-root bin at the hardware store. If there was such a thing as a rose called Calliope, he asked me when he came home with it, was it possible that there might also be a Thalia and a Clio? Yes, it was. There were. We had to look for them, but there were. It took careful nurturing to get them to thrive, but after eight years – four times as old now as the babies whose souls they represent – all three are well-established, gracing the Garden in summer's full bloom: The Calliope, an apricot floribunda as stunningly beautiful as Callie herself once was; the Clio, a blushing pink Hybrid Perpetual, sweet-scented, long-stemmed, and armed with thorns, so appropriate for feisty little Clio herself; and the Thalia, a white multiflora spreading magnificently over the pergola set at the Garden's entrance and resuming its climb each spring along the little wrought-iron perimeter fence. Of the three girls, Thalia was always our climber.

Now Willow has joined our babies, to watch over them. Teddy says the tree is too far from the rest of the Garden, but I know that when it matures, it will expand the Garden's scope, watching over the scene as a big sister should. Its branches will float on the breeze, looking almost like rain, and it will balance the roses and the flowering crabs already anchored by my brightly-colored stained-glass garden stakes and the little cherub fountain trickling its perpetual watery lullabies. I spend most of my time out there, entering always armed with rose dust or neem oil, red as blood, to protect and defend my babies.

"They're gone," Daphne says, pouting. "Why don't you protect *me*?"

I don't know how, I tell her silently. I have a terrible track record. But I say nothing. She tosses her head and takes refuge in the stable. She's become a pretty good rider, and Winston likes her. I think Magic would too, if she gave him a chance.

We got through three. We can survive one more. Mama buried two and survived it by crocheting endless piles of little Polish booties. It became such a habit that she kept doing it for sixty years straight, until she died, in every color of the rainbow and in every possible size, not caring at all that she didn't know who would one day wear them. We're still wearing them. She's been dead herself for twenty years and we still haven't run out of booties. Callie and Thalia and Clio never even met her, and they died wearing her booties, pink and blue and green.

I'm not sick, I think to myself again. Teddy should understand my need to create. I've become an expert with gold leaf, and several of my garden stakes are gilt, topped with colorful globes of stained glass, a hobby I took up after the last time I stopped painting. I used to sell my art pieces at local art shows and craft fairs, but this summer I've been loath to part with any of them. The ever-growing collection of stakes sprouts around the front yard, the paddock, the stable, the Garden, and the pool area like wrought-iron apologies.

Teddy doesn't have episodes. He jogs daily around the pool, ten times round clockwise, then twenty the other way, trying to restore his heart per doctor's orders. Me, I paint and read poetry to my weeping angels in the Garden, and he calls it an episode. I learned from Mama, first when Josephine died in her infancy when I was twelve and then when Luke passed when I was sixteen, that out of the pain and vacancy of death, one must create something that will live. That the love must become a legacy worthy of your embrace. I do understand why Teddy can't compliment me on this painting; he's coping in his own way and doesn't comprehend mine, and I have to give him that, so I vow to myself that perhaps the next angels I paint will be dancing.

But right now I stand before the canvas with brush and palette in hand, deciding where to add the blood that will represent the inescapable agony that has become my life. As I regard the painting, the image blurs and my eyes focus instead beyond it, just in time to see Daphne mount a tacked-up Winston, turn his head away from the barn, and give him a savage poke in the ribs with a booted foot. Just for a moment, my mind, confused, instead sees Willow and Magic in the snow, starting off on their ride six months ago, though today I'm standing at a different window. I resist an urge to run after them, hollering not to go.

Magic makes no such effort. He neighs after them almost frantically, trotting back and forth in his beautiful swinging loose-gaited stride along the paddock fence.

He hates being left behind.

The poem is by Edgar Allen Poe from: "The Conqueror Worm." Lounsbury, Thomas R., ed. *Yale Book of American Verse*. New Haven: Yale University Press, 1912; Bartleby.com, 1999. 26 March 2013

Memory Book
by Vanna Smythe

Brynd squinted from the blinding light of the sun reflecting in the puddles left by last night's storm. The main thoroughfare of the town was packed with people; all and more seemed to have come to make their purchases on this first spring day.

It suited Brynd perfectly.

He'd already chosen his target. A rich-looking man – his heavy cloak adding at least two stone to his already formidable girth – haggling with the crone who sold the porcelain dolls. Brynd couldn't imagine what girl would want a doll that could break so easily. But girls were all dumb.

The man's velvet coin pouch hung off his wide belt, attached by a thin string. One slash would free it, and likely the man wouldn't even notice the lightening of his load.

Brynd tucked his curly brown hair under his hood, then tied his kerchief over his mouth and nose, so only his eyes showed. When Brynd looked back at his target, an old blind beggar seemed to stare directly at him. A thin cloth veiled the beggar's eyes, yet still Brynd felt the man's gaze pierce him.

No matter. The man can't see.

Brynd edged closer to the rich man, squeezing between two younger men who stood a step behind him. The man's face was crimson, and he was flapping his arms around wildly, explaining something to the crone.

Brynd took out his small knife and pretended to stumble beside the man. He fell to the ground under the man's thick cloak, slicing through the cord that fastened the coin pouch to his belt as he did so.

He failed to catch the falling coin purse.

It clanked loudly as it hit the cobblestones.

Brynd scrambled to pick it up, but not before the old man turned. "A thief! Get him!"

Brynd found his feet as only a lithe boy of eight years old can, and ran. A glance back showed him the two young men giving chase. Their long legs would make it a short one. He'd be lucky to keep all his fingers if they caught him.

"Stop, thief! You can't escape us!" one of them yelled, and Brynd imagined he felt the man's warm breath against his neck.

The blind beggar stood in his path. Brynd couldn't avoid jostling him. The blind man stumbled and collided with the first of Brynd's pursuers. The other one couldn't stop in time, and tumbled to the ground too.

Saved!

~*~

Deep in the forest and certain no one had pursued him, Brynd untied the pouch to check how well he had done. More gold than silver coins spilled from the pouch.

This would have been ample to buy the biggest blown glass vase that Mam so liked. If only Brynd had not botched the stealing so, he could be carrying the gift home to his mother now.

At least he could pick some flowers for her on the way home. Mam'd like that. Maybe she'd even stay in this night.

The sun was well over the midpoint in the sky before he reached the small wooden hut that was his home.

"Where have you been?" His mother's sharp voice greeted him from the shadows that hid her bed.

She is cross.

Brynd untangled the pouch from his pocket and set it clanking on the simple wooden table where they shared their meals. "A small trouble getting this…"

His mother approached slowly, still wrapped in the blanket, her black hair greasy with sweat.

She hefted the pouch and whistled appreciatively when she opened it to see all the gold.

Brynd held out the flowers to her. "I had meant to buy you a vase for these, the violet one of blown glass you liked so much, when last we were in town."

She didn't reach for the flowers, just looked at him with her mouth open. Then she snorted. "Good. Why would you spend coin on a thing like that?"

She spilled the coins on the table to count them, ignoreing the flowers.

"You said you liked it…"

"No, son, you were gift enough for me." She didn't mean a true gift, Brynd was sure. She meant he was a gift she didn't want. Often she said so, but not always.

Sometimes she smiled, tussled his hair, and hugged him. She did on that day, when she admired the vase. But that was ages ago.

Today her hands shook and there was no kindness in her muddy green eyes.

She dumped her blanket across the table and put the coins back into the pouch. At the door she slung her violet cloak across her shoulders. "Don't wait up."

Brynd started after her. "You mustn't go out with all that money."

"You will not tell me what to do, boy. Never will you tell me what to do!"

She turned and slapped him, then left and slammed the door behind her.

Brynd's cheek burned. He clutched the flowers still.

She'd been worried about him, he was gone so long. That's what made her cross.

He filled a mug from the bucket of water by the hearth, placed the flowers in and set them beside her bed. She liked the flowers, she was just too cross to tell him so right then.

The Disciple watched Brynd's mother sway along the thoroughfare. He approached her and grabbed her arm.

His particular talent as a Disciple lay in awakening compassion and love in the hearts of men and women, but the magic worked much better if the people he touched had an innate store of it. This woman did.

He pulled off the cloth covering his eyes and looked at her. She sighed and her eyes widened, as she met his turquoise-colored eyes and the full force of his magic hit her heart.

"Your son was born with the magic of the Disciples. Soon I will take him from you, make him forget all so that we may train him. Create for him a memory book. Do so with love, care, and warmth." The Disciple fortified his words with images set directly into her mind explaining the process.

"How?" She asked, tears welling in her eyes. "I have forgotten my love for him."

"Find a way, do not let drink steal it. Make the most of the time you have left with him. I will come for him at dawn tomorrow."

The Disciple released her, unwilling to overwhelm her with his magic.

A mean glint appeared in her eyes almost immediately. "Old man, get out of my way."

"After I take him, he will remember nothing. A memory book is all that will help him remember once his training is complete. If you do not make it for him, he will never again know you."

"As if I believe that you are a Disciple, or that Brynd is special enough to become one!"

Her laughed echoed shrilly across the street as she walked away.

~*~

Smelly old man, what was he even talking about?

Brianna entered the tavern where the ale was cheap and the company made up of folk she knew well. How they'd all laugh when she told them of a Disciple wanting to take

Brynd away. Disciples could stop time, turn iron into gold, heal with the touch of their hands, and speak to wild beasts. They were always taken for training while still children. The smith's daughter was collected for training when she was only seven years old. Now a woman of twenty, she was a Disciple and sometimes visited her family.

Would Brynd visit me?

Nonsense. The man was likely just another lying old beggar.

Besides, Brianna didn't know how to make a memory book.

Yet there was knowledge in her mind of a leather-bound book filled with drawings, souvenirs and trinkets, scraps and locks of hair. In her mind, she and Brynd were filling it.

The main room of the tavern smelled of spilled ale, vomit and unwashed men. Despite the early hour, more than half of the tables were occupied. The baker waved her over to join him, but Brianna didn't want company.

She sat down at an empty table, and the serving boy brought her a large mug of ale without being asked to.

The papery sold leather-bound books. Brianna had enough coin to get a good one, with brass buckles and paper stitched in well, so it wouldn't unravel. She still had a box of souvenirs of happier times at home. From before she began to drink daily, and coin always ran short.

She stood and ran from the tavern.

If I hurry I can still catch the paper maker before he closes his shop.

Rain began to fall as she walked to her shabby home, clearing her head. Brianna clutched the book to her chest, covered well by her cloak.

~*~

Brynd sat at the table, carving a spoon from a block of wood, working a bear into the handle.

"You are so good at that," Brianna said as she tussled his hair. The warmth and love in his bright brown eyes seared her chest. *Will the Disciples make his eyes turn turquoise as they trained him?* Surely it would be so, just as the old legends claimed. *Where will his magical talent lie?*

"Come, put the carving away now. We must do something." Brianna set the book on the table and went to collect a box of souvenirs she kept in a cupboard by the far wall. Dust and dirt had formed a thick paste over the box.

She brought it to the table and wiped off the filth.

"What is this, Mam?"

"A box full of memories, enough to fill a book … I hope."

A lock of his hair, taken while Brynd was still in swaddling clothes, a locket he'd carved for her not so long ago, bearing a single flower. Pages filled with her own clumsy writing, detailing Brynd's first step, his first word. It was "Mam," she remembered now.

Hot tears streamed down her face.

"Put it away, Mam, if it makes you cry," Brynd urged, an edge of fear in his voice.

She cupped his cheeks in her hands. "Fear not. I will never be cross with you again."

Sobs threaten to overcome her, but she stifled them.

Creating a memory book should have no sadness to it, only joy and love. How she knew this, Brianna couldn't say, but know it she did.

"Bring water and flour. We must make glue." She rose to get the quill and ink. Some water would reawaken the dried powder and make enough ink to write with.

On the first page she wrote, "Brynd's Memory Book" in bold and shaky letters, hoping she got them all right. She hadn't set anything down in writing for a long time.

She stroked the lock of Brynd's baby hair, then told him to put a blob of glue down so she could set it into the book. He looked at her questioningly, but obeyed.

His tiny head cover went below it. Under it, she wrote of the day of his birth. It was late spring, the flowers all in bloom. She had picked one, and dried it to remind her. Tears choked her as she set it into the book now.

"What did you write, Mam?"

"Of your birth and all the happiness I felt when first I held you."

She wrote of his first steps then, his first words.

"Do you remember how I would call 'bread' 'dough' for so long?" Brynd asked, smiling.

"I do."

Brynd took one of his drawings from the box. It was of their old cat.

"I wonder what became of him," Brynd said.

"He left, as is the way with cats," Brianna assured him.

She glued in the drawing. "Here, you will remember him always now."

One of his carvings went in next.

"I cut my finger when I was making this," Brynd said, memory of pain marring his eyes. "You cleaned the blood and wrapped it up in a flowery paste, and it didn't hurt so bad afterwards.

"You remember that, do you?"

The first letters he set down went into the book next. She had never taught him all of them. The Disciples would, she was sure.

Coins were hard to get. Brianna had no man, no trade. She'd been just a girl when she got pregnant, shunned by her family for the shame. Left alone. Brynd was a ray of sunshine, but soon the thunderclouds had set in.

Brianna had been forced to steal, and she made Brynd steal for her now.

She had done so much wrong. How could this little book of what she did right outweigh that? How could she have forgotten her love for him when it threatened to take away her air now?

Soon, too soon, all the souvenirs of good times were fastened into the book.

She dipped the quill into the ink and wrote of her love for him. Brynd would remember all again, once. The man he would become might not look so forgivingly on her transgressions against him, his unconditional love and trust.

She sought his forgiveness with those words, tears marring them in places.

Gray light began appearing on the horizon as she made the final token for him – a collage made of the flowers he had picked for her.

"Don't destroy them!" Brynd cried.

"I'm not destroying, I am creating that which will last," Brianna assured him with a smile. Then she wrote how she would always cherish the last flowers he picked for her. She kept one whole, to dry and keep.

~*~

The Disciple stood in the doorway, the sun rising behind him. "It is time."

Brianna clutched Brynd to her chest. "No, not yet!"

The man shook his head. "You know it must be so. Your son must be trained as a Disciple."

She hugged Brynd tighter, and then covered his face and head with a thousand kisses. "I love you, my sunshine boy. I have forgotten, but will never forget again. Go now with this man. When you return, I hope you love me still."

She led him to the man.

Brynd squeezed her hand. "I don't want to go!"

She pried his hand open gently and set it into the old man's. All recognition was gone from her son's eyes when he looked back at her.

"Did you make the memory book?" the Disicple asked. She ran to the table to fetch it.

"Do not expect him back soon," the old man said, then turned to the boy. "Are you ready to leave?"

"Yes, I wish to go home to the mountains," Brynd responded.

So quickly he forgets. Tears ran unchecked down Brianna's cheeks as she watched them walk across the meadow and disappear in the trees.

Glass

by Thea van Diepen

Isabelle took off her glasses, squinting in an attempt to see the hand she held outstretched in front of her. All that her eyes presented was a great blur. Frustrated, she returned the glasses to their accustomed place and stared at her fingers thoughtfully.

'How could you think they are artist's hands?' her mother's voice echoed through her mind. 'It is quite obvious that they are a pianist's hands. Anyone could see that.'

'It's true,' Isabelle's father had said, adjusting his glasses. 'No one could mistake it.'

"Well, I obviously could." Isabelle said now. "Why can't they see what I see?" She sighed, picked up her pencil, and began to draw. In the town of Vue, each and every person wore glasses, which they received on the week of their first spoken sentence, and which were buried with them when they died. All of the glasses were the same, from the style of the frames to the colours painted on their metal. Even the irregularities on the surface of the lenses were identical.

Because of this, not a single person noticed the presence of their glasses in any particular way, just as no one would really notice that another person had two eyes. It was how people were, from generation to generation.

Isabelle was unique among the rest of the town. She had started speaking quite late and so, unlike anyone else, could remember slightly what it was like to see without glasses. This meant that she did not think much of removing them every so often to use only her eyes, but she never did so in public, where the absence of glasses would be noticed like the loss of a limb. No one would understand her actions because no one could remember that there had been another way of seeing. But Isabelle could no longer see that way. The blur in front of her face was evidence of that.

Then why? she thought. *Why do my parents and I see so differently? All I want to be is an artist, but no matter how well I can draw, no matter what kind of art I create, Mama always frowns upon it. She thinks it's silly, and she doesn't care if I know. The only thing she has wanted from me is that I become a pianist, just like her. Never mind that I can barely tell one note from another, or that those black dots mean nothing to me beyond splotches of ink on a page.* Isabelle drew angrily, having to stop and erase each time she accidentally made a line that was too dark or too thick. The slowly developing image on her page was that of a girl sitting in a dark room, her head flowering, glowing with ideas and impressions.

You can't make me, Mama, she told herself fiercely. *You can't make me.*

'They are pianist's hands,' repeated her mother, followed again by her father's affirmation.

No! Isabelle threw her pencil onto her desk with such vigour that it nearly broke. Unable to focus, she stood, ran her fingers through her hair. Repositioned her glasses. *Why can't they see what I see?*

Outside Isabelle's window, a gentle sunset delicately painted the sky a pink that was slowly deepening to purple, then to black. It mocked her with its very tranquility. She made a face at it and turned away. Everyone else in her family had gone to sleep earlier, and Isabelle wondered if she should do the same. Staying awake was accomplishing nothing but frustration. *Why can't they see what I see?* For some irrational reason, Isabelle felt she would be unable to go to sleep until she could answer that question.

"Go away," she told it, hoping that, by doing so, she could ignore the problem. She tried to turn her mind to sleep, to drawing, to something that would not take hold of her mind in the way this question had. Instead, Isabelle found those seven words growing in her mind, disturbing her attempted self-distraction. It seemed incomprehensible that she and her mother could look at the very same thing, and yet see it in so completely different ways. They both had eyes that worked, they both wore glasses; the world should look no different to them. Even if they switched glasses – A wild thought entered Isabelle's mind and, without a word, she left her room, tiptoeing down the hall to her parent's bedroom. She eased the door open and slipped in, her eyes scanning the room for her mother's glasses. She spotted them at once and picked them up as silently as she could.

This is preposterous! her mind cried. *Looking through her glasses won't change things in the least! You idiot, they're exactly the same!* Isabelle ignored it and returned to her room with the glasses, her entire body almost shivering, her emotions on the brink of both excitement and fear.

"Okay," she said, "now," and put on her mother's glasses. Immediately, she noticed a change in the room. All the things her mother had scorned now seemed scornful. Isabelle's most cherished drawings had become colourless, insipid, worthless. She looked down at her hands, limp at the shock of what her eyes were showing her. Pianist's hands, to be sure. Her very fingers seemed able to conjure beauty out of even the most out of tune upright.

Moving slowly so as not to disrupt the fragile new idea unfolding in her mind, Isabelle replaced her mother's glasses with her own and sat down at her desk. Picking up her pencil, she drew until her picture was completed, then returned her mother's glasses, changed, and went to bed. The drawing still showed the girl sitting, the same thoughts growing out of her mind.

But she wore no glasses.

New Life
by Thea van Diepen

The seed burst open, sending out nanobots to start building the roots. Following paths already hollowed out in the metallic dirt by a special solvent, some nanobots constructed tiny rubber tubes. Others followed along behind, building suction motors, and the roots began to pull up the material-rich solvent. Reaching the end of the tunnels, the nanobots travelled back up, making wires along the way, eventually connecting them to a complex of microchips within the seed that served to detect the need of new materials.

The solvent, having reached the processing compartment within the seed, began to undergo a complicated process by which the seed extracted the materials. Once the solvent was again pure, a detector informed the microchip complex in charge of materials, which opened a release valve and sent the solvent down the roots to pick up more materials from the dirt. The microchip complex informed the central microchip of this development, which sent the root nanobots back down.

The engineer peered in at her work, noted down the growth hopefully, then went to lunch. She danced a little in the hallway before she closed the door, unable to contain her excitement. After years of work and failure after failure, she might have finally created the plant that would make it.

During lunch, the energy-detecting microchip complex informed the central microchip that energy reserves continued to drop. The material-detecting microchip sent a report saying that material reserves now held enough for some leaves. In less than a second, the stem nanobots rushed from their storage, eager and ready for work.

By the time the engineer got back, a small sprout proudly displayed two new solar panel leaves. The engineer adjusted the lamps so that the light level remained high and watered around the sprout with material-laden solvent. Then she noted down all pertinent information, went to her computer and, having nothing to do but wait, began a game of solitaire. Her fingers drummed on the desk in an effort to keep her from glancing back every few minutes, her excitement having morphed to anxiety.

The young plant drank in the light, sending the energy down a network of wires and into stations to charge the nanobots. Eventually, all the nanobots had enough energy, and the excess went to the seed. Detectors along the roots had already discovered the engineer's solvent, and now the seed could finally create more nanobots to create the roots that could gather the sudden abundance of materials. The plant's network of roots became ever more complex, growing outwards and downwards in an effort to support the rapidly developing stem.

Just before the engineer left work for the day, she took a picture of the plant, now about four inches tall and looking sturdier all the time. As she turned off the lights, she smiled in an attempt to ignore the twisting in her stomach. Only a handful of her previous attempts had made it this far, and none had lasted through the night. She wanted to stay, to nurse it through till morning, but that would be interference. Much as she wished otherwise, the plant would have to succeed or fail without her.

When the plant's leaves detected the dimming, they relayed the information to the microchip megacomplex, which ordered the nanobots to slow and begin entering night mode. All excess energy diverted to the newly made stack of batteries. The roots pulled up every trace of solvent and nanobots transported all the new materials into the specialized storage compartments within the plant's core, the tuber that the seed had become as it enlarged.

Once all the lights in the facility had turned off, the plant had entered into full rest mode, sending only a few nanobots to build some extra leaves in preparation for the new day.

The next morning, the engineer opened the door gingerly, keeping her face turned away from the plant as she turned on her computer, steeling herself for the possibility of yet another failure. As her computer started up, she took a deep breath and turned around.

The plant still stood.

Holding her breath, the engineer checked the readings from its enclosure, emotion swelling within her as each piece of information pointed towards life. There were even buds growing near the top, the flowers within them developing perfectly. The engineer looked back at her creation, the grin on her face straining her muscles with its size, feeling like she could burst into song and no-one would think it odd.

As the day went by, the plant continued to grow, doubling its size and number of buds. The nanobots within each of these buds built tirelessly, swelling the casings until they had done all they could and split open the rubber to reveal the vivid flowers, coloured by bits of dye found within the metallic soil. Two of the flowers had grown close to each other and they rubbed together when they opened, quietly beginning the process of fertilization as the engineer was distracted by an email from her boss.

She had to read through it three times before its words cut through her fog of happiness. The company she worked for had unexpectedly lost some of its funding and so would have to abandon certain portions of its project.

Her boss then informed her in no uncertain terms that she was laid off, and would have a few days to collect her things.

The engineer deleted the email, biting back a scream the entire time. She broke a pencil. Then another. Then she threw her garbage can across the room and covered her face with her hands.

After a few minutes of tense silence, the engineer uncovered her face and looked at the garbage strewn across the floor. She sighed, tidied up, and left the room, turning off the lights before she went. A few days later, she returned, packed up her things and tore down the plant's enclosure. Then she pulled out the robotic plant, dead of too much darkness, and brought it to an incinerator in case any of the nanobots still functioned.

As the flames rose up and began to consume the plant, its tiny, fragile seed case managed to sneak itself into one of the engineer's pockets.

I Need a Story
by Russell Adams

The Hunter

Hey, Stosh, I really need a story. You're our clan's *nori*.
You've got more stories than anybody except Yowi whose
head is full of spirits screaming stuff that scares the *cacarache*
out of me.

You won't believe my day.

My boat tipped over and the icy river soaked my furs
and nearly dragged me to the bottom. I lost that axe I spent
a whole moon fine-chipping. By the time I got dry, I was
starving so I roared like a cave bear to steal berries from an
upriver clan girl.

Then the bees resented my borrowing those measly
couple handfuls of honey to go with the berries, so I was
covered with stings when the woman's whole clan spotted
me and I had to drop the rest of the berries to run for my
life until I ducked into the river again breathing through a
reed just to avoid getting -

What are you chuckling at, Old Man? After a day like
that, *I'm* the one needing the laughs. Yeah, the sun's still up.
You can't tell a story while it's light? Tell me a funny story,
Old Man, or my club's going to bash your head down so far
you'll be pissing out your nose!

Okay, don't get your loincloth in a twist. I'll sit, *I'll sit,* but I'm not letting go of my club. This is the one I used on that sabertooth three moons ago when I saved your giblets--remember *that?* Tough about the hand, but at least you only use that one to wipe your ass. I bashed that sabertooth, remember? Ai-yey! Just like that, *Ai-yey! Oops.* Sorry about the water pot, Stosh. I'll have Yula make you another. A couple fat marmots will cover his time.

Glad *you're* in such a good mood! I want to hear The Dwarf Who Fell on His Head When the Cliff Collapsed. Eh? You don't remember that one but hum a few bars and you'll fake it? *Sheesh*, you better duck, Stosh. Mr. Basher has killed hoarier graybeards than you. That joke was ancient back when the first Australopithecine thought of it and got hooted away from the tribe's stash of ripe maggots.

Yeah. I just told you. Flipping the boat was how it started. Next, losing my axe. Then the berries and the-- What are you making me repeat all that for, Old Man? You going senile that I have to tell you all over again? You gotta tell me a story, Stosh. Can't you see how badly I need a good laugh?

Okay, okay! Then came the woman's clan charging across the meadow. The only good part about that was when one of them tripped and landed face-first in a fresh pile of rhino shit. *That* was really funny! Even the rest of his clan forgot about me for a moment to point and laugh at that shit-covered *bugho*.

So then the chase started up all over again. What the *Bromeliad* do you want from me? I'm telling you. *I'm telling you.* You've seen hunters running for their lives from another clan. You can't remember how that goes? How'd you like to be reminded by me chasing you with Mr. Basher? *Gingko,* you're getting senile, Stosh.

Okay, okay, I'll do it all for you just like it happened. It was like this. I'd just killed the last of the stinging bees and was sitting in the tall grass *like this.* Happy now, Stosh? I'm stuffing down my hard-won honied berries like this. *<lick>, <lick>, <lick>, <smack>, <smack>. Oh, this is sooooo tummy rubbing gooOOD!!! <yummy>, <yummy>, <yummy>.* You like that? You see? *Now you see?* I *told* you that's how it was. What I just did was what I told you before. What are you laughing at, Old Man? You just smiled when I told you the first time.

What the *Baobab* is so funny? I could have been stung to death. I know, I know, I *tell* you everything and then I have to *show* you because you can't imagine what I'm telling you. You actually have to see it happening. What's wrong with you? You're supposed to be good with words. Why do you always have to be *shown* everything. If I tell you I *accidentally* pissed on a wild dog's puppy and then had to climb a tree to get away from mommy's teeth, that's not enough for you? I actually have to go piss on some momma's pup just so I can get chased up a *fontakratz* tree for you to actually *see* how it happened?

If that woman's clan had caught me, it've been my radishes for lunch. Come on! That's not funny, either! If you think having your oysters eaten is funny, you're as out of it as Yowi, Old Fellow, and somebody ought to put you out of your misery. What's that, Mr. Basher? You're volunteering? *Helligins*, no! I'm the one that's had the bad day. *I* get first crack at cracking this senile old man's nut wide open.

Hey? Where the *weaselberry* did you all come from? What are you all looking at? Go back to your hunting. Go back to digging up yams. Yama, you're holding a filthy baby and there's water running down your leg. That's nasty. Go wash it off. The baby and the leg. Stop laughing. Stop laughing. *Stop kraking laughing.* All of you. Now there's water running down Fia and Huma and--suffering mynahs!--you too, Milo? All of you have water running down your legs and none of you are even holding babies. What's so *truckling* funny?

What's that, Old Man? The axe? I chipped that axe for a whole moon like this, one stone on the other, one flake at a time. <clink>, <clink>, <clink>. You've seen me working stone more times than you've spanked your monkey – filthy, vicious beast. I'd take a stick to her or add her in the *pot au feu* just to be done with the biting.

No, not like that, Nori! That's how children and baboons chip rocks. You gotta do it right. Like this. No, no, no...like *this*. <*Clink*>. With *finesse*. Your way you'll eventually smash your thumb between the rocks. That's what happened when I didn't listen to Zog when I was just a – *That's not funny, Stosh!* It really hurt.

Am I living in a troop of *blatting* baboons?

Aaaaaaaaaaaaaaaaaaaaaaaaaaaaaaack! Look at me, everybody! I'm a baboon, too! See me jump; see me scratch, see me mate with all the females. Stop laughing, stop laughing, stop *fruncking* laughing!

I'm Uka, best hunter in this tribe, best stone tool maker. I have *uh, uh, uh, uh, uh*--that many--boys and *nuh, nuh, nuh, nuh* girls. You're laughing at *me?* You're laughing at your most important clan member? How many of you made *uh, uh, uh, uh, uh, nuh, nuh, nuh, nuh* brats? At least *tell me* what's so *frenicky* funny about me having such a horrible day!

The *hellicate* with all of you. I'm going fishing upriver where the other clan's girls bathe when it's hot. I'll come back when I decide to--if you're lucky. You *bughoes* don't deserve me, none of you!

The Storyteller

The stone kettle still simmered as the sun set. Meat and vegetables, herbs and aromatic grasses and leaves, and more than a few flies and assorted insects that had gotten too close to the smoke constantly bobbed to the surface and sank again.

After an evening stuffing themselves with stew, mastodon jerky, rabbits, meerkats, bad-tempered snakes best eaten alive, and a variety of birds, fish, assorted eggs, and birdlings straight from the shell, the clan had stuffed themselves into the narrow story clearing.

Stosh the Old Man visibly grew in stature as he became Nori the Storyteller, "We have all now eaten until we can eat no more. The children's bellies are so round, they can't even walk. Their parents will have to roll them down the path to their furs. It's been a long day. What else is there to do now but sleep?"

"A story!" little Meeri, the nuh, nuh, nuh, nuh, nuh, nuh-th daughter of Umti and Dola called out.

"A story, a story!" all the unsleepy children called out together.

"A story, Nori, a story," the mothers and unmated girls pleaded in chorus.

"Nori," the warriors chanted in unison, "the night stretches long before us, and there will be ample time later to fill our women's bellies in return for them having filled ours. A story, or our spears will make you regret your stinginess." At this, all the children and the women and girls and Nori himself were laughing. Even the serious warriors and Metasse the Shaman were doubled over.

"So, after considering the ways of his clan all day, an old man is not to be permitted sleep until he has been extorted to tell a story? But which?"

"The story of Benek the Fisherman Who Hooked Only His Own Big Toe," Tilset the master fisherman called out.

This was hooted down by the warriors who demanded The Story of The Three Warriors Who Destroyed All the Surrounding Clans With Their Big Hard Clubs.

"All you men care about is fighting and hunting," called Tata, the headwoman, who was known to be unhappy with her sons' mates. "Tell the Story of Mela, The Son's Lazy Wife Who Was Eaten by Morfed the Crocodile Because She Refused to Move Faster Than a Mince."

"Yuni! Yuni!" the youngest boys shouted, calling for yet another story of Yuni the bad-tempered water buffalo.

Then Nori lifted his arms, each densely covered with raised tattoos. The left hand was missing three fingers-- which everyone agreed was appropriate for the clan's master *storyteller,* though none could say precisely why. "Those are all fine stories I have told many times before. Generations have grown up on those stories. But tonight I refuse to tell any of them."

Women, children, boys, girls, even the warriors, groaned. "Are you angry with us, Nori? *Please* tell us a story." Each pleaded so earnestly that the *nori* raised his arms again.

All fell silent except Swoota who had only joined Jalks' household as a junior-wife a moon ago, much to his mother's consternation. "Do you know The Yam That Thought He Was a Squash?"

An annoyed stir rose up. Swoota was forever asking for stories only she had ever heard of. Whenever she tried telling one, she got the details so tangled the story always ended with Jalks leading her off in tears into the bushes for a bit of consoling, a conclusion that secretly satisfied everyone. By consensus, only baboons could care about vegetable stories.

"No, but if you hum a bit of it, I'll fake it," Nori said with an eye-twinkle so bright everyone except Swoota laughed and applauded his cleverness. "While I will not tell you any story you have asked for, nor any story you have heard before, tonight I will tell you a story."

The shouting of his name and pounding of clubs on anything near at hand (resulting in a few pained yips and outcries) made it impossible for Nori to continue. Whispers of "A new story, a new story," raced around the fire.

Everyone hushed as Metasse the Shaman threw aromatic leaves into the flames. His peacock fan spread purifying smoke over the gathering which resulted in widespread coughing and sneezing, but most of the sacred smoke found Nori who knew enough to hold his breath.

"Just as clans disappear when night spirits withhold children," Metasse intoned, "so, too, our own spirits shrivel without new stories. Nori has the blessing of the rocks and trees of this gathering place. Has your new telling a name, Nori?"

Each member of the clan leaned forward.

Of course, it had a name. Just as there could be no story name without a story, there could be no story without a name.

Nori sat back on his telling stone. "I searched all afternoon for the name that belongs to this story. This is The Story of the Mighty Hunter Who Fell in the River, Lost His Prized Axe, and Stole Berries From a Woman of Another Clan Whose Relatives Pursued Him."

Metasse stood quietly. "I'm sure that is a fine telling, Nori, but the name feels somehow incomplete. What happened to the mighty hunter in the end?"

"Bees stung him to punish stolen honey."

When the laughter had subsided, Nori stood like a hunter poised in his boat with spear ready to let fly at a fish. He began his chant. "The hunter waited, spear poised. Mandalbloke, great river fish, swam by untroubled, dozing, dreaming his wet dreams."

Humming dramatically, Nori inched his spear forward. The children, the women, the warriors, and Metasse held their breath for the strike. Suddenly, he toppled, making with his mouth and hands the sound of splashing water. He shrieked like a young girl who had just placed bare buttocks on the hot coal set under her by a mischievous brother. Everyone around the fire dissolved in laughter.

~*~

The clan was large enough for the bright sound to reach the river and travel a ways upstream, but not nearly so far as the place where, along with fine fishing, all the other clan's young girls were wont to bathe deliciously naked when heat and mosquitoes got to be too much.

Nor had it any reason to go so far.

In a cluster of dense growth within sight of the story clearing, Uka the unlucky hunter of the story, attentively watched Nori's antics and listened to his chant. The two young girls he'd abducted from the upriver clan that afternoon understood not a word, but they giggled at the old man's antics and at the distracted way Uka fondled them, which tickled.

Uka jerked a thumb toward himself. "Me. That *me*. My story!" But the girls merely smiled at his words, at what he was telling them in a language they didn't know.

The *nori* with his performance pulled Uka's attention toward the clearing, but the girls with two sets of friendly, inquisitive fingers and two soft, moist tongues pulled it in quite another. Uka turned from the storytelling and drew the girls down onto soft grasses to make clear what he'd had in mind by their not-too-unwilling abduction. This, they had no trouble understanding and in the end seemed satisfied that his vigorous showing was ever so much more convincing than any mere explanation.

Neither Uka nor the girls had yet noticed the silent shadows converging on them from upriver.

Make a Sound
by Liz Schröder

Greg charged into the studio without so much as glancing at the red "ON AIR" light.

From behind the dusty, beat-up sound board, Jen speared him with a withering glare but continued reading her news report.

"And finally, Island Elementary School is holding their third annual bake sale this afternoon. School officials hope to raise enough money to refurbish the school playground. For RMNW, I'm Jen Roulade. Next up, it's two hours of oldies. Here to start you off is some crazy band from England."

Jen started a song by the Beatles, shut the mic off – careful not to bump it, lest the improvised swing arm fall apart – and brushed her headphones off. "What's up, Greg?"

Greg smiled smugly. "A new contract. A good one this time."

"Who's the client?"

"That new store on Ketcher Island."

"Sven's?"

"Yep."

"What are they asking for?"

Greg sighed and took a swallow of his coffee. He passed the papers over the sound board and watched as Jen flipped through them.

"Standard... standard... that will work..." She glanced up at him. "Where's the catch, Greg? This looks like exactly what we've needed! One good client, one good contract. Sign here and send me a check; we need some new equipment."

"Page nine." Greg's voice echoed in the mug.

Jen flipped more pages. "Oh, here – contest?" Her voice went higher as she read the contract aloud. "Prize package to include backyard... patio furniture? National commercial spots?! What is this?"

"Conditions. No spot, no deal."

"Who the he – hockey pucks do you think they are? We can't promise them a great spot! You can't control the audience's responses, you *know* that!" Jen glared at Greg.

He just... stood there, like part of the battered furniture. Stalwart, unflinching. He must have an advantage hidden somewhere in the contract. She checked again.

There it was. "You already signed this." If the mic hadn't been right there, Jen would've thrown something at him. "You signed it, and figured *I* could deal with the consequences. *Jen* couldn't get a decent-sounding winner, so it's not *your* fault when the station goes under!"

"Jen, stop. Listen a minute. If anyone can get useable sound bites out of this audience, it's you. Besides, I – "

Jen pushed the microphone off to the side and grabbed the pen mug. Before she could throw it, the repurposed lamp swing arm groaned. With a loud *sproing* the hinge collapsed. The microphone sank lazily towards its base, stopping two inches over the sound board.

Jen and Greg stared at it in shock.

"We can't go on like this, Jen," Greg said quietly. "I know this station is your dream. It's mine, too. But dreams cost money, and sometimes, you have to take the money and then work in the dream."

Jen sighed. "You say something like that when the mic is hot, you'll induce mass suicide in our audience. 'Positive radio for positive people,' remember?" Greg nodded, and Jen went on. "I'll find some way to make this work. But I can't guarantee an excited contest winner."

"You don't have to. I talked to Jeff at Sven's. What he really needs is a good story spot. Just record all the calls. We can cut it together for Jeff later, and it'll be fine."

"It'll have to be. Just – what if Ed Richter wins it? That guy wouldn't smile if his life depended on it, but he calls for every single contest."

Greg set his coffee on the countertop. "You can't control that. Prize pigs are prize pigs, and sometimes they win. Just pray he doesn't. You've got this, okay?"

"Sure. Do you have air copy for this, or is it improv?"

"Last page. Mary's in Memphis for a timeshare this week, so I wrote it. Be sure to say "Sven's Home Improvement Super Center – coming to an island near you!' a couple of times." The studio shook as the door thudded shut. Greg was gone, coffee and all.

Some dream job this was turning out to be. "Owner and operator of my own radio station by age thirty," sounded like a big accomplishment, but it wasn't a glamorous job, and the pay was lousy. A few decent contracts would keep RMNW on its feet, though. Jen would hold the station together with cable ties if she had to. She stared at the drooping mic. "How am I going to fix you this time?" Rummaging through her supply drawer, Jen came up with a ruler and some electrical tape. Thirty seconds and some creative taping later, the mic was back in a useable placement just in time for the quarter-after weather update.

"...and that's your RMNW forecast, Lake Michigan! You know, I love a good surprise, don't you? Not the kind where you come home and the cat's left a hairball on the rug – that's disgusting. But a good surprise. Like this." Jen hit play on the contest song, then turned it down to talk over it. "Surprise Prizes! Someone listening this hour is going to be the lucky winner of a great prize package from Sven's! I've got all the details coming up in just a few minutes, so be sure and stay tuned!" She turned the contest music all the way down and started the next song.

When the little red "MIC ON" light on the control board winked out, the white flashing light on the phone began to blink. Jen hit the red "REC" button on the 360 Studio Recorder and answered.

"Hello, this is Ryan White," the familiar voice said. "Did I win?"

"Hello, Ryan. No, the contest hasn't started yet."

"Oh. All right, I will call you back. Bye."

"Bye, Ryan." Jen hung up, stopped the recording, and grabbed the contest rules sheet. During the next ten minutes, she announced two more sixties songs, refilled her own coffee, and checked Greg's air copy. He'd written it in pen on a piece of notebook paper. Jen couldn't make out a single word of it.

Without the scripts, Jen knew she'd say something that would set the callers on edge, and then she'd never get decent sound bites. It would be a stream of Ryans, all wanting to know if they'd won, and not caring that they didn't because they could always call again. The five hundred or so occupants of the islands in northwest Lake Michigan were as close-knit as any small town, and RMNW was the only station with intentional broadcast coverage on the lake. If even one of her listeners got mad enough to call the FCC, her dream would be over. FCC fines were the death of radio stations across the country. Jen couldn't afford an unhappy audience. Quickly, she worked out a basic script for the prize breaks and jotted it on the back of Greg's notes.

The phone strobe flashed again, and Jen winced. She'd been staring right at it. "RMNW, this is Jen, who's calling?"

"Ed Richter. Did Evelyn win already?"

"I haven't even played the contest call tones, Mr. Richter. Nobody's won yet."

"Right, right. Call you back." The line went dead.

Jen cut the phone, checked her notes, and switched back to the mic. "You know, folks, great music just never dies. We've got more headed your way, but now it's time to tell you about today's Surprise Prize! Today's prize is one of two entire prize packages, courtesy of Sven's Home

Improvement Super Center – coming to an island near you! Today's winner will also be featured in Sven's national advertisements! How about that? Just listen for the telephone ring – that's your cue to call and win!"

With the mic off again, Jen did some quick airtime math. She needed to know when to play the call tones and how much music she'd need to cover the time she would spend on the phone. It was twenty after. If she played the call tones too early, there would be no suspense. Each call usually took thirty seconds to answer. Call-backs would use up at least six calls. An even dozen call spots would avoid contestant bias. Jen needed at least an eight-minute break to get the winner's reaction. She would play the call tones at the end of the 10:30 commercial break, then, and have the winner on air near the top of the hour.

Minutes ticked by. Jen played the call cue, crossed her fingers, and waited for the phone light to flash. It didn't. It sat dark for fifteen seconds … thirty … forty-five. Maybe *it* was broken. Jen swallowed nervously, and knocked gently on the desk's wood trim.

As if waiting for this more personal cue, the phone light flashed. Jen punched the record button and answered.

"This is Evelyn Masse. Has Mr. Richter won a prize this month?"

"Hello, Evelyn. I can't share information about other callers, but you're caller number one for this contest."

"Is that so? Well then. I'll be sure to call you back." Click.

The phone continued to flash, and Jen counted off the caller numbers, giving each a variation of "Sorry, you're not the winner just now, please call again." Callers four and seven were both Ed Richter, and caller six was Evelyn again. Caller nine was Ryan White again, who requested a song in place of winning.

Twelve seconds were left on Jen's second song. She needed to stall. "Keep calling, folks – be caller number twelve and win a fabulous prize from Sven's!" She played Ryan's song. The phone's strobe light was starting to give her a headache.

"Ed Richter here again. Say, what kind of prize are you giving away, anyway? Free dirt?"

"That's why we call it a Surprise Prize, Mr. Richter – the prize is a secret until someone wins. You're caller number ten this time."

"Right, right. All right then." Click.

Flash.

"Jen, hi, it's Mary Stevenopol. Can you hear me?"

Jen smiled. "Hi, Mary. I can hear you just fine. I thought you were in Memphis this week."

"Oh, I am, but I thought I'd give my favorite radio DJ a call and see how things are going."

"It's great. Greg dropped a Surprise Prize giveaway on me as part of a contract from Sven's, and you're caller eleven. I'd love to chat; can I call you back after the show?"

"Oh, sure. Make some interview questions up and we can do a morning show segment."

"Sounds like a good plan."

"If I'd been caller twelve would I have won?"

"Ah, no. Sorry, Mary, but employees can't win the on-air giveaways."

"Oh, well. Give me a call later on. Bye!"

One more song. It was getting late – ten till, and no winner yet. But the phone flashed.

"RMNW, this is Jen, and you win!"

There was static from the phone, and voices with distinctly southern accents in the background. "Elliot, you give me that phone back right now!" Laughter. A seagull called. A loud beep – someone must have hit a button.

Jen held her breath and counted to five. It figured. It just figured. The phone call with the sound that was going to save her dream job, her station, and her reputation was a butt-dial from some tourist on a boat out in the lake somewhere. "RMNW, this is Jen, and you win!" she repeated into the mic, loudly.

"What the – ah, hahaha! Hey Maureen, it's for you!"

"You called someone?!"

At least they knew she was there. Just to be sure, she turned her mic down slightly. Then she straightened her shoulders, pictured a large auditorium, took a deep breath, and projected her voice straight into the mic. "This is Jen on RMNW. Congratulations, you're the winner!" She winced slightly when the meters pegged, but they couldn't have *not* heard that.

"Hello?" The woman – Maureen? – had the phone in hand now. Her voice was much clearer.

"Hey, this is Jen at RMNW. You're caller twelve, and you've won!"

"I did?! Well, how about that! What did I win?"

"You've won the Surprise Prize: a fabulous prize package from Sven's Home Improvement Super Center – a full back yard remodel featuring your choice of either a new patio including patio furniture, or a three-tier modular children's play equipment set. You've also won a spot on Sven's national advertisements! Congratulations!"

"Oh... Oh my..." the caller sounded shocked. "Oh my word! Hun, that is just the most amazing prize, but I can't take it. I'm from Tennessee and my back yard is all mountain. I'm just up here for the week on a house trade."

Horrified, Jen closed her eyes. She could almost see her little station crumbling to nothing.

But then Maureen continued, "Is there some way I could pass this on to someone in the area who can use it?"

Frantically, Jen checked the contract pages. "What's your name again, please?"

"Maureen Finch."

"Thank you, Maureen. Actually, the usual no-transference clause has been removed... 'Due to the nature of the prize, winner may transfer the prize to one other person.' You could give it to anyone you wanted."

"Well then, suppose we surprise someone with it."

~*~

Jen recorded a thirty-second contest wrap-up, with Maureen's shocked "Oh my word!" as the main contestant response.

"We've got surprises all around today!" she added. "I'll have another one coming up later this afternoon, so keep listening!" Then she dashed out of the studio. Greg was sitting at the reception desk. "Greg, I need the boat keys. Can you babysit the board for a bit?"

Greg nearly spilled his coffee in surprise. "Uh, sure – why?"

"That contest. If you want any good sound, I'll have to go out and get it. Hand me the recorder kit, please."

Greg passed her a padded box, a microphone in a zippered pouch, and a set of keys. "Good luck."

~*~

Jen ran a finger over her new mic stand. This mic didn't even have dust in the corners yet. She played the next set of commercials and grinned when she heard the Sven's Home Improvement ad.

SCRIPT – SVEN'S HOME IMPROVEMENT SUPER CENTER NAT'L RMNWCW010000RC

SFX: CHILDREN PLAYING OUTDOORS

ANNOUNCER
THIS IS JEN WITH RMNW – RADIO FOR NORTHWEST LAKE MICHIGAN. I'M HERE AT ISLAND ELEMENTARY SCHOOL WITH MAUREEN FINCH –

MAUREEN
HELLO!

ANNOUNCER
--AND ELEMENTARY SCHOOL PRINCIPAL ED RICHTER –

RICHTER
HI THERE.

ANNOUNCER
AND WE'RE HERE TO GIVE AWAY JUST AN AMAZING PRIZE FROM SVEN'S HOME IMPROVEMENT SUPER CENTER! MAUREEN

ORIGINALLY WON THIS PRIZE IN A CONTEST ON RMNW –

<u>MAUREEN</u>
BUT I CAN'T USE IT! SO I'D LIKE TO DONATE IT TO THE STUDENTS AND FACULTY AT ISLAND ELEMENTARY SCHOOL.

<u>ANNOUNCER</u>
THIS ONE-OF-A-KIND PRIZE PACKAGE FROM SVEN'S INCLUDES A FULL YARD RENOVATION, WITH TURF, A THREE-TIER MODULAR CHILDREN'S PLAY SET INCLUDING SWINGS, SLIDE, ROPE BRIDGE AND MORE!

<u>RICHTER</u>
THIS IS UNBELIEVABLE! THANK YOU SO MUCH! WE'VE BEEN SAVING MONEY AND HAVING BAKE SALES FOR PLAYGROUND RENOVATIONS FOR THREE YEARS. YOU'VE MADE OUR DREAMS COME TRUE!

<u>SFX:</u> CHILDREN CHEER LOUDLY

<u>ANNOUNCER</u>
THIS MOMENT OF DREAM FULFILLMENT IS BROUGHT TO YOU BY SVEN'S HOME IMPROVEMENT SUPER CENTER AND RMNW – POSITIVE RADIO FOR POSITIVE PEOPLE!

It sounded perfect.

This is a work of fiction. While attempting to remain faithful to radio broadcasting, I have made up the station, its call letters, its broadcast area, and just about everything else. The 360 is a real piece of equipment, however, and I couldn't quite write it out entirely. I have no affiliations with the company that makes 360s, although I do perforce use one at my day job.

Just Add Copper
by Connie Cockrell

Mervin Hightower pulled his hat lower over his face. It was risky to be out after curfew but tonight, he had to meet his contact, Benny. He took shallow breaths. The alley reeked of old cooking oil and excrement.

He slid around the corner of the old brick building, stepping into an oily puddle, and swore under his breath. Hightower shook the slime from his shoe and moved forward in the dim glow of a nearby light. This was crazy. Security could be by any time. As he frantically steadied a stack of toppling crates, a cat ran screaming between his legs and into the dark. Mervin's heart pounded. Where's Benny?

His foot hit something soft. He recoiled. Jumpin' Juniper, what now? Squatting down he reached out in the dim light. Rags? Something sticky. He held his hand in the dim light. Blood! He rolled the bundle over and his stomach heaved at the sight of Benny's neck sliced wide open.

Mervin stood, bile rising. Poor Benny. But where was the copper? He needed that copper. A quick circle around Benny proved it was gone. Holy Guacamole! No one deserved to die over copper. At a sound from the street his head whipped around. He had to get out of here. The aliens sent anyone useless to them to the feeding pens, dinner for the overlords. A last glance at Benny and he left.

~*~

Mervin burst through his lab door. His friend Ernest nearly dropped the measuring cup he was drying.

"What's the matter?" He set the cup down and hurried over to the door.

"Benny's dead! Blood all over him and the alley." Mervin threw his coat and hat onto the folding chair near the door. "The copper was gone."

Ernest's face went white. "Dead? Great night!" He took a step toward his friend. "What'll we do now? We need that copper or we won't win the competition."

Mervin paced around the lab table. "I don't know. I don't want to end up in the feeding pens. We have to win."

He stopped at the table. Everything was cleaned, dried and laid out for their next experiment. Ernest stepped to the other side, face worried, fingers drumming.

That's when the door crashed in.

Ernest spun around as three men came charging into the room, the door splintered into toothpicks.

One of them held a stunner. Mervin ducked as the armed man fired, the stun blast passing by him close enough for his skin to tingle. How the blue blazes did he get one of those? He crawled to his left, crouching behind the table, leaping at the first man around the end.

They fell into a cart with a crash, pans flying in every direction. Mervin didn't know his opponent, so he felt no remorse for slamming the guy's head into the floor as the man tried to knee him in the groin and punch his head. As Mervin rose from the stunned man, a kick in the ribs sent him flying into the overturned cart. His head smacked into the edge of a shelf, his eyes watering with pain. He could hear Ernest, involved in his own fight, out of sight on the other side of the room.

His attacker kicked him in the ribs again. "Stay out of the competition, Mervin. I'm going to win, and you're going to stay home." His eyes cleared enough for him to see it was his chief rival, Aldous. He was kicked again, in the stomach. Mervin panicked. His diaphragm in spasm, he couldn't breathe.

He heard the intruders trashing the lab, implements hitting the floor, glass breaking, drawers being pulled and tossed aside. He blacked out for a second, waking to hear them leaving. With a painful, ragged inhale, he rose. "Ernest? Ernest? Are you alright?"

A moan sent Mervin to the other side of the room. He found Ernest in a pile of broken desk pieces. Kneeling beside his friend, he ran his hands over Ernest's legs and arms. "Anything broken?"

Mervin was concerned. Hospitals were only for the human servants of the overlords. A broken bone was now a life threatening injury.

Ernest moaned again, struggling to sit up. He shook his head. "I don't think so, just my pride."

Mervin helped him up and sat him in an undamaged chair, then looked through the remains of the desk.

"Aldous took the data crystal," he said as he sank to the floor. He tossed the piece of desk he was holding back onto the pile.

Ernest opened his eyes and wiped blood dripping from his forehead. "All of our work, it's gone?"

Mervin shook his head. "I made a backup, just in case. Can you walk?"

Ernest nodded.

"Good, let's go."

~*~

They had to walk; there was no transportation running during curfew. Two hours later the pair arrived at Mervin's house. They went to the back door. No sense letting the neighbors know I'm out during curfew; any one of them would sell me out to the Overlords in a heartbeat.

Mervin quietly turned the key but the door was stuck; he shouldered it open. They slid inside, crunching over things on the floor. Closing the door, Mervin's skin prickled. Something was wrong. He found and lit a candle, hoping his daughter, Jane, had remembered to pull the curtains. The kitchen was covered with broken dishes, spilled food, table and chairs overturned. He picked up the candle and moved as fast as the flame would allow into the living room. The same destruction was here. He hurried upstairs to her room, Ernest close on his heels.

Jane's bedroom door was open, the bed empty. He called out in panic, the room's only disarray was the disheveled bed. "Jane! Jane?"

Ernest followed him into his bedroom. It was destroyed too. Mervin turned a chair upright and sat down. The candle tipped to the side, wax dripping onto Mervin's pant leg. Ernest stood in the doorway. "Maybe she stayed at a friend's house."

Mervin shook his head. "No, she was here last night. I'll bet Aldous took her. The beating was a warning." Mervin shot out of the chair, running his free hand through his hair. "It wasn't enough that he destroyed my lab, he had to make sure. He had to take Jane." He looked wild-eyed around the room. Thrusting the candle at Ernest, he dashed over to his dresser. "Bring the light," he commanded.

Ernest stepped over dresser drawers and spilled clothing. "What are you doing? There's nothing left in the dresser, all the drawers have been pulled."

Mervin tipped the dresser back and twisted the right front leg. It unscrewed and he let the dresser drop. He twisted the leg again. It came apart in two pieces. Inside the bottom was a data crystal. He plucked it out, the leg halves thudding on the floor. "They didn't find it," he said as he held it up. "They'll kill her if we compete. We have to get her back."

Ernest looked from the crystal to Mervin's face. "How will we do that?"

Mervin looked around the room. "I'll bet he left a note." He dashed out of the room, Ernest following as fast as he could without putting out the candle.

Mervin was in Jane's room. A note was on her dresser mirror. Ernest held the candle up to the paper stuck there.

Jane is safe. Don't try to rescue her. She'll be returned unharmed day after tomorrow if you stay out of the competition.

"Where would he keep her, Mervin?"

Mervin's eyes went cold. "I don't know. Let's find out."

Creeping along the dark city streets, they visited friend after friend, time ticking away. It was the sixth person they awakened in the early morning hours that had the answer. They arrived at a decrepit warehouse in the poorest part of town, just before sunrise. It was just dark enough to see a glimmer of light from a second floor window. Mervin whispered, "Aldous is a cheapskate, I'm betting he only hired one guy to watch Jane. Let's go."

The pair crossed the dark street and entered the building. On the second floor, they paused where dim light was leaking out from under the rotten-looking door. Mervin flashed his fingers; one, two, three, and they both kicked the door in. Mervin's first glance went to Jane, tied to a chair in the middle of the room, still in her nightgown.

His plans went south as they realized there were two guards. One got out of his chair, stunner in hand. Ernest raced across the room and kicked the stunner from the guard's hand and delivered a roundhouse kick to the guard's head. He fell unconscious to the floor.

Mervin went for the second guard, and was punched in the head. He woke a moment later with Ernest and his daughter kneeling over him.

Mervin sat up and hugged her. "Are you alright? They didn't hurt you did they?"

She had her arms around his neck. "No dad, they didn't hurt me. I was just scared. Are you alright?"

"I'm fine now you're with me." Mervin turned to Ernest. "We have to find a place where Jane can be safe."

Ernest scooped the stunner up from where it had landed after he'd kicked the guard in the head. "I know just the place. Carol's."

Mervin's eyebrows went up. "Will she do it?"

Ernest grinned. "Oh yeah, I think she will."

~*~

Jane safe with Carol, Mervin and Ernest stood on a corner. It was daylight and people were moving around the streets, looking for something, anything they could do or sell to keep body and soul together another day.

"What now, Mervin? Where will Aldous have his lab?"

Mervin rubbed his unshaven face. "At other competetions, I've heard Aldous' assistant talking about the crappy neighborhood they worked in. I'm guessing it's in the neighborhood of the warehouse where we found Jane. Let's go back and look around. I'll bet we can find something that will lead us to his lab."

Ernest shrugged, "OK by me."

In the warehouse district they strolled up and down the streets, pretending to scavenge, keeping an eye on the surrounding buildings. It was an hour before they found what they were looking for. Aldous' assistant was going into a three-story brick building half a block from the warehouse. "Gotcha," Mervin growled.

They crossed the street and examined the door. There didn't seem to be any traps. Just then, two human Security Officers came up behind them, an alien supervisor trailing behind. "Hey, you two! What's your business here?" The lead Officer tapped his baton against the brick wall.

Mervin, his heart in his throat, turned to the Security team and their alien overlord. He pasted a smile on his face. "Good morning, officers. We're just going in to work."

"Really? Looked to me like you were trying to break in." The second Security officer moved behind Mervin and Ernest. The alien waited behind the first officer.

Mervin tried to swallow but his mouth was too dry. "Not at all officer," he stepped to the door and, heart in his throat, turned the knob, almost wishing the door would blow and take the alien with them. The door opened. "See, not locked."

The officer scowled. "Get to work then. Mind yourself." He glanced meaningfully behind him at the alien. "There's always room in the feeding pens."

Mervin bowed, "Of course officer. Have a nice day."

The Security officer snorted, but pushed on by. Mervin and Ernest backed up to the wall, eyes on the ground, to let the long-legged alien pass. It wasn't until they rounded the corner that Mervin and Ernest relaxed. They hustled into the building.

"I thought we were goners for sure," Ernest whispered.

"Me too. Damn bullies. Always targeting those of us who don't have protection," Mervin responded as they climbed the stairs. "If we win this competition, we won't have to worry either."

They stopped on the open stairwell at each level, barely breathing, listening for sounds or smells of work in progress. They found their goal on the third floor. Creeping to the door, halfway down the hallway, they could hear two voices and the sounds of a lab in full production.

Mervin slowly opened the door halfway. They bent low and slid into the room, Ernest softly closing the door behind him. They could hear two men talking on the other side of the room, their backs to the door.

Mervin heard Aldous say, "More sucrose, that's what's needed, more sucrose," as they crawled under the table between them. Mervin and Ernest leapt up, Ernest grabbing a knife from the table now behind them.

"Stop right there!" Mervin shouted.

Aldous whipped around, mouth gaping open.

Mervin pointed the recovered stunner at Aldous as Ernest moved to the assistant. "You couldn't beat me in the kitchen before the aliens came and you're not going to beat me now. Give me my bowl!"

Aldous laughed as he tossed the bowl he was holding on the table. "You are a pitiful excuse for a chef. I, I am the best chef. The copper bowl is mine."

Ernest forced the assistant to a chair and was tying him to it with an apron. "The bowl's back here, Mervin."

Aldous' face fell.

"Get it."

Mervin shook the knife at Aldous. "Kidnap my daughter will you? You killed Benny, didn't you? You don't deserve it. I won't destroy your lab. I just want my bowl."

As Ernest moved toward the door with the bowl, Aldous howled. "That's mine! You fourth-rate hack!"

Mervin backed up to the door Ernest held open for him. "Enter the competition, Aldous. I'm not afraid of your cooking."

~*~

In a borrowed lab and with the analysis from the data crystal of the aliens' body chemistry, they worked their way through several recipe possibilities. The next day, Aldous glared across the room as the judging proceeded. Mervin, eyes gritty from lack of sleep, smoothed the front of his chef's jacket with damp palms.

Ernest rocked gently. "Do you think the theories on how they taste their food are valid?"

Mervin gripped the hem of his jacket. "I hope so. The copper from the bowl should help. The chemical analysis seems to indicate we're on track. Who knows?"

A trio of aliens worked their way around the room, and Mervin held his breath as the aliens sucked up the chemical and protein brew they presented. It took half an hour for the aliens to make a decision. A team of humans bowed to the overlords, one of them picking up the winner's medallion and striding to the microphone.

Mervin's blood was beating in his ears so loud he could hardly hear his and Ernest's names announced. They pounded each other on the back. They were on the right side of feeding pens, for now.

The Mistake
by Jennifer Johnson

Harper's fingers danced over the lute strings to a lullaby she hadn't heard since her mother's passing. The notes swirled with the magic, feathering a plump little songbird into existence. She let the final chord ring out, then gently damped the sound to cut the magic.

The new songbird ruffled its blue-green feathers – the exact shade of the ocean – and echoed her mother's lullaby. The other birds she had created joined their voices. Even though they were created from different melodies, the notes intertwined like a symphony. Harper basked in the music of her new friends.

"I didn't know you could do that," said Isabelle from the doorway. She seemed wary of interrupting.

Harper beckoned her to a neighboring cushion. "I just learned. They're tiny echoes. Go on," she urged the birds.

A brave jig darted to Isabelle's shoulder. She giggled as the bird plucked at her curls. A waltz glided over next, and then half the flock followed.

"They're precious." Isabelle examined the waltz on her finger. "Are they real?"

"Real enough," Harper said with a shrug. She hesitated, unsure if she wanted to share her magic. But Isabelle was a good friend, and this might make her happy. "Would – would you like to try?"

"Oh, I couldn't! I don't know how to do the spell."

"The spell's on the instrument," Harper explained. "You could only play one note, if you wanted, it'd still work. Just might not make a bird." She held the lute out.

Isabelle bit her lip, but she reached out for the lute. Her hand bumped the body, and Harper's fingers slipped. They brushed against the strings just as Isabelle's hands tried to catch it and struck an ugly chord.

Harper's ears rang painfully. She clapped her hands over them. The lute fell, pulling another smattering of wrong notes from its depths.

Isabelle slapped the strings to smother the sound, but it was too late. The magic had already taken hold.

"Ugh!" cried Harper.

It could hardly be called a songbird. It was dusky gray, with an uneven, spiky shape to its body, like the scribbles of a bad pen. It opened its deformed beak and shrilled back the notes that had created it.

Harper yelped, clapping her hands back over her ears. The proper songbirds raised a melodious storm, whirling around the room. Even Isabelle flinched, but she scooped it up and cradled it to her chest. It kept screaming.

"Make it stop!" Harper shouted, even though she could see Isabelle trying.

Isabelle's soothing voice and caresses finally managed to calm it. The songbirds quieted as well, choosing perches far away from the mistake.

The ballad Harper had first created settled on her knee. She put a hand on its head for comfort.

"We have to get rid of it," said Harper.

"No." Isabelle's eyes widened in shock. "How can you say that?"

"It's a mistake, it shouldn't even be here."

"But it's here now."

Harper sighed. "It's mine to do with as I–"

"It is *not* yours!" hissed Isabelle. "We made it together, we both hit the strings. By law, it belongs to both of us."

174

Harper had never hated that law more. That …thing was musical pain. Her ears hurt just thinking about it.

"And I will not let you destroy it," Isabelle finished triumphantly. The effect was ruined when she gasped in horror.

Harper followed her gaze down to the ballad on her knee. Her hand passed right through the bird. She snatched it back as if she'd been burned. The bird sang a line from its ballad, completely unaware that Harper could see straight through its body.

A shiver trickled down her spine. "Echoes fade."

Isabelle glanced at her, eyes dark with worry. "Harper…"

But she only shook her head and watched the ballad fade out of existence.

~*~

By the next day, Harper had lost most of the flock. Only a few birds remained, including the lullaby imbued with memories of her childhood.

She tried to take that as a good sign.

She whistled a few notes, and her echo birds joined in, singing as they flew around the garden. Since they probably only had minutes or hours left, she thought they'd enjoy the sunshine and flowers more than a dark sitting room. So long as the mistake kept its beak shut, at least.

It had managed to hang onto its existence as well, hiding behind Isabelle's pity. She didn't know what was taking it so long. It should have known it wasn't wanted. Shame engulfed her for thinking that, but it was true.

She glanced to where Isabelle sat with the mistake, pretending to read. "You don't have to do that, you know."

"Hmmm?" Isabelle made a show of marking her spot with a finger.

"Hover like that."

"I'm not hovering," she said too innocently. "I'm enjoying the beautiful day."

"You're hovering," Harper insisted. "Now take that thing inside, before it starts trying to sing."

"That's not fair –" she started, but Harper cut her off.

"I don't care about fair. I care about my ears. And not having them ruined."

"He's not going to ruin your ears, you're being too harsh."

"Easy for you to say, you got a full night's sleep." No matter how many times she had shoved the mistake into Isabelle's room, it always found its way back to hers and started squawking. From her pillow.

"I'll buy you some beeswax, then," said Isabelle, her voice tinged with frustration. The mistake in her lap puffed out its spiky feathers.

"Why bother?" asked Harper. "It'll be lucky to last past sundown."

Scowling at her songbirds, she didn't notice Isabelle had moved until she laid a hand on her shoulder. Harper shrugged her off, but her friend didn't move away.

"I know you don't like him," she said softly. "But he's a living creature, the same as you or me. Exactly the same. I can't condone destroying him any more than I could condone someone destroying you."

She didn't answer, preferring to watch the echo birds scattered across the garden. The lullaby pecked at her fingers, the edges of its wings already starting to fade. It seemed memories weren't the answer to escaping oblivion after all. Even now, it gave the mistake a wide berth, hopping away as the other bird neared Harper's knees.

"You want to know why he keeps going to your room?" asked Isabelle.

"Not particularly," said Harper. The lullaby's tail was barely an outline now.

Isabelle stroked the mistake's spiky head, and he trilled off-key. "He's lonely. He wants to be with others like him."

Harper raised an eyebrow. "But they don't even like it."

She shrugged. "Doesn't matter, I guess. They're the closest thing he has to a family. It's not a great family, but it's what he has."

"And you still don't want to put it out of its misery?"

Isabelle shifted uncomfortably. "You could help make his life less miserable," she said.

176

But Harper was straining to hear the last notes of her mother's lullaby before it disappeared forever. ... *and she drifted away, past the shore. She drifted away, fading away.*

"Harper?"

She wrenched herself out of her memories. She couldn't go down that path again. The lullaby chirped one last time and vanished.

"Harper!"

She jumped. "What?"

Isabelle watched her closely, searching for something in her face. "Are you okay?"

"I'm fine."

"Are you?"

Harper didn't like the sound of that doubt. Or the hinted promise of a sympathetic ear. "Yes. I'm fine."

"But the echoes..."

"Are fading, yes. I wish they weren't," she admitted, "it's sad, but I'm okay. I'll deal with it."

Isabelle didn't say anything. Not that she had to. They both knew it was a lie.

Harper stood, brushing off her skirts. "Just...keep that thing away from me, okay? I'm going inside."

She stalked off, pretending not to hear Isabelle crooning, "Stay with me, sweetie. She'll be right back."

~*~

That night, she awoke with a start. The mistake was shrieking. She moaned and pulled the pillow over her head. No good. It still sounded like it was screaming inside her skull. She sat up, shouting, "Will you be quiet?"

And stopped.

The mistake was on her windowsill, screaming in terror because it had started to fade.

She blocked her ears. None of the other birds had made a fuss. They'd gone quietly. They'd gone without a fight. Why couldn't he do the same? A chill dragged down her spine. She couldn't accept it either.

She leapt out of bed. Opened the door. "Isabelle!" she yelled, fear rasping her throat. She couldn't do this. Not like this. "Isabelle!"

No answer. Except the mistake, crying for all it was worth. A jumble of emotions swelled in her chest, and she was at his side, her hands cupped around his spiky body. "It's okay," she whispered, "you're okay. Don't be scared."

He started trembling, but it only felt like butterfly wings.

"It's not going to hurt, I promise." But she didn't know that. She couldn't know that.

"It's okay, I've got you," she cried, but she didn't, he was slipping through her fingers.

He keened as his gray feathers got lighter and lighter.

"You're not alone." Her voice cracked. "You're not alone, I'm here. The others are waiting for you." It was a lie, wasn't it? There wasn't anyone waiting. Not for him, and not for her. Nobody waited for an echo.

He shrilled. She winced, but refused to move. She wasn't letting him die alone.

"You're so brave," she crooned.

His eyes were bright with terror, but she smoothed the spiky feathers on his head.

"I'm sorry I wasn't there for you," she cried. "I'm so sorry. But I'm here now, okay, I've got you." Her fingers went right through him. "It's not your fault. I shouldn't – I shouldn't have done the spell. I didn't know this would happen. I didn't know we'd fade away. No one told me I'd fade away. No one told me. I don't want to fade. I don't want to – but ... but I'll be with you soon, I promise. Just hold on, I've got you."

But he was already gone. He'd faded. He'd faded away and she hadn't noticed. Her hands fell to the windowsill. And then her tears.

She didn't know how long she sat there before arms encircled her. She ducked her head against Isabelle's. Isabelle was real. Isabelle was solid. Isabelle wasn't going to disappear one day when her echo magic faded. She sobbed into her friend's shoulder. "I don't want to fade away," she cried. Her hands fell uselessly into her lap. "I don't want to fade away."

Isabelle tightened her hold. They stayed like that all night, her arms wrapped around the echo of a girl.

Some Other World
by A.E. Kalquist

Zoe's gloved hand shook as she held it over the withered plant. She took a deep breath, filling her lungs with the chill air, crisp with the taste of the damp earth and rotting leaves under her feet. The charge raced through her, starting at the earth and rushing up through her body until she felt her cheeks flush. *Come back.*

The moisture returned first to the leaves of the plant and they unfurled. A green tinge appeared at the tip of each leaf, moving down and spreading away from the veins. The stem came next, fattening up and losing its woody appearance. Zoe exhaled and stepped back on to the brick pathway to examine her work. Her plant stood out, vibrant in the midst of the rest of the dead potted plants in this section. She shivered and pulled her hood up around her face.

Footsteps sounded on the other side of the hay bales. Why was anyone even out in this cold? She hadn't seen anyone enter the maze.

"Mommy?" the fearful voice of a small child called out from behind the bales.

"Right here, love," a woman responded.

The child giggled and the sound of their voices faded as they moved away, deeper into the maze.

Zoe bit her lower lip and blinked back tears. No more crying. She whirled to face her plant, ripped it from the soil, and flung it away. It hit the ground and withered, as dry and dead as it had been when she'd found it. She turned, fists clenched, and waited until the sick feeling subsided. Why did her father have to bring them here, over that stupid bridge to this freezing place?

"Zoe!" Her father was walking down the path, waving a small brown bag. "I bought some chestnuts for us for later. How about we do the hay ride? It's happening in five minutes."

She just wanted to leave, but she could see the pleading in his eyes. Besides, he'd taken her out of school under the false pretense that she had a doctor's appointment. The only other place to go was home and anywhere was better than that. "Okay."

A wagon, piled with hay, but empty of riders, stood in front of the pumpkin patch near the entrance. Two horses stamped in front of it, their warm breath fogging the air. Next to the wagon, an old woman with a patterned kerchief knotted around her head held two steaming mugs. Zoe's father climbed onto the wagon and pulled Zoe up after him. The woman passed him a mug and he turned to find a seat. Zoe reached down for her mug, but the woman gripped her arm, stopping her.

The wrinkles creasing the woman's dark skin deepened around her eyes as she peered up at Zoe. "There is no death, child, only a change of worlds," she said in a soft voice. Then she smiled, handed Zoe the mug, and rounded the wagon to take the driver's seat.

Zoe turned, her stomach churning, and sat down across from her father in the straw. *There is no death. Only a change of worlds. Did she see what I did? No. I was alone. I made sure.* The scent of apples and spices wafted up from her mug and she took a sip. The warm liquid calmed her. They jolted forward and the clopping of the horses' hooves filled the silence.

Zoe leaned against the side of the wagon, sipping her cider and looking out at the pumpkin patch. A crow alighted on a scarecrow and plucked a piece of straw from it before flying away again. She smirked at the incongruity of the sight and looked over at her father. He was staring into his mug, wearing a distant look. Zoe set down her own mug, empty now, and cleared her throat. He looked up and gave her a smile, but the smile didn't reach his eyes.

The fields stopped at a line of thick fir trees and the wagon continued on, following a winding path through the forest. Zoe didn't know how she did it, brought things back to life, but it had something to do with the charge of a place. Here, it was strong.

The sound of rushing water reached her and she leaned forward to look at the wooden bridge they were nearing. A black blur sped by her face, so low and close that she felt the breeze it made in passing. She jumped back. The crow landed on the railing of the bridge ahead and cawed several times, as if laughing at her.

The charge vibrating within her grew stronger as they neared the bridge and she struggled to keep her breathing even. The horses led the wagon onto the wooden planks. Energy bolted up her legs, danced through her torso, and sped back down her arms. She felt powerless to push it away or contain it. Terror and excitement warred within her. She focused on the rocks below the bridge, water swirling around them, and took a deep breath, willing herself to stay calm.

The crow cawed once more and took off ahead of them, disappearing into the trees. Then the wagon was over the bridge and the overwhelming energy surge she'd felt receded. But a small crackle of it stayed within her, thrumming in time with the beat of her heart. Zoe smiled with the thrill of it. *This is new.*

"Having fun?" The sound of her father's voice brought her back. She met his sad eyes and despair washed over her again. It didn't matter how many plants she brought to life or how many birds with broken wings she healed; nothing would fix their broken family. Nothing could bring her mother back. She gave her father a weak nod and turned away.

The wagon circled back to the pumpkin patch and a man approached to help them down. The ever-present gray sky finally let loose and fat droplets of water began to fall on them. Zoe bent over to retrieve her mug and saw the woman's patterned kerchief lying next to it. She looked up at the driver's seat, but the woman was already gone.

Zoe's father jumped down and she followed, taking the mug and kerchief with her. The man collected their mugs, gave them a smile, and began to walk away.

"What's that?" Her father was looking at the kerchief in her hand.

"The woman driving -- she dropped it."

Her father glanced around and then called out to the man who had taken their mugs. "Sir?"

The man turned, head cocked.

"That woman dropped this," her father said, gesturing to the kerchief.

The man walked back over to them and examined it, brow furrowed. "What woman?"

"The elderly woman driving. Native American, maybe?"

The man shook his head and gave them both a strange look as he handed the kerchief back to Zoe. "No one like that works here."

"She just drove the wagon," Zoe said, her heart speeding up.

The man gave a nervous laugh and backed away a step. "It was only me up there, folks. Don't think you're the first ones to pull that joke."

"What joke?" Zoe's father said.

"The old Duwamish burial ground there," he said, waving an arm toward the tree line. "I've heard the old stories about how Chief Seattle's mother, Sholeetsa, still walks those woods. Only she doesn't, or I'd have seen her by now." He laughed louder this time, and tipped his hat in their direction. "Have a good day." Then he turned and hurried away.

Zoe exchanged a confused look with her father and he shook his head. "I dunno, kid. I saw her, too, and she was most definitely not a ghost. That guy," he paused, circled his finger next to his head and made a goofy face. "Let's head home, okay? Looks like the rain might get worse."

Zoe stuffed the kerchief into her coat pocket and nodded. The charge she'd felt during the ride still flowed through her. It hadn't faded. Her father might not believe in ghosts, but grown-ups doubted lots of things she knew existed. She followed her father back to their car and got in. She tensed as he pulled onto the winding dirt road. They would have to cross that stupid bridge again to get home. *How do I do it? How do I bring things back to life? Why couldn't I do it for Mommy?* She'd tried. She'd held her hands over that brown box, but nothing had happened. *There is no death, child, only a change of worlds.* What had the woman meant? Was there a world, a place, where Zoe's mother still existed?

Her father turned right and the metal bridge loomed ahead. As they drew closer, the charge running through her intensified. It pushed against every fiber in her body, begging to be released. The rain was falling harder now and the few cars ahead of them seemed to melt into the windshield as the wipers swept back and forth. Zoe squeezed her eyes shut and inhaled, feeling new power well up within her. *Come back. Come back. Come back.*

She peeked through one eye. They were on the bridge. Nothing had changed. Despair filled her again. The charge was still there, a warm tingle, teasing her. She looked out at the blurred metal railing and the eddying river below. She took another deep breath and concentrated on the memory of what she'd felt in the wagon when they'd crossed the wooden bridge. *Only a change of worlds. Come back.*

She felt a release. The energy was still there, but the pressure was gone. She looked ahead. Nothing. Anger started to rise within her, but then she saw it. A few cars up, a flash of blue. She leaned forward in her seat, straining to see better through the rain. The car switched from the left lane to the right lane and her heart jumped. It was a blue sedan. Just like the one her mother had died in when it had slammed into the truck on this bridge.

The world slowed. A truck traveled ahead of the sedan. It began to swerve on the slippery road and crossed into the right lane in front of the sedan. The truck slammed into the rail and the sedan tried to stop, but failed. She watched it crash into the side of the truck and heard her father gasp. The other cars in front of them slowed to a stop and her father stopped, too. Zoe ripped off her seat belt and opened the door.

"Zoe." Her father grabbed her arm, but she pulled away from him and ran out into the rain. She slipped once, caught herself, and stumbled forward. *Please don't be dead.*

The front of the sedan was crumpled, the windshield shattered. A bright red smear along the driver's side window obscured the figure within.

She pulled the door open. The woman inside was unrecognizable. Zoe averted her eyes from the mangled face and blinked back the icy rain flooding her vision. She held a shaking hand toward the woman.

Zoe could hear her father calling her name as he came after her, but she blocked out his voice and focused on the charge. She took a deep breath. The energy gathered, a vibrating weight in her chest, and she willed it to flow out through her hand. *Come back, Mommy, come back. Heal. Please don't die.* Then the power was gone and she slumped down onto the wet pavement, exhausted.

She heard her father speaking, as if through a long tunnel. "Oh my god. Denise." She lifted her eyes and saw her father leaning into the car. "No. No. Don't move. Just wait. I've called 911. You're bleeding."

Zoe stumbled to her feet. "Mommy? Mommy?" She pushed her father out of the way. Her mother sat in the driver's seat, a dazed look on her face. She was still covered with blood, but there was no sign of the damage that had been there moments earlier. Zoe launched herself at her mother and embraced her. *She came back.* "I thought you were dead."

"Zoe? I'm right here. I'm OK."

The sounds of sirens filled the air and the bright lights cut through the sheets of rain. The paramedics moved her mother to the ambulance to check for injuries and gave the driver of the truck a blanket and ice for his head. Then the rain began to lessen. Zoe felt lightheaded with relief and confusion.

"Zoe, come on. We'll follow your mother back to the hospital. I think she's going to be fine," her father said, placing a hand on her shoulder.

She looked at him and started. He was wearing shorts now. She gazed down at her own clothes. Shorts, her lion t-shirt, and a windbreaker. The clothes she'd been wearing the day Mommy died. The air wasn't freezing anymore, either. "Daddy, Mommy was dead."

He stooped down to make eye contact with her. She could feel his hands shaking on her shoulders. "Mommy wasn't dead. Mommy will be fine."

Then he led her back to the car. The brown bag from the farm sat on the floor under her feet and she grabbed it. Chestnuts. There would be chestnuts inside. She opened the bag and looked in. "Blueberries?"

"Sure. Eat them now if you're hungry," he said, "but save some for your mom. She loves those."

Zoe settled back into the seat as they followed the ambulance to the hospital. *Did I dream it all?*

There is no death, child, only a change of worlds.

She sat up and dug her hand into her coat pocket. A soft cloth met her touch and she pulled it out. It was the patterned kerchief the old woman had left behind.

"Where'd you get that?" her father said.

She smiled. "Some other world."

Finding Light
by Amy Padgett

It all started in a cave, in the dark.

We were just exploring – spelunking in this cave that we'd known about forever. I'm not sure exactly how it happened or what came first. My light went out. I got separated from my friend. I must have gotten turned around and headed the wrong way in that darkness.

You know how the sun can make your eyes hurt on a bright day? That's what this was like, only with the dark. It consumed everything. Completely closed in. My eyes ached from the strain of trying to see... something... *anything*.... But there wasn't anything to see. Nothing but black.

At least it wasn't cold. If this had been a wet, clammy cave, I might have panicked. Instead it was kind of exciting. Here I was, having a *real* adventure. I admit, though, that I was also a little afraid. It crossed my mind that I would die here, alone, in this hole in eternity that didn't lead *anywhere*. But at least I would die in an interesting way, not as mister boring nobody from nowhere. I almost laughed at that, but it's hard to laugh in the dark.

As I felt my way along, trying to find something that would take me back to the real world – the place where light existed and hope was a possibility – I began to realize that there was a kind of glow. It was almost like the air itself was lit up, making it possible for me to see... just a little. It wasn't a lot of light, but in that blinding blackness a single candle would have seemed like golden daylight. I couldn't tell where it was coming from – it seemed like it was suddenly everywhere all at once. I kept moving forward because I knew that behind me the dark was still waiting.

I kept going for what might have been minutes, might have been hours. Eventually, there was enough brightness that I could really see. And what I saw was nothing short of miraculous.

There in front of me, in the middle of a cavern that felt bigger than it looked, was the most beautiful statue I had ever seen. A warm glow radiated from its surface, although that surface seemed to be made from gold.

I'd never seen glowing gold before, but there it was. The statue had dark eyes that looked like jewels set into a delicately featured face. Dark hair cascaded down its back, perfectly lacquered in place. The torso was covered in rich folds of fabric, the light from the statue seemingly dressed in yet more layers of light. It almost reminded me of Egyptian artifacts I'd seen, only more beautiful, more exquisite, more perfect.

I started to approach it, hoping to get a better sense of what it was made of. Finding some lost treasure was what I had always dreamed of, and here it was.

I froze where I stood when it turned and spoke to me.

~*~

That voice. That magnificent voice. It sounded like a thousand bells tolling. It was the thundering of a thousand storms. A thousand angels lifting perfectly pure voices to their Creator; a thousand demons screaming in agony from the recesses of hell.

Momentarily, I realized that I was on the ground, my body overcome by convulsions at the beautiful, terrifying sound of that voice. I don't know how long I lay there, unable to move, to think, or even to care who or where I was. Eventually, though, I managed to sit up and found the *whatever-it-was* looking at me.

"Have you recovered, traveler?" The sound still reminded me of bells, but more like tiny, tinkling bells than the peal from a church tower. I decided I must have just been startled before... overreacted.

"I... I think so." I could barely whisper the reply from my parched throat as I struggled simply to stay balanced. I didn't trust my legs to stand. "I'm sorry for... for what happened. I was just so surprised. I thought you were a statue, but then you..." I trailed off, forgetting the words before they formed on my lips as this small, golden creature held up a hand.

"You have come to me. You alone have found me. You shall be rewarded beyond measure."

I may have screamed as the fire enveloped my body, consuming me from the inside, interrupted only by icy pinpricks of pain running through me. Had I thought it was dark here? My vision was overwhelmed by the blaze that burned through me, filling my eyes with a sea of white, even as the darkness had once enveloped me in eternal blackness.

It seemed to last an eternity, but when it subsided, all my weariness was gone. My time of wandering, lost and alone, through endless caves, blinded by that perfect darkness, seemed a distant memory.

"What do you see now, friend?" Again that voice seemed to sparkle with subtle music.

I wasn't sure what he meant – everything was exactly the same as it had been. But even as I began to reply, I realized that a vision was welling up inside me. Not in my sight, exactly. It was more like something behind my eyes – more than a thought or a dream, but less than the substance of reality. Except that it was growing, becoming more real, filling my senses.

In moments it was the cave that seemed a dream. Somehow my reality was changing... had *changed*. Where there had been shadows and hard stone, now I saw a deep, black sky, a million tiny lights scattered across its depth, one edge of that darkness bleeding with the light of a still-invisible sun. I could hear leaves rustling as a slight breeze danced across my skin. I could smell the fresh scent of a brook that cascaded over rocks just out of sight from where I stood.

Though I didn't remember standing, I now stood in a meadow looking out at the deep purples and greens of a forested valley, just starting to glow in the first rays of the morning sun.

~*~

I turned slowly, taking in the wonder and beauty of it all. I forgot, even if only briefly, the cave where I had been only moments earlier. I could have stood forever, staring out over that view, taking in the majesty of every detail.

"Are you enjoying your creation?" I jumped as my eyes fell on a young man with long black hair, sitting on a perfectly flat fragment of a boulder, just up the slope from where I stood.

"Wha...?" I looked around, confused. "Who are you? Where did you come from?"

"Don't you recognize me?"

I gasped as I realized I did; that musical voice could belong to no one else.

"Yes," he said, smiling. "I'm that one. The statue." He chuckled and his laughter sent a shiver up my spine. I turned my eyes back to the brightening landscape below us.

"You may call me Adam." He smiled slightly, seemingly speaking only to himself for a moment. "Yes. That should do nicely."

"What happened? What is this place?"

The man stepped up beside me and I glanced sideways at him as he surveyed the valley.

"This," he said, "is exactly what you wanted it to be." He turned towards me, his expression neutral. "This is what you created. You are a god, or near enough.... It is the gift I promised."

~*~

"What do you mean, I'm a god?" My voice sounded breathless and slightly hysterical to my own ears. "You brought me here. *You* did this, not me!" My mind raced through my memories of the last hours (*days?*) since I'd gotten lost in that cave. What was going on? I must have hit my head – this was all a delusion. I had to be somewhere injured, maybe dying. This was what my subconscious had created to help me cope.

A smile played across my companion's lips. "It is no delusion. You are more healthy than ever before in your life." I didn't feel healthy. In fact, I might have felt a little sick.

"Tell me again," I finally said to my – what was he, my host? "How did we get here? What on earth is happening?" I looked at him in what I hoped was an insistent way, trying to understand what I was experiencing.

His dark eyes caught mine and I felt self-conscious under that unblinking gaze. "As I said before, you now have all the powers of a god. In this place, *you* are the creator. You make the rules. As for how we arrived here," he looked around, clearly indicating the whole of the mountain, the valley, the forest, the field, "you wished it, and it became so."

And as he said it, I realized that indeed, it was true. I was in that cave and dreamed of seeing the sun rise again. As much as I had wanted to explore the things underground, I wished for exactly the opposite, there in the dark.

And here I was, on a mountaintop in the light.

~*~

My mind raced with the possibilities. If this was really real, I could do anything. I could *make* anything.

I closed my eyes and thought for a moment of the dreams I'd always had. To travel, see the world. To have enough money to never worry about money again – maybe to have enough to make a real difference for others. To finally do something that made me feel like I was worthy to be breathing God's air.

When I opened my eyes, Adam was still staring at me. "You're thinking too small," he said. "Worthy to breathe God's air? It's *your* air now." He laughed again and I shuddered at the sound.

He was right – I needed to do something great. I needed to *be* great. How could I not?

I needed to fix something. Fix it *all*. Everything that was wrong with the world... I had the power to make it better.

"Peace," I said. "World peace! Total harmony... *right now!*" By the end, I was shouting. "And equality," I added. "Perfect equality. All men –and women too –are created equal. *So there!*" I felt a little petulant saying it out loud that way. Then again, peace and equality were the top non-selfish wishes most people ever wished for; just ask Miss America. And now, as their benevolent deity, I fulfilled their greatest wish.

"Peace? How boring." Adam sighed as he turned to me. "Shall we go and observe your creation?"

I felt myself grinning foolishly. I'm sure I looked ridiculous, but I couldn't help it. I just fixed *everything* for *everybody*. Why shouldn't I be happy? "You bet!" I felt absolutely giddy. "Let's find out how it changed things. Maybe the Middle East first? They've been at war for*ever*."

~*~

Even as I said it, I felt the world shift around me. As suddenly as we had appeared on that mountaintop, we were now standing on a street corner in what was obviously some Middle Eastern town. Maybe it was Afghanistan, maybe it was Israel. I could probably have figured it out, but it didn't matter. I could *feel* the peace. There was no animosity anywhere. I'd done it! But as I started to notice the people walking down the street, I realized something was wrong. There was no sense of conflict, but there was also no sense of joy, no excitement. I stopped a man walking towards us and asked him, "Where are we?"

He looked at me a little oddly, then answered, "Gaza."

Of course, I thought. *Gaza*. "Are you Palestinian or Israeli?"

"What do you mean?" he asked. "We are all one." The reply was absolutely flat, devoid of any emotion.

"That is very *peaceful* of you," Adam interrupted. "You may go." The young man smiled and nodded, then turned placidly and walked away.

"That's weird," I said as we watched him go.

"Not really. You took away the possibility of conflict – of judgment even – by declaring all are equal." Adam raised an eyebrow. "What did you think the result would be?"

I watched the blank faces on the people all around us, looking for some spark of... something. Hope for their future, maybe, that they hadn't had in the middle of war. "I thought they'd be happier, I guess. Happy for peace."

"When war is not a possibility, peace has no meaning." He looked almost annoyed as he said it.

"Oh." I felt ridiculous for not realizing it before. "I hadn't thought of it that way."

The fine features of Adam's face were not improved by the scowl he now wore. "Do you have another plan?" he asked. All the music was gone from his voice.

~*~

I opened my mind to potential outcomes, and felt a dread settle over me. I saw dozens of scenarios, one by one, and I realized that whatever I did would have similar consequences.

My declaration of perfect equality? It removed all hope of achieving something better. I thought, too, of ending poverty, but the effect would have been the same. With nothing to work for, no reward for a job well done, there would be no innovation, no enthusiasm, no *hope*.

I tuned my consciousness to the children then. Ending hunger. Ensuring education. But no matter how I altered my focus, no matter how light my touch, I could find no way to improve life for everybody without somehow stripping them of their humanity. Everything I did rendered hope meaningless.

Without an element of random chance, without the freedom to choose their own path and make their own decisions, the lives of these people – *my* people, the human race – became flat. Boring. *Adventureless.*

That was the key. Without adventure, without challenge and conflict, effort and work, there could be no meaning to these lives. Or to *my* life.

I looked back at Adam. "I undo it all," I said, and a wave of sadness washed over me as everything disappeared back into the darkness of the cave.

My awareness of the world faded. I felt the ordinary settle over my consciousness, my deity exchanged for simple humanity once more. I felt small, sitting here again in the dark.

"Why?" I asked, not expecting an answer.

He shrugged. An odd gesture on his form. "An experiment, I suppose," he said. "To test what I could not. Only a man can change mankind." I realized as he spoke that he was becoming like a statue once again. "And you have not changed. You still require free will."

And with that, even the statue disappeared.

There I sat, lost in a cave. But as I began to lament being lost in the dark, my hand closed on a cold, cylindrical object. I switched on the flashlight, and as hope flooded the cavern, I rose and turned to find my way back home.

The Interview
by Vanessa Wells

"Do you have any idea how many applications I have for this position every year?"

Ethan swallowed in a vain attempt to wet his mouth. "I'd guess that it was equal to the number of graduating wand wielders, sir."

The Magus narrowed his eyes and gave him a tiny nod. "Three of the applicants are grandchildren of Greatlords. Another will undoubtedly test into Great status. While your grades are top notch, and I'm sure you are very good at whatever it is that you specialize in…." He flipped through a thick stack of neat pages. "Ah yes … Creation … well, I must admit while these marks are impressive, school work alone will not gain you a place as my apprentice."

He looked deep into Ethan's eyes. "All I see is a penniless orphan in a second-hand suit with a rather daring amount of ambition. Can you show me something more? A reason I should give a plum position to you, and offend people with families that I'll have to appease later?"

Ethan's hands were shaking as he pulled out his wand. What would be impressive enough to win him this apprenticeship? Was there anything he could do that would surprise the leader of the entire city, the man to which every

Greatlord bent a knee? The man was genius; it was why this apprenticeship was so hotly contested every year. With it, Ethan knew that he'd stand a good chance at attaining Greatlord status himself… Without it…well, without, being the top of his class would help him a bit, but he could easily end up sweeping floors for some half-mad wand wielder for the next three years. There were more than enough horror stories floating around the dorms.

His mind raced. He'd studied the old texts, he had achieved a great deal. He could make silks and satins, wool, and cotton… objects in glass and even some metals.

Something crystal perhaps; crystal was rather difficult to create. Or should he try something new… some original element? No, the chances of actually pulling that off without preparation were slim at best, catastrophic at worst.

What would the Magus need?

He took a deep breath. "I know how to create quite a few things, sir, but I want to study with you because you know things I would like to learn. If you'd assign me a task, I'll do my best to show you what I'm made of …"

The magus smirked slightly. "You already have."

He raised his wand and his secretary walked into the room. Ethan looked down, calculating how many other applications he could put in before the college let out for the summer and he no longer had a place to live.

"Mr. Ainsley, I'd like you to meet Ethan Fain, my new apprentice. See that the others are informed… cancel the remaining interviews, and arrange quarters for him to move into directly after graduation."

Ethan ducked his head, almost faint. "T-thank you, sir."

"Thank you Ethan. I enjoy teaching … when I have a worthy student. Go … enjoy the last few days of freedom. When you come here, we will get to work."

Trial of the Magideem
by Ted Atchley

Pain. Burning in his cheek. Mark tried to move, but strong ropes bound his wrists behind his back around a thin pine. The old man stared at him with the same angry expression his uncle had whenever he caught Mark daydreaming instead of working. Pain always followed.

Images flashed before Mark's memory: saying goodbye to his friend Barnabas, trailing the old man – a Magideem, losing sight of him near the woods, and then blacking out. The dull ache in the back of his head helped fill in the missing details. "Where–"

The Magideem slapped his cheek. "I will ask the questions, boy. You will answer them, and your life depends on the truthfulness of your answers." The Magideem crossed his arms while he let that thought that sink in.

Mark swallowed hard and nodded.

"Why were you following me?"

In a blink, Mark had considered a half dozen explanations. At home, he often needed to come up with lies to explain unfinished chores. But this time, he tried a new approach he told the truth. "I wanted to find your home. Somewhere inside you hide the secret of the Magideem's power."

The old man rolled his eyes. "Magideem are forbidden to teach their secrets to any but their apprentices. You could have searched everything I own and it would have eluded you."

Mark bowed his head. Of course, it could never have been so simple. The Magideem walked behind him and he heard the distinct sound of a dagger being pulled from its sheath. An unexpected calmness flooded his soul. Fear he had expected, but he dreaded only the pain rather than fearing death itself. Ever since his parents died, he had lived as a prisoner to his uncle's temper. Death would liberate him. At least he would never cower from another beating at his uncle's hands. Mark felt the bonds around his wrists loosen and fall away.

"Go home, boy, and thank whatever god you worship that I spared your life."

Mark's feet refused to budge. He simply couldn't go back to his uncle. Instead, he spun around and locked eyes with the Magideem. "Teach me your secret."

The old man's wrinkles creased in a surprised expression. "You? A Magideem?"

"Please, sir. I have watched for you every spring for the last five years. I sit at your feet in the tavern and listen as you recite the great tales. I am transported into your world. The magic grabs me, and for a few short moments I am your mighty hero saving the kingdom and winning the heart of the princess, or your clever bandit overthrowing the evil tyrant."

The old man's expression soured. "Farmer's boy. You think the Magideem lives a life of ease. We do nothing all the day while you toil in the hot sun, only to drag ourselves to a tavern in the cool of the evening to tell our stories. We make it look oh so simple, so easy. You are sure you could do it. I tell you this, boy, my soul knows of torments yours cannot even begin to fathom. Find something, anything else to do with your short life. I wouldn't wish this miserable existence on anyone."

Mark dropped to his knees. Like a drought destroyed harvest, his one chance forsaken. "I came to you to be

Magideem. It is all I want. I will not leave, I will not stop following you, and I will not stop begging until you agree to take me on as your apprentice."

The old man pointed his gnarled staff down the road.

Mark didn't move. The Magideem couldn't treat their apprentices worse than his uncle treated him. How hard could this old man hit?

"Please, sir. I'm not seeking an easy life. I will do whatever you ask. I'm not afraid."

At that the Magideem raised an eyebrow. "Not afraid, eh?" The Magideem bore an expression that reminded Mark of his friend Barnabas when Barnabas held a winning hand and Mark had made too large a wager.

A moment of silence passed.

Then the old man slipped his backpack off his shoulders. "Do you have a name, boy?"

"Mark from Chatshire."

"Very well, Mark of Chatshire. I agree to take you on as my apprentice." The Magideem handed his backpack to Mark. "And you can start by carrying my pack."

Mark stood and took the pack with a sharp, "Yes sir!"

"My name is Silas, but in public you must refer to me as Master or Magideem."

Mark nodded.

"And you will be afraid, my boy. In ways you can't even imagine!"

~*~

Mark's life changed little once they reached Silas' cabin, deep in the woods. He had simply traded one set of chores for another. He painted, cooked, cleaned, and whatever other menial task crossed Silas' mind. Mark never complained – his uncle had taught him as much.

About every other night Silas would travel to a nearby village and delight the crowds with his tales. Mark played the role of pack mule and waiter. After the second performance Mark heard Silas mutter something about how he should have gotten an apprentice long ago.

After about two weeks, Silas called Mark to his room after supper. The Magideem unfurled a scroll across his desk. Mark's mouth hung open. Only Temple priests owned scrolls, but Silas had a shelf full of them.

The scroll contained unintelligible lines and circles.

"You were not born with a Magideem's gift."

Mark's gallant attempt at keeping his face expressionless failed. For two weeks he had waited on Silas hand and foot, and all along Silas had known he didn't have the ability to be Magideem! As the initial shock wore off, a burning from deep inside his gut worked its way up. Mark clenched and unclenched his fists.

Silas' face morphed into a sly, knowing smile.

"And neither was I."

The surging anger crashed into a returning shock like waves against the rocks. Mark's mind spun, trying to make sense of the Magideem's words.

"What I do is not magic, and it's not natural born talent. You have already demonstrated the desire, and that is the first step. Now you must exercise the discipline to turn that passion into skill. No one is born a Magideem; you choose to be one."

Silas had stripped off Mark's defenses. He could only reply, "Then I choose it."

"There are three trials you must pass to become Magideem. The Trial of Discipline begins now."

Every night Silas taught Mark how each line and circle and squiggle translated to a sound, and sounds into words. Mark devoted himself to the exercises Silas taught him, but at every turn he encountered another archaic rule. This squiggle made that sound unless it was next to that other squiggle, but if both squiggles were next to that line then it made an entirely different sound!

Mark ran his hand through his hair. How would he ever learn to make sense of it all?

~*~

One evening, they returned to Chatshire for a performance. At Mark's request they arrived early. Barnabas, Mark's best friend, waited for them at the tavern.

Mark and Barnabas found their favorite spot in the shadows behind the tavern. They played cards as the boys talked. Had it really been less than a month since Mark told Barnabas his crazy idea of becoming the Magideem's apprentice? Barnabas caught Mark up on the local gossip, and how angry Mark's uncle had been after Mark ran away. Even though the Magideem had sworn Mark to secrecy, Mark divulged the struggles with his training.

Barnabas embraced him. "You're smarter than you think you are, bud. You study it just like you learned cards from me. I know you can do it."

When Mark arrived back at the cabin, he rededicated himself to learning the scrolls, and every night he could decipher a little more than the night before.

~*~

Months passed and the forest transformed into an artist's palette of beautiful colors. Mark finished washing the dishes from supper, but Silas had put his traveling cloak on.

"Isn't it a bit late to head out for a performance tonight?" Mark asked.

The old man's face bore a somber expression. "Grab a torch. Tonight, you face the second trial."

The two traveled even deeper into the woods. The sun dipped low, and gave everything an eerie twilight glow.

Silas pointed at a cavity next to a giant fallen tree. "In you must go."

Mark recognized it as a burrow, hopefully long abandoned, of some huge animal. "Is it safe?"

Silas shook his head and chuckled. "It wouldn't be much of a Trial of Fear if it was."

Mark lowered himself down into the hole, his mind racing. Silas must have survived this trial, how bad could it be? The chamber gave him enough room to stand, and his torch illuminated a passage at the other end.

"MARK!"

He knew that angry voice. He'd know it anywhere.

His uncle!

How?

Before Mark could consider the question, his uncle emerged from the passage, liquor-fueled hate burning in his eyes.

"You never should have run! Now I'm just going to have to straighten you out again." Mark's uncle marched toward him.

Mark tried to scramble back up the entrance of the burrow but it had mysteriously closed.

"You can't run this time, runt. You are getting what you deserve."

Mark wanted to curl up into a ball, but his body froze in fear. He closed his eyes and braced for the blow like he had so many times before.

Another voice, remembered from his conversations with Barnabas. *"It's not your fault he beats you. You don't deserve it, no matter what you've done. Good people don't beat their kids like that. One of these days, you gotta take a stand."*

Mark opened his eyes. He stood tall and stared down his uncle. "No. I'm not taking your abuse anymore. Not today. Not ever again!"

His uncle charged, fists flying.

Mark yelled and swung his own fist, but it passed right through his uncle, and his uncle vanished.

Silas reached down the again-opened entrance and helped Mark out of the burrow.

"My uncle – I saw him."

Silas nodded. "I know."

~*~

Mark's lessons continued through the fall and into the winter. One night in early spring, as they traveled to a performance, Silas asked Mark to recite the beginning of the story he had picked out for that night.

Mark delivered the first twenty lines, not missing a single word.

"You are doing well."

"One day I will be greatest Magideem in all the land! They will sing my name from the mountains to the seas!"

The old man frowned.

Mark cocked his head. "Is there something wrong?"

"You have been with me all this time, yet you still do not understand."

Mark didn't even try to hide the puzzlement in his face.

"This isn't about you, or me. It's about those farmers and merchants who come to hear our tales. We take them out of their miserable reality. We bring just a whisper of joy into their lives, and if we do our jobs masterfully then for just a few moments they may forget the labors of their day, and the ache in their backs. We do this to make *them* heroes, boy. Not the other way around."

~*~

Over the next month Mark noticed changes. They traveled less, and the old Magideem wouldn't wake until midday. A hacking cough had become Silas' constant companion. That made it all the more strange when Mark found Silas packing their wagon one morning.

"Are you well enough to travel?" Mark asked.

"The time for the final trial has come. Pack something warm."

A day's travel north found them at the base of the Heaven's Reach Mountain. Mark and Silas made camp at the base of a sheer face.

After doubling over with a coughing spell, Silas straightened and pointed toward the cloud-shrouded summit.

"Climb it."

Mark looked up in awe. He had had no training, and no net. He just stood there, mouth agape. "I... I can't."

"Doubt," Silas wheezed, "is the Magideem's greatest enemy." He paused to catch his breath, and then finished his thought, "Welcome to the Trial of Doubt."

Mark looked over at Silas. Barely half a season had passed since they first met, but Silas looked ten years older now. Mark wondered just how long Silas had been a Magideem.

Turning his attention back to the wall, Mark noticed small indentations, and outcroppings. He reached out and tested one. His hand fit over it well. He pulled his legs up and hung there for a moment.

Satisfied it would hold him; he took a deep breath, and started his climb. Each hand-hold and footrest led to the next. He had to plan out two or three moves ahead or he would find himself at a spot where he couldn't continue.

His hands and feet ached. He wondered how much farther he had to go, so he made the mistake of checking his progress by looking down.

Silas and the wagon looked so small. Mark looked back up, and he still couldn't see the summit. Pain shot through his fingers and his heels. He couldn't hold on much longer. *I'm never going to make it. I can't do it. I was a fool to ever think I could become a Magideem.*

But another voice told him a different story. The final encouragement Barnabas had given him. *I know you can do this. As long as you don't quit, you'll succeed.*

Mark steadied himself, and took several deep breaths. He reached out a tentative hand to the next hold. The pain never relented, but his fingers held.

He reached the summit and found Silas already standing there to help Mark to his feet.

"How – ?"

Silas pointed a sheepish thumb toward a cave behind him. "There's an entrance on the eastern face. It's quite a pleasant climb."

~*~

They made the long journey back to the cabin. Silas wheezed louder every mile.

Mark helped the old Magideem into bed, and Silas bid Mark to sit down next to him. "I have taught you all that you need to know, and you have passed every trial. Once, only the Council of Six could designate a new Magideem, but they have become corrupt, and spend their time fighting each other. Now, an old Magideem must appoint new ones, and today, Mark of Chatshire, you have joined our ranks."

Silas paused for another wracking cough.

"Now, my boy, tell me a story."

A Splash of Art
by Katharina Gerlach

Mia put down her paintbrush and looked at her picture. It just didn't look like the one she had in her head. Why couldn't she get it out the way she wanted? It was as if the paint fought her just like hammer and marble had done in the course before or the wood she used for carving before that. She ground her teeth and glanced at the other kids in her class. In their drab, gray uniforms they melted into the gray walls as if nothing but their easels and the colorful pictures filled the room.

Footsteps approached from behind, but Master Ryan's shadow never fell on her canvas due to the bright overhead light.

"What's that supposed to be? A holy lady in under-wear?" His voice held more than the usual contempt.

Mia swallowed and ducked, not daring to answer.

Her teacher walked on, leaving snide remarks at every pupil's creation. Nothing pleased him.

"I bet his application for Artist status has been turned down once more," Jenna whispered from the easel behind Mia. "I don't get it, though. Why is it so darn important to belong to the crème de la crème? He earns a lot more as an art teacher than what he would get in the temple."

Mia didn't answer. For one, she was scared Master Ryan would hear, and secondly, she understood his ambition all too well. If she dared to daydream, she always found herself in a circle of artists talking about themes, ideas, colors, words, or melodies.

"It's unfair to vent his frustrations in the classroom," Jenna said.

Fast as lightning, Master Ryan's pointer slammed into Mia's painting. The crash made her wince.

"No talking. All of you are untalented, lazy, and too stupid for your own good." Master Ryan's voice echoed through the classroom as if they were in a giant cave. "None of you has an inkling of the golden ratio or the balance of asymmetry. I'm stuck in a class of imbeciles posing as artists."

He turned his easel, and Mia gasped. Tears shot into her eyes as she contemplated the Lady with the Child he had painted. The picture's proportions were perfectly balanced, and mother and child looked nearly real. If it hadn't been for the modern architecture in the background, it could have been one of the old masters.

"If you refuse to give it all you've got, why do your parents still bother to pay for the course? They might as well burn their money." Master Ryan's face had turned purple, a shade he wouldn't lose for a while, Mia knew. She lost herself in the composition of his picture.

His rant ended as abruptly as it had started. With a cold, flat voice he announced, "The whole class is on kitchen duty for the rest of the week."

Mia groaned inside but didn't dare to complain as others did. When the bell went off, she packed her things as fast as she could. With a little luck, she'd be able to go to the library for a few minutes before someone fetched her class for duty. No such luck.

"The old grumping miser. If I didn't love working in the kitchen so much, I'd complain to my parents. After all, they pay for his wages too." Jenna grabbed her arm and pulled her out of the school toward the community's kitchen compound, the ugliest building of their community. Mia often wondered what the architect had in mind when he planned a building that looked like a giant water kettle. She would have liked to ask him, but he lived in the temple with the other True Artists. She sighed, but Jenna never noticed. She was too busy ranting about Master Ryan's unfairness.

They had to wait for nearly twenty minutes before all members of the class had arrived, some escorted by a community guard. The assistant of a subcook told them what to do and handed out white aprons. Jenna and Mia were paired, and another assistant led them to the food serving area. Mia had seen more of the stainless steel kitchen than she cared to remember, but this was work she'd never done before.

"Your task is simple," the assistant said. "Just put one helping of everything on the plates and push them onto the conveyor belt. It will take it into the warming facility and dispense them one by one to the hungry people in the lunchroom."

Straightforward and boring as hell. Mia slipped the last of her brown curls under the obligatory hairnet. The white of the walls made her itch. They reminded her of fresh snow on a winter morning, and she longed for colors to splash all over this biggest possible canvas in the community.

"Ooh, I'm so excited." Jenna's eyes sparkled. "I wish father would relent and let me work here permanently. Did you see the third subcook from the right? I met him in the shop the other day. He's the cutest boy ever. I mean, you can't see it with those white overalls, but his muscles... I bet he goes to the gym every day."

Mia didn't bother to point out that everyone went to the gym every day. It was obligatory unless a doctor pronounced you unfit. She sighed and let her friend ramble while she grabbed the spoons and ladled rice, beans, salad, and meat onto the plates with a small helping of cranberry sauce on the side. After the tenth plate, her mind decided to take a break from reality. Her hands worked automatically, Jenna's voice blurred into a monotonous melody, and the conveyor belt took plate after plate into the gaping maw of the warming tunnel.

"Did it ever occur to you that the food has a texture no ordinary paint can match?" Part of her wanted to dig her fingers into the cranberry sauce. "With a little imagination, you could produce something quite nice," the voice in her head insisted. "It wouldn't be spectacular since you haven't got all that many colors to work with, but it wouldn't be bad. The food's texture would help."

Mia shook her head. Now, she was really going crazy. Master Ryan had been right all the time. She would never make a good Artist. Not when that crazy part of her insisted on playing with food like a toddler. She looked at Jenna who had stopped talking a while ago.

When her friend noticed that she had returned to the world from her imagination, she grinned. "I really wish I could lose myself in thought the way you do. I would hide inside my mind until Master Ryan's visit is over."

Mia smiled. "Did I miss him?" She hoped against better knowledge. Master Ryan always inspected them close to the shift's end to make sure everybody stayed.

"If only." Jenna laughed and slapped another helping of green beans onto the third to last plate.

"Come on," the voice in her head urged. "It's only two more plates. Do whatever you like. Master Ryan will never know. They'll be inside the tunnel before he'll ever make it to here."

One more plate was gone before the temptation was so strong, Mia couldn't help herself any longer. She held up her hand as Jenna prepared to slap more food on the plate.

"Wait. I want to try something." She grabbed a handful of rice. "Make sure that the Master isn't coming to us first." Jenna stared at her open-mouthed, and Mia realized that it was the first time ever in their friendship that she had uttered something akin to an order. She grinned at her friend. "I'll let you peek if you keep him out of my way long enough."

Speechless, Jenna nodded and scurried toward the kitchen's only entrance.

With the rice, Mia created a base for her picture. She had something in mind already. Gently rubbing cranberry sauce into the right places, she shaded a basic face. She sliced meat for hair, and the beans, if neatly aligned, would make a splendid vest. She worked like a maniac and finished just as Jenna returned.

"He's on his…" Jenna's jaw dropped as she gazed at the face made of food. "That's incredible, Mia."

Mia blushed and pushed the plate onto the conveyor belt, when she heard Master Ryan's heavy footsteps coming closer. All of a sudden, she sweated. The conveyor belt seemed to slow down deliberately. *Go faster, please.* Mia didn't dare to turn. Her ears burned as if her teacher had already smacked her. *Please hurry.* Mia stared at the tunnel wishing the plate to move faster.

"So, how are you doing?" Master Ryan's voice sounded friendlier than before, but the plate would change that any minute, Mia knew.

"You can't imagine how much I enjoyed this, Master Ryan." Jenna spoke faster and more high-pitched than ever. "Can't you talk to my father and tell him what a failure I am as an up-and-coming Artist? I'd love to work here more often. It's my dream job."

When Mia turned, her best friend clung to the teacher's arm, imploring him with wide eyes. She could look so puppy-dog if she wanted.

"Well, if that is your wish…" Master Ryan stared at her with disgust. Then, he looked up at Mia. "Do you want to quit the course as well?"

Mia shook her head and glanced at the mouth of the tunnel once more. Luckily, the offending plate was gone. A weight tumbled from her heart, and she smiled timidly.

"Well, don't you have a mouth?"

"No. I mean … yes sir, I do have a mouth. And no, I don't want to quit, I love art."

"It's not as if I've seen anything worth looking at yet. Nine A.M. tomorrow for both of you, and bring your parents," the Master said and turned to go. Jenna and Mia followed him. At the kitchen door, they all took off their white coats and put them into a drop that led directly down to the washing room. They neared the exit, when a stocky cook came running after them. Mia stared. A real cook – not an assistant or a subcook. His white chef's hat wobbled as he sprinted.

"Wait, girls, don't go yet." He panted heavily and wiped his brow when he reached them. "You were the ones servicing food dispenser seven five?"

Jenna and Mia nodded in unison, and Master Ryan's face clouded.

"I knew they'd cause trouble."

The cook took both girls' arms and dragged them along.

"Hurry up, the Great Master of Arts wants to see you."

Mia's heart dropped into her feet that became nearly too heavy to lift, but the cook dragged her along.

"We didn't do anything wrong. And we've got the right to demand our parents to be there if you take us in for questioning." Jenna's protest sounded sophisticated. Sometimes it was useful to have a friend with a judge for a father.

She kept complaining the whole way along the corridors to the small private serving room of the temple members.

Inside, the cook pressed the girls to the floor and left. Master Ryan knelt, pulling the girls down with him. Surprised, Mia glanced up at a middle-aged man who didn't look much different from other men his age she had seen. Except, he wore a robe covered in words printed onto the fabric. Her breath caught. With an insurrection like this on her slate, she'd never get a place in the temple. The palms of her hands grew wet in the silence.

The Grand Master mustered them and pulled up an eyebrow when he saw Master Ryan.

"Whose idea was this?" He pointed to the table where a telltale plate stood.

Mia blushed and lowered her gaze.

"We're not going to say a word unless our parents are here." Jenna folded her arms in front of her chest and pressed her lips together.

From below her eyelashes, Mia observed the man. He seemed nice enough, and at Jenna's words, his eyes widened.

Master Ryan got up. "Please excuse whatever mischief they caused this time. My students are not worthy of your attention. May I see what trouble they caused this time?" Without invitation, he walked to the table, bowing to the Grand Master several times. Two yellow-clad body guards stopped him, but he was close enough to see Mia's artwork. He paled.

"It seems he's not very pleased to see his likeness in food." The Grand Master smiled at Mia. "I'm not accusing you of anything. I was only surprised to find an artfully done face on my plate." He walked over and helped them up. "I would love to convince the artist that her place is with us at the temple." He held Mia's hands, and his eyes bored into hers as if he knew who had created the face on the plate. "Will you come with me for proper training?"

Mia nodded. This was the chance of her life, and she wouldn't miss it for the world.

My Soul To Take
by Amanda Tompkins

The fire escape gave an ominous creak as I scrabbled rather desperately for the brick ledge that hovered just out of arm's reach. Gritting my teeth against the urge to swear rather spectacularly, and in multiple languages, I finally managed to drag myself to the window of apartment 701's bedroom before I plummeted the seven stories to the unforgiving road below.

Sweating and – if I were being totally honest – wheezing at the exertion, I dragged my knees under myself and vowed to reconsider entering some cardio into my daily schedule. Crumbling bits of clay broke free and rained down from the outcropping. Not particularly wanting to follow them, and not wanting to make any explanation to any bystanders that might witness my unplanned descent, I reached into the Aether and wove a tiny bit of power through the ancient mortar and pigeon droppings that more or less held the ledge together.

Sweat made my hair cling to my forehead, and I pushed it back impatiently. The stuff was the bane of my existence; I should have just cut it off already, but I never seemed to get around to it. Pressing my face against the window felt good, and I rested there for a moment while my eyes adjusted to the dark bedroom. After a brief time, I could finally see well enough to make out more than just dim shapes, but then I kind of wished I couldn't.

The dark pink coverlet had been discarded in a tangle on the floor, and two bodies lay entwined on the bed, moving together rhythmically. The fact that one of the bodies happened to be transparent was pretty much the only thing preventing me from gouging my own eyes out.

Don't get me wrong, I have a healthy sex life, or at least I used to. I'm not a prude or anything, but I didn't like to watch strangers bump uglies. Though I suppose I didn't have much of a leg to stand on to support my displeasure, seeing as how I was peering through a window, of an apartment that wasn't mine, at midnight. Really, I was just lucky no one saw me and called the cops.

The window was locked, which was irritating but not entirely unexpected.

Condensation beaded on the glass as I exhaled slowly, and then dragged a finger through the resulting moisture in a brief pattern, which caused the window to crumble into a torrent of sand of equal mass.

I felt smug about my tidy conversion right up until I tried to stealthily slide my leg down into the apartment without alerting the inhabitants, and managed to step on the cat that was squatting like a loaf of evil pumpernickel as it glared at the people on the bed.

The resulting shriek of outraged fury woke people in the next time zone, I'm sure. It also surprised me enough that I stumbled and went sprawling face first into the carpet, and knocked over a teetering pile of paperbacks, bringing dozens of little sharp corners down on my head and back.

I hate cats. Smug little furry bastards, always acting like they know something I don't. And the worst part is, they usually do.

There was a kind of imploded squeak, and the two figures on the bed separated while I scrambled back to my feet. I could feel the blood in my cheeks, and knew I was scarlet all the way to my hairline. Pasty skin inherited from my Irish grandfather meant I was prone to freckles *and* blushes that could be seen from outer space. I won the genetic lottery on that one.

Light flooded the room, making me throw one arm up to cover my eyes at the sudden glare of the bedside lamp. The thirtyish-looking woman fumbled hastily for her glasses while the obscenely pretty man in the ruffled shirt and leather pants hovered two inches above the floor, glancing back and forth between us.

The woman peered at us both, mouth working silently for a moment before she squeaked again. "I'm not dreaming!" Diving for the comforter on the ground, she hastily wrapped it around herself, which I thought was a little unnecessary since she was already in a full pair of flannel pajamas. "What are you doing in my apartment? I'll scream!" Her voice kept climbing higher; in short order only dogs would be able to hear her if she did manage a scream. I didn't think it was a real threat though, since once she truly focused on the dark-haired Adonis currently flexing on the other side of the bed, her voice trailed off after a garbled, "You!".

"My dear one, my butterfly, come back to bed and let me love you, *Cherie*."

The woman stood, gaping at him long enough for me to actually say something.

"To answer your question, he's a manifestation that's here to drain your life force, and I'm here to save you."

They both turned to stare at me for a minute, before she managed to croak out a few more words. "You're here to save me?"

"You see anyone else here?"

"Well, no, but … wait, drain my life force? How could you!" The thrown pillow sailed harmlessly through the manifestation's chest and thumped lightly against the wall behind it.

"I would never! I love you, *Cherie*! I have crossed oceans to be with you!" It even spoke in purple prose. There is no mercy in the world.

"Alright, look I hate to break up this little love fest, but... well, actually no, I don't. Yes, he's here to drain your life force. You dreamed him up, you summoned him here with your wishing, and he needs to feed. So he's got to go so you can go back to bed, and I can get on with my life."

The woman sat down on the bed abruptly, her cheeks scarlet. "I did not wish for –." She coughed and tried again. "I mean, I dreamt of... But that doesn't mean anything!"

"Yeah, well, a dream is a wish your heart makes, to misquote a Disney princess." I toed over another stack of paperbacks whose covers were plastered with half-dressed young women with big hair and Hollywood's version of historical dresses, some in clinches with improbably groomed men sporting enormous chests. "And it means you might want to branch out in your reading habits."

"Who *are* you?"

"Aisling O'Reily, Magi."

She blinked rapidly, and for a second I was afraid she'd pass out on me. It had happened before.

"Magi?"

"I'm a will worker. A Mage. A seeker of knowledge. I wield the potential power of the Aether."

"So you're like, a witch? A sorceress?"

It was a kind of simplified, but whatever got her through. I didn't really want to explain myself anyway. Just in, banish, out, and then I could go get some waffles. "If you like."

"What I'd *like* is for you people to get out of my apartment!"

I sighed, and fished a piece of blue chalk out of the pocket of my jeans and knelt down to start tracing out the formula I would need, ignoring her squawk of protest. Some Magi didn't need the words, the symbols, to do what they did, but I liked them. They reminded me of my old life.

"Look, Sherry." She jumped and stared at me, both put at ease and more frightened that I knew her name. "I can go, but then the manifestation will keep coming back. Over and over, until it drains you to death and it takes on its own physicality. You gave it form, your belief gave it shape, it won't leave you alone now. I'm not sure if that will impact my Karma, but I don't really want to take the chance."

"No, *ma petite*! I would never – "

Its words were cut off as I dismissed its mouth with an angry gesture. "That's enough out of the peanut gallery, thank you."

Sherry stared at the outraged manifestation, and then turned back to me. "You really are a witch."

"Magi. And I said as much, didn't I?"

"Well, yes, but – " Her eyes trailed over me, and my hands rose to tug at the hem of my sweatshirt self-consciously before I could stop myself. I hoped she didn't see the coffee stain. Flustered and trying to hide it, I turned back to my formula. The sweeping arches and arcane squiggles began to take shape, and maybe I got a tiny, petty thrill from pressing the chalk harder than necessary into the white carpet.

There was an awkward pause while Sherry watched me work, still bundled up in her comforter on the bed, and the manifestation pawed at its face and glared at me with smoldering dark eyes. I tried not to laugh.

"So, how do you become a Magi? Are you born that way?"

The sound I made in response was bitterness personified. "Not a chance. A year ago, I was a perfectly normal woman, working on my thesis in experimental physics."

From her expression, Sherry didn't agree that being interested in physics let me claim the classification of normal, but I let it go. I'm magnanimous like that.

"So, what happened?"

Sitting back on my heels, I sighed a little. "Have you ever thought about a word over and over again, until it loses all meaning and stops making sense to you?" I waited for her to nod before continuing. "I did that with reality."

Both of them stared at me, clearly unable to wrap their minds – or a reasonable facsimile in the manifestation's artfully coiffured head – around this, and all my old resentment started bubbling up to the surface.

"Our universe is governed by theories and laws that really make very little sense when you get right down to it. If quantum physics doesn't alarm you, then you don't understand it well enough. Energy and vibrations and molecules in transition; I hear some people awaken to magic in some blinding light of illumination. Mine was more like a nervous breakdown."

I stomped over to Sherry, who flinched back and yelped when I tugged out one hair from her head. "So there I am, suddenly realizing that I can manipulate the world in ways others only dream of, and *bam*! Up shows Cornelius Abernathy, my new 'Master.' You'll have to forgive the sarcastic air quotes. He tells me he's been sent by the council of Magi to teach me the mysteries of the universe, and, like a sucker, I believed him."

She was hanging forward now, intent on my story. "He didn't teach you?"

"Oh sure, the old goat showed me a few things. Then, get this, he and the Council get together to cast a spell to 'protect all mankind' from the weakening barrier of the Aether. Twenty seven of the world's most powerful will workers, coming together to save shmoes like you from the crap they call through across the barrier. Um, no offense."

"And yet, I'm offended."

"Anyway, someone chants when they should have conjured, and *whamo*! The whole spell goes up like a tornado, and storms over the world, ripping holes in the Aether and making everything *worse* than it was before! And the best part? The pompous old jerks aren't even around to deal with it!"

"They died?"

"How the hell would I know? They're gone. They vanished when the Mage storm hit. Poof! Left the handful of apprentices behind to take care of their freaking mess! I signed on to learn the mysteries of the universe, not to clean up metaphysical bed-wetting!"

The manifestation's gestures were getting more frantic and I finally released his mouth with an impatient snarl. "What?"

It worked its jaw for a second before responding. "You have quite the little red-headed temper, *non*?"

"Make one ginger joke, Le Pew. I *dare* you."

Though it was only a couple of hours old, apparently the manifestation knew when it was being mocked. I also discovered that it had absorbed enough energy from starry-eyed Sherry to be able to affect the physical world, when it howled and darted across the room to wrap surprisingly strong fingers around my throat.

Sherry shrieked, and started pummeling its back with a pillow. "Get off of her!"

I choked, and tried to pry it off while I reached for the Aether. "I don't need your help! I'm a Magi of the Seven Spheres!"

"What does that even mean?"

"I don't know! They never got a chance to tell me!"

The lamp she smashed over its head proved to be far more effective. I dropped to the floor, hoping to complete the pattern before it regained its sense, but a strangled gasp snapped my head up.

The manifestation had wrapped itself around Sherry, one arm anchoring her, the other covering her mouth. It glared at me balefully, and its features lost some of their chiseled prettiness as it began to feed.

"I heard you correctly, *mademoiselle sorciere*. If I take it all, I will become real. I will have life, and not be bound to one room under the cover of darkness. I will be free to have as many women as I desire."

Sherry looked a little indignant at that, but I just sighed and sat back on my heels. "Too bad you wished for handsome and vast expanses of man-boob instead of, like, smarts or loyalty."

The manifestation made a warning hiss, and Sherry's eyes fluttered behind her glasses as her skin went pale.

"You must not have been listening well, boy toy. I said Sherry could feed you initially, because she's the one who created you. You're just raw Aether shaped by her belief."

I saw the spark of recognition behind her glasses, and a wave of relief surged over me that I hadn't overestimated her. Sometimes even smart people go totally useless in dangerous situations, but Sherry wasn't going to let me down.

The manifestation hesitated, and I used my will to complete the pattern and open the barrier enough for Sherry to send her deadbeat dream man back to the beyond.

Instead, I felt an energy *drain* as Aether got pulled into the world.

There was a small implosion and a burst of light. When it cleared, I picked myself up, full of fury at her stupidity. "Why in Hell – !"

Then I paused. And looked down. Way down. The black teacup poodle seemed at least as surprised as I was.

Sherry blinked at me, waving away the last of the smoke. "I thought you wanted me to reshape him! That's what you said, isn't it? That my belief gave him form?"

"I thought you'd banish him." A miniature yap trailed off into a whimper. "Why'd you pick this form?"

"You said it yourself; smarts and loyalty." She shrugged. "I always wanted a dog."

All I could do was shake my head. "Ain't love grand?"

The Forest King
by Amanda Tompkins

There once was a girl who lived at the edge of a forest, whose mother loved her very much. This forest wasn't like others; it was thick and lush, and had never known a blade. Oak and yew grew to towering heights within, and pine and spruce perfumed the air year round. There were places within it where the canopy was so thick, the light could not so much as peek through.

Though the woods teemed with animals, and the bushes were heavy with berries, the people never went there. In fact, most seemed to forget that the forest was there at all; their lives consumed by town and field. But the girl never forgot.

The girl's mother warned her never to set foot in the forest, as it was full of wolves and bears and any number of other dangers. And the girl obeyed, but she could not forget the forest as the others did.

Sometimes she would stand at the edge of the woods, and look as far into the trees as she could. She'd listen to the sleepy twitter of songbirds, and the slow drip of water onto the ground. It always seemed so cool and soothing, especially in the summer when the sun seared everything around it to a uniform brown. The shadows were thick under the branches, spun out like cobwebs until it was as if night never lifted from within the forest.

The girl would stand at the edge of the trees, where the shadows lapped like the cool water of a pond, but she dared not stick so much as one toe inside, her mother's warning still in her ears. One day, the frustration became too great.

"I'm not afraid of you," she called into the woods, and the birdsong stilled. The shadows took on a mocking quality.

"Then why," they seemed to ask, "do you refuse to set as much as one toe inside?"

The girl didn't know how to respond. The only answer she had to give was that her mother was afraid, but that seemed like no answer at all.

So she turned and walked back to the house, the mocking laughter of ravens harsh in her ears.

~*~

For days the girl managed to stay away, but eventually her feet drew her back to the forest's edge where the shadows hung heavy and the wind sighed through the leaves. She heard the raven's call, and the frogs singing somewhere deep under the trees. She could smell the green of the foliage, and the musk of animals, all mixed with the rich scent of loam. A fox ghosted out from the bushes, glancing back at her, as if expectant, before disappearing again.

Finally, the girl let the wind tug her into the trees, to where the berries grew thick on the bushes, sweet and tart.

"See?" she said to herself. "Nothing to fear." And so she strayed deeper. And there were nuts fallen on the ground, their meat firm and sweet. And so she strayed deeper. She walked until the world grew quiet, and the light faded. She wandered deeper; until the ground was carpeted in moss so thick it silenced her footsteps. She walked until the shadows rose up and blocked her path.

The girl stopped then, for the shadows became a man, tall and strong. Great branching antlers crowned his brow, and his eyes were golden, as a wolf. The shadows reached for her, but the girl ran.

She ran, and the shadows followed on her heels. She heard the cry of the owl, and the mournful howl of the wolf. She heard the call of the raven, and the voice of the wind that spoke her name in hushed tones.

She ran past the trees and the bushes, past the edge of the woods, and over the field. She ran until she reached her house, and shut the door on the shadows that chased her still, locking them outside.

But the shadows didn't go away. She saw them in corners, hiding in tiny nooks. They stretched out behind the people in the village, lingering near her before being pulled away. And the other people in the village began to look at her as they did the forest, with fear and mistrust. Eventually, they simply ducked their heads and hurried past, as though they had forgotten her as they had the trees that were their neighbors.

At night, she heard the mournful song of the wolf, echoing over the fields and roads, calling her back. It was a sound full of loneliness, of sadness and fading hope, and it made her toss in her bed.

The girl again heard her mother's warning, but her feet led her back to the trees. The shadows were waiting for her, and again became a man with branching antlers that seemed to grow into the canopy, and then the man became a wolf.

The wolf sang to her a song, a song about a woman who had wanted a child so badly that she had traveled deep into the forest, and had stolen away a piece of it. The shadows reached for her, but the girl was frightened and ran away, locking the door once more to keep the darkness at bay.

The people continued to forget her, bound by their lives to town and field. The shadows never left; she saw them everywhere now. So the girl went to her mother, and asked her if the wolf who was a man spoke true. And her mother tried to deny it, but the lie would not pass her lips. So she wept, and clung to the girl.

"I wanted a daughter, more than anything. I love you; I did everything to keep you safe. I moved us away from the forest, to a place of sun-browned fields, far from branch or leaf."

"But we live at the edge of the forest," said the girl in confusion. "We have always lived next to the forest."

"The forest follows us, daughter," her mother sobbed. "It follows you."

The girl returned to the woods, and she heard the wolf and the owl. She heard the birds, and the sighing of the wind. She walked past the bushes full of berries, and past the places where the nuts fell to the earth. She walked on moss so thick it silenced the world, to where the shadows waited.

The shadows became a man with branching antlers and golden eyes like a wolf. The darkness reached for her, and this time she stepped forward to meet them. Shadows embraced the girl, wrapping her in a protective cloak of night, and she spoke to them with the voice of the wind in the trees.

"Father."

There once was a girl who lived by the edge of a village, whose father loved her very much.

The Wish

by Martha Verlander

"If you could have one wish – a wish guaranteed to come true – what would it be?"

Lilla was the third classmate Jerriette had asked today. She'd thought about journaling the answers, but if her classmates saw her write it down, they'd be less likely to answer. Instead she tucked their answers into the corner of her brain that remembered pretty much everything.

Lilla cocked her head, long blond hair falling forward over her shoulder. "To be the most popular girl in school, of course."

Jerriette should have known. Lilla had a brain – a good one – but preferred not to use it. She'd have to push a little. "Why?"

Lilla stared at her, totally perplexed. "Well... everybody likes you!"

"Why is that important?"

"Why *isn't* it? I'd always have someone to hang out with, to do things with..." Her voice trailed off, as if she'd exhausted the limit of her ideas.

"You know, some won't like you just *because* you're popular."

Lilla shrugged. "What would you suggest?"

All kinds of things, but that really wasn't the point.

"I think you said the first cool thing you thought of. Maybe you'd choose something else if you thought about it more. Why don't you give it some thought and tell me tomorrow what you'd wish."

"Why?" Lilla said. "It's not like you could make my wish come true. So who cares?" The bell rang for sixth period. Lilla shrugged. "Gotta go. Ol' Danyluk is a terror when you're late." She leaped to her feet and escaped.

Jerriette sighed. Not very promising. No more than the other two she'd questioned. She needed a good answer. Soon.

By day's end, Jerriette had spoken to seven kids. Answers ranged from money to popularity, to straight As, to a new car, to... whatever.

She'd have thought surely someone – Lilla seemed like-lyest – would ask for world peace, or abolition of hunger, or something important like that. Everything depended on it.

Her own wish wouldn't count, because she knew the stakes. She walked away from school as the final bell rang. How could she be expected to find an appropriate wish in time? She couldn't afford to lose. Mankind couldn't afford for her to lose!

Unable to make herself go home, she instead walked to the riverbank two blocks from the school. If she couldn't think of something, she could always throw herself into the current and drown. Better than watching everything crumble around her.

Luckily, no one was making out on the riverbank today.

Sick with worry, she sat cross-legged on the bank, watching the water. Superimposed over the surface she imagined an old woman's craggy face, speckled with liver spots, with deep-sunken, watery eyes.

She seemed an old woman, but Jerriette still couldn't be sure if she'd been a witch, a sorcerer, or an angel of death.

"Look! What do you see?" the old woman had asked. She passed her hand above the wide, shallow bowl of water.

Jerriette looked, expecting to see the bottom of the bowl through the water.

Instead, the water flickered with color and cleared, leaving a vision across the surface. She didn't recognize the view at first.

A war-torn city of shattered streets, crying children, filth and debris everywhere. A man with eyeballs melting down his cheeks ...

Horrified, she began to cry in big, gulping sobs. The picture disappeared from the water but not from Jerriette's brain. Never from her brain.

Even now she felt the tears on her face, remembering. "Who are you?" she whispered. "*What* are you?"

The old woman laughed – a young woman's laugh, but no less disturbing for that. "Do you know what you're seeing?"

Jerriette shuddered. "Something awful! A world war? The end of the world?"

The woman stood, age sloughing from her face like melting wax. Smooth, unlined cheeks. Full, rosy lips. Eyes bright and knowing. "You see the times to come. I have been sent to find one person to save the world. You are the one chosen. What you do within the next day and a night will determine whether the earth lives or dies."

Shocked, Jerriette had argued for the earth, begged for mercy, and even tried a temper tantrum.

The woman disappeared, after giving specific instructtions. The ones Jerriette was trying desperately to follow.

What are *the priorities of human beings?* she wondered. She wasn't allowed to tell people that her questions were a test. She could only find out what they truly valued, more than anything else. The question was important, but she had been warned to do nothing to influence the answers.

"Why me?" she cried to the birds and squirrels by the riverbank. "Why did the old woman bring this to me? I'm just a kid!" The old woman should have gone to the president, or the pope, or someone like that. Someone who would know what to do, to find a way out of the trap she felt closing in.

Why me? she asked again. *Am I the first one she saw? Or was I singled out?*

225

The birds had stopped singing. The sudden quiet drew her attention and she looked around, uneasy.

The old woman stood nearby, though Jerriette could have sworn no one had been there a minute ago.

"You have been busy," the woman said, "working hard to accomplish great things. Come closer, so you may see what you have achieved."

The crone sat on the ground before her scrying bowl – that hadn't been there until she sat – and gestured for Jerriette to sit across from her.

Reluctantly, she took the place indicated and bent forward to see what the bowl showed. She saw Poppy, the first classmate she'd approached. Poppy's wish? Money.

Jerriette watched as the wish came true, burying Poppy in a sudden avalanche of gold coins. The image of Poppy shrieked and ducked out from under the onslaught, but within moments she bore cuts and bruises on face and arms from the shower of heavy coins.

Jerriette shuddered.

The old woman spoke again. "The weight of her desire has borne her down." She passed her hand above the bowl again.

Susan had wished for a dog, and she got one. The sheer joy of having a furry playmate shone from her face as she played with it in her yard. Then the dog bit her, mangling her arm badly.

Jake, the captain of the high school football team, had wished for a car – a really cool sports car! The day he got it, he got into a drag race and crashed. The car had been totaled and Jake was still in the hospital from his injuries.

Such a simple trap. Find out what people really want most. Give it to them. Magnified. Let them see for themselves the true value of whatever they yearned for.

And don't let them change their minds. No do-overs.

"We are responsible for the choices we make, and for the consequences of those choices," the old woman said, sorrow edging her voice.

"Don't we ever get good consequences?" Jerriette cried, her heart tight with grief and anger.

"Yes. We choose the consequences by choosing the action. The two cannot be separated."

"These are my fault, then, for I chose to do as you told me to, without knowing what would happen."

"These are not your fault. I am the one who commanded you, and I knew what the consequences could be, though I'd hoped for better." The voice and the ancient eyes held compassion.

"Why? Why would you do such a thing?"

"These lessons are for you. What have you learned?"

"Never to trust a stranger." She'd learned more than that, but spite felt better at the moment.

"And?"

The words dragged out of her mouth. "To think ahead. To consider consequences, to imagine the worst scenario." She lifted her chin. "Not to trust a stranger whose motives I don't know."

"These are not wishes I have made. They're the wishes of those you spoke to. I do not control your world's future. You do. I'm simply teaching you some tools to make the outcome more to your liking."

Jerriette sat abruptly on the grass. "You're saying that *I'm* responsible for everybody's future? When I can't control any of the people?"

"Tell me, Jerriette. If *you* could have one wish – a wish guaranteed to come true – what would *you* wish for?"

"I didn't think my wish counted."

"It does now. One wish only. No do-overs."

She opened her mouth to say, "I wish I'd never met you." And closed it again without speaking. "How long can I think about it?"

"Until midnight tomorrow." The woman passed a hand above the bowl again. She and the bowl disappeared.

Jerriette turned and walked away. Too little time. It wasn't fair. She savagely kicked a rock, sending it into the river with a small splash.

Think of the consequences. Some clue that was! Agitated, she walked along the river, watching sticks and debris in the water.

What if she refused to make a wish? The old woman couldn't force her, after all.

Consequences. Failure to make a choice was still making a choice. Her heart sank. That would set the world on the path to the destruction she'd seen in the bowl.

So. What kind of wish could change that future? She closed her eyes and pictured the world as she thought it should be. Everyone in her scenario got along. Everyone was happy. They all had enough money to live on. The land was peaceful and civilization was eco-friendly. Dogs and cats played together and never bit or scratched people. She concentrated on imagining a world as perfect as she could.

The next step: Consequences. This felt like the key to everything, if she wasn't overreacting to the woman's lecture. What could be the consequences of having a world like the one she imagined?

People could be bored with everything so perfect. Who would try to make something new, if the world was already perfect? Who would try to solve a problem – assuming they found one to solve? If everything was perfect, would all desire to create disappear?

Or would people be so bored they might try to destroy the perfection, just for something different to do? She could think of a lot of things that could go wrong, given human nature. So maybe she should wish instead for a change in human nature? So that nobody would be greedy or jealous or …

Jerriette walked until she became tired, then sat again, still thinking – playing the "what if" game.

And then she walked again, this time to public places to observe. After that she visited neighborhoods, looking for ideas. *Good thing Dad can't see me now, in this part of town! He'd be so angry!*

Why? Not because she was disobedient. Because he feared for her. A lot of crime happened in this part of town.

Her mind twisted around that for a bit. Love, and hate, and conflict. How could one wish remove all anger, all hate, all inequality, all pain? And what would the consequences be? Would it be worthwhile to have that world?

Jerriette's stomach growled. She'd forgotten to eat. And her folks would be worried because she hadn't come home from school.

She turned her footsteps toward home, suddenly more worried about them than about a perfect wish. Walking as fast as possible, she still struggled with questions and responsibility, fairness and consequences…

Could perfection even be possible?

And then she stopped. She had an answer. She knew what to wish.

~*~

Jerriette had gone over and over her choice, lying awake all last night and skipping school today to think it through one more time. She couldn't think of anything else, let alone concentrate on her studies, so she might as well not be there. The crone waited for her on the grassy verge of the school's football field, her scrying bowl in front of her and a satisfied look on her face.

Jerriette saw no one else, not even kids in phys. ed. classes or on their way home.

She'd asked no one what they wished for since her last talk with the old woman. She didn't need answers anymore. Either what she had would be enough – or it wouldn't. She'd done the best she could, tried hard to examine consequences and find the right path forward.

Without a greeting, Jerriette folded her legs and sat across the bowl from the crone.

They sat quietly, each sizing the other up. Jerriette met the old woman's gaze calmly and waited. Strangely, she felt no fear or trepidation. She no longer worried about her answer. A quiet acceptance ran softly through her veins. Because she knew her wish to be the correct one?

No. Simply because she had an answer. It was all she had to offer.

"Tell me," said the crone, "if you had one wish, guaranteed to be granted, what would you wish for? No take-backs, no do-overs. You know the stakes."

"This is a good world, with people who argue and fight, love and hate, build and tear down. People are wonderful, and they're awful. They rub off on each other, their lives influenced by all those they meet, by all their own experiences. The future cannot be decided or determined by one person, only influenced. We're all doing the best we can already. Most of us, anyway. I can't think of any way to make the future better by myself. We haven't done such a bad job so far, have we?" She took a deep breath before continuing.

"I wish for the world to continue as it has since the beginning.

"I want all of us to have the chance to live our lives the best we can, for the earth to follow its own course, with all the ills and healing, the good and the bad. I wish for us to be who we are. Nothing more, nothing less."

The old woman smiled, the corners of ancient lips curving up just a bit. "You were well chosen, Jerriette. One of the foibles of humans is always to desire what they cannot have. You are wise to choose simply to be who you are." She passed her hand over the bowl and disappeared.

In Jerriette's head, words rang softly. "There is no better future you could have envisioned."

And the world grew still, just before the birds began to sing again.

The Café
by Faith Boughan

I felt like I was about to throw up. Or fall over. Or both.

The noises and smells of the *souq*, however intoxicating, overwhelmed my senses and I felt an urge to escape, to reconnect with something familiar. I turned a corner, vision beginning to spin – though now I wonder whether it was just the first stage of dehydration – and my eyes landed on the first words that had made sense since entering the world-famous bazaar.

Arabic lettering announced in its flowing script what was written in blocky English letters below: Naguib Mahfouz Café.

Thank God, I thought. *Or should that be "praise Allah?"* My feet stumbled over the doorway's lip, and I only narrowly regained my balance before my knees buckled anyway and cracked against the floor. A few patrons at tables with mahogany tablecloths turned to assess the newcomer who had disturbed their murmurings with his intrusion.

I pretended not to notice.

A white-aproned waiter gestured that I sit down. I chose a seat in the far corner, opposite the kitchen entrance, and waited patiently while the waiter placed a worn, laminated menu on the small table.

"Sir? To drink?" His heavy accent meant I needed a few seconds to parse the strange sounds.

I coughed, stared at the menu for a moment, and replied, "Nescafe. No, scratch that, I'll have a karkade … cold, please."

The waiter nodded and smiled, turning on his heel toward the kitchen.

The hush of the café provided a stark contrast to the bustling, noisy, crowded atmosphere of *Khan al-Khalili*. I'd been warned to expect impatient tourists and pushy salesmen, but nothing could have prepared me for the actual experience of being here. In fact, I couldn't quite place a finger on why I'd bothered coming to Egypt in the first place. Social boredom? Career fatigue? Misguided romantic notions?

The waiter set down a thin glass of red liquid and folded his hands together. "Anything else, sir?"

"Not for the moment, thanks." He began to walk away, but I raised a hand just as his gaze slipped from mine. "Actually, would you mind turning the music down a bit?" I hadn't noticed it until just now – cymbals clanging amidst a repetitive phrase of drumbeats. The sudden awareness brought a throb to my temple.

He nodded and walked away. I sat for a minute, listening to the beat of the cymbals and drum, waiting for the music to soften. It got louder.

doum doum tek-a-tek doum tek-a-tek

A sip of the karkade brought a flush of calm from head to toe. I wondered what my boss would think if he knew where I was. I'd at least left a note for the woman who'd shared my bed the night before… before what?

Before I'd come to my senses and realized the waste I'd made of my life. Dull, boring, uninspired. Was that how I would spend the next thirty years? Thirty-five, if I got lucky?

One cab ride to the airport and one plane ticket to the furthest available location that night, and I'd landed in Egypt. Exotic, foreign Egypt, where I'd hoped to find out what it meant to live.

But forty minutes in the *souq* and all I'd learned was that people were people, no matter where in the world you found them. And that when it came to pistachio *hawala*, you really could have too much of a good thing. I might as well have stayed home and taken calls from telemarketers. At least you could hang up on them – in the bazaar, the merchants just followed you.

"Sir?" I hailed the waiter again. "The music?"

He nodded enthusiastically, smiled, and walked back to the kitchen. I got the point.

doum doum tek-a-tek doum tek-a-tek

I glanced around the room to find the speakers – maybe I could switch tables, find a spot less… rhythmic.

I saw no speakers. Were they hidden? No, that would require a significant cash flow and a willingness to make upgrades to the facility … something which the owner obviously didn't make a priority, judging by the cracked floor tiles and the black streaks of chipped paint along the walls from where patrons pushed their chairs back with too much force. Quaint, yes. Affluent, no.

So where were the speakers?

The more I strained to see them, the louder the cymbals chimed in my ears. I felt the first flush of migraine creep up the back of my neck, and I drained the rest of the karkade in hopes to stave it off. It didn't work.

I slapped five Egyptian pounds onto the table, though no doubt the drink cost far less. I'd come to the café for escape – I'd come to Egypt for escape – but it was clear that I'd come to the wrong place.

doum doum tek-a-tek doum tek-a-tek

"Good Lord, does no one else hear that?" I spoke aloud to no one in particular.

A man at a neighboring table gave me a quizzical look.

"Those … cymbals. The drums. Don't you find it a bit loud?"

He shrugged, and I wondered if he didn't speak English. Until he did. "I can't hear a bloody thing, friend. In fact, I was just commenting to my wife that the silence in here was rather delightful compared to the noise in the street."

I stared at him. "Are you deaf?"

His eyes narrowed. "Pardon?"

I shook my head and pressed two fingers to the bridge of my nose. I wasn't ready to face the *souq* again, but the clanging hurt my ears. I had a problem that demanded a solution. But wasn't that why I'd come to Egypt? To solve the problem of existence?

I shoved back from the table and the chair slid easily, bumping against the wall to add yet another streak of black. My signature. I stepped around the tables, vision blurring once more as the rhythm pounded through my skull and slipped down into my belly, churning the remains of my beverage.

Would it be louder, outside?

I touched the door and the drums changed.

They were softer. Sweeter. The cymbals rang with a welcoming chime.

The rhythm pulsed through my fingertips as relief surged through my shoulders.

But then came the voice.

"...faat omry seneen wa seneen, shoft aleel a'sheen elly beyeshky haala lahaala..."

Somewhere in the café, a woman *sang*.

"You've got to be kidding me."

I rubbed my face with both hands, feeling the hot flush of sunburnt skin that had only begun to ache. Why hadn't I worn a hat? Or brought sunscreen?

The doorway's lip taunted me, so I pushed on the door and raised a foot to cross the threshold – without incident, this time.

"Sir?"

The waiter. Hadn't I left enough money? Everyone in this country wanted more, more, more.

"Left the cash on the table," I called over my shoulder, but froze when I saw him.

He stood rigid by the kitchen doors, one arm extended toward a hallway that I swear didn't exist when I'd entered the café. Not that I had been particularly observant, as my aching knees could attest.

The waiter's gaze slid from mine to the hall.

"This way, sir."

That way? Into a mysterious hall, led by a stranger in a country where I didn't speak the language, knew nothing of the customs, and had only traveled to because it had been the first flight that could take me away from the reminders of life's mediocrity?

The people at neighboring tables said nothing, did nothing, heard nothing.

"Sir?"

I don't know why I turned around. I don't know why I took my hand off the door, and I don't know why my feet carried me across the room to where the waiter stood, arm outstretched.

"I already paid." He shrugged and looked toward the hallway. A set of double doors, just like the kitchen's swinging pair, stared at me. "Is this about the music?"

"There's no damn music," muttered the man who'd spoken earlier.

Of course there wasn't.

My feet crunched on crumbs, broken tiles, and roach carcasses as I walked toward the double doors.

~*~

Egypt, land of wonder and mystery, said the website. I'd booked my ticket without hesitation or sense. Who the hell was Naguib Mahfouz, anyway?

"...yamal hob nadah ala albi ma radish albi gawab, ya ma ash shouq hawaal yahaayyelni..."

doum doum tek-a-tek

The doors swung open easily. As if they'd been waiting for me this whole time.

I shook my head, blinked once – twice – three times, waiting for my vision to clear. I thought I'd escaped the bazaar by entering the café, but apparently no one could escape the bloody thing, no matter how hard they tried.

The doors had brought me inside a large, square-roomed tent. Fabric draped across the ceiling, walls, and floors – patterned with vibrant red, deep blue, rusted orange, black and white and green. Cushions of various sizes lined the edges of the tent, and in the far corner sat an elderly woman in a dull, gray kaftan. Her eyes were closed and she swayed back and forth, rapturous, to the sound of the drums that brought me nothing but irritation – and on the ends of both thumbs and index fingers, arms raised toward the center of the room, were tiny cymbals. She clanged them together. I gritted my teeth at their harsh ring.

To her left, a man sat with head bowed, *doumbek* between his knees. He pounded on the drumhead with a fury that matched the one growing in the pit of my stomach. What the hell was I doing here? The café patrons were bloody liars. Of course they could hear this.

"Excuse me? Sorry to interrupt – no, scratch that, I'm not – but I was trying to have a moment's peace – "

The words died in my mouth as I turned to point at the swinging doors back into the café, intending to make a point about relaxation after the madness of the *souq*. The doors were gone. Heavy fabrics covered the space where I'd entered, and I pushed my hand through to find the doors... and met air.

"You've got to be kidding me." I stuck my head through the fabric. No café. Just an empty, dusty street. No people. No waiter. No anything.

Impossible.

There must have been something in the karkade. Or I'd fallen asleep, been kidnapped and woken up here, or...

"*...wa a'olo ruh ya azab...*"

"Hello?"

I spun around. A woman had entered the tent, from the other side. Dark, furious hair contrasted with her pale skin, a spot of pink at the end of her nose that revealed a moment too long in the sun. She looked around the tent with wide eyes and a half-open mouth.

"Well, this is unexpected." Her voice had a musical lilt, as though she existed within the cadence of the music that surrounded us. "And here I thought I'd just ask the manager to turn down the volume."

My vision blurred and spun as her words took hold. "Who... how did you...?"

"Oh!" She saw me and smiled, and the dizziness faded. "Sorry, I didn't mean to… I mean, there were drums pounding in my ears and no one seemed to want to do anything about it."

I nodded and swallowed, throat drier than the desert I'd flown over early this morning.

"Are you all right?" She stepped toward me and I found myself retreating backward. "I didn't mean to startle you. Oh, do you not speak German?"

German? Of course I didn't speak German, but what did that have to do with anything?

doum doum tek-a-tek doum tek-a-tek

"I don't. And I'm not. I'm from Winnipeg, Manitoba. Canada?"

She frowned, glanced at the musicians, back at me, and behind her. And did the exact same thing I had. She pulled her head back through the curtains, face drained of all color. "Of course you're speaking German. My English comprehension is terrible, though I'm learning."

We stared at each other as the drumbeat continued to pound, the woman's voice wailing her song as though nothing else in the world mattered. Maybe it didn't.

"This is impossible," my opposite said.

"I know." I rubbed my forehead for a moment before yanking my hand away. The sunburn bloody hurt – so I couldn't be dreaming.

"The music … I don't know why I came here. Hell, I don't know why I came to Egypt in the first place. What a mess."

"Being here?"

"No." She squeezed her eyes shut and we stood facing each other in silence. When she opened them, they were rimmed with red. "Me."

I knew that feeling. If I knew anything, any truth in the moment, that was it. "I'm starting to think that's why we're here."

She snorted and crossed her arms. "It's not why I'm here. I'm here because … it doesn't matter. Who are you, anyway?"

I almost laughed. The absurdity, the unlikeliness, the misguided notion I'd held that Egypt might somehow, in some way, hold the key to my re-creation …

"I'm someone who's searching for something that can't be found. I don't know why I thought I'd find it here. I admit, I don't know why I'm here either." Her frown reversed like a slow-motion playback, until the barest hint of a smile crested her lips.

"… fel donia mafeesh abdan abdan ahla min alhob …"
doum doum tek-a-tek

She nodded toward the singer. "Do you know what she's singing?"

I shook my head. Did it matter? "I don't speak Arabic."

Then she sighed and I sighed, and I thought back to the woman I'd left behind after a long night of pleasure and guilt. I shouldn't have left her like that. It was a cruel gesture, given by a part of me I'd hoped to leave behind.

She shrugged. "Many years of my life have passed, … something … something, many times love has knocked on my door and I didn't answer – "

"What?"

"The song. I tell the pain to go away … uh, I think it's that nothing in the world is sweeter than love … gotta say, I'm not missing the irony here."

Her words pulled me out of the memories. "You, too?"

She nodded, speaking softly. "Yes."

A flood of relief, sprinkled with hope, surged into the place where the drumbeats pounded their endless rhythm. "Maybe this is it. Maybe … look, I don't know who the hell Naguib Mahfouz was, or why I chose to get on a plane to Egypt, or how I ended up in this room at this moment, but … I woke up the other day and thought, this can't be it. I need change. To … recreate myself. To find who I am."

Her smile could have warmed a village. She shrugged and stretched her hand toward me. I hesitated only as long as it took for the drums to beat their rhythm one final time.

"Together?"

"Sure." I said. "Why the hell not?"
doum.

The Definition of a Superhero
by Taven Moore

Second Place Winner

"There are two kinds of people in this world," Sophie's dad used to say.

The loan officer approached with a grim look. The hard lump of fear that Sophie had been nurturing just below her breastbone for the last six months took a nosedive, slamming into her stomach and shattering into exactly ten thousand glittering shards. One shard for each dollar she needed to keep her little bookstore afloat.

Sophie swallowed against her spreading panic. *There are two kinds of people in this world,* she reminded herself. *Those who control their fear, and those who let their fear control them.*

I decide which one I am today.

Sophie lifted her paperwork from the desk, noticing with no small amount of irony a plaque which proudly proclaimed "We Insure Your Money For Up to $10,000 in Supervillain-Related Damages!"

She stood and forced a wooden smile to her lips, fifty page business plan held out like a shield.

The officer did not return the smile. "I am sorry, Miss Rivera."

Sophie stiffened her spine. "I will revise the business plan and have it back to you tomorrow."

A pained look spread across the officer's face. "Miss Rivera, please stop. It's not your business plan. It's your *business*. Nobody's buying paper books anymore."

A flicker of anger curled in Sophie's belly, glinting dangerously over the sharp landscape of fear. "They *are* buying books; they just can't reach me. On page seventeen, I outline the significance of the battle between Black Frog and Windy City this spring. As soon as the damaged light rail station re-opens, my business will double! I just need to add more graphs to clarify the situation."

Sophie's hands tingled. Clutched in her white-knuckled fingers, the pages of her business plan fluttered despite the stale air of the office. A different kind of fear crept into Sophie's gut, neatly extinguishing the anger.

No. I get to choose, and I choose to rule my fear.

The tingling faded, the pages in her hand stopped twitching, and she exhaled.

"This is the loan department's final decision."

Final decision.

The words dropped into her soul like stones through hot oil. What would she say to her father's grave on Sunday? That she'd lost everything he'd worked for – no, everything *they* had worked for?

And her customers. What would she say to Mrs. Henderson, who came in every Thursday to pick up a knitting magazine and the newest romance novels? Or Teddy Billingsly, who skulked in whenever his dad had been drinking and stayed till she couldn't find another reason to keep the doors open?

Yet this was the bank's "final decision." Despair and anger intertwined.

Tingling raced through her fingertips. A crisp sheet of paper escaped her grasp and shot into the air. Immediately, it folded itself into a paper airplane whose every edge presented a papercut arsenal.

No! Sophie barely had time to snatch the missile out of the air before it swooped to attack.

The officer's face shifted from confusion to fright, then all the way into fury.

Sophie closed her eyes and despaired.

Only fully-trained superheroes were permitted to use powers, and Sophie didn't have a license. When she'd taken Power Control 101, Torch Guard had still been an instructor. He had sneered at her trembling paper airplane before destroying it with an offhand gesture. She'd run from the room as he called out that he would notify her if the city ever needed someone to fold paper. The fact that he was a supervillain now did nothing to alleviate her humiliation. Papercrafting was a stupid, useless power.

As if conjured from her memories, a familiar voice boomed from the lobby. "Everybody on the ground!"

Shocked, Sophie turned to see the red-spandexed Torch Guard stride through the bank's heavy double doors, index fingers pointed like fake guns.

Cute, until she remembered the news footage of him setting cars on fire using those "finger pistols. "

"This is a robbery!" chirped a female voice. Sophie looked up to see the gray-caped Windy City twirling through the air of the domed cathedral-style lobby.

Torch Guard pointed his finger at the front desk and a jet of orange flame leaped from his index finger, splashing against the bulletproof glass used to protect the bank tellers from robberies. That's when the screaming started, as the shock of the villain's appearance rolled through the room.

"Everyone move to the side and get on the ground. Now!"

Sophie's heartbeat sped up, pounding against her throat with a panicked tempo. *This can't be happening.*

She and the loan officer scurried to join the group of hostages. Terrified people pressed themselves against the wall, trying to look as small as possible.

Through it all, a pragmatic voice in the back of her head whispered, *Just how stupid is he? Melting bulletproof glass is nearly impossible!*

A man in a gray business suit stood to address the villains, arms outstretched. "Now, see here – "

"Naughty!" Windy's voice called out. "Torch said to stay on the ground!"

Windy gestured and the man lifted into the air.

A gout of fire licked upward to envelop his shrieking figure, meeting the whirling winds and flaring into an inferno. Sophie closed her eyes and crushed her hands against her ears to block out the sound.

A minute passed, and her breath scraped harshly against a raw throat. Had she screamed? She didn't remember screaming.

There are two kinds of people in this world, her mind taunted her cowardly heart.

"Yeah. Dead and alive," she whispered, but shame forced her to swallow past the lump of fear in her throat and open her eyes.

Torch's fire jetted at the bulletproof glass, flames shifting from hot yellow to blue. He wore a manic grin, sweat slipping down his cheek with the effort.

Above him, Windy aimed her palms at the point where fire met glass, her winds spurring his fire to white-hot brilliance.

To Sophie's shock, the glass actually melted.

As soon as Torch stopped his fire, Windy swooped through the ruined glass and began looting the tills, shoving fistfuls of bills into a black canvas bag.

Torch Guard pointed at one of the cowering tellers. "Open the vault."

The subject of his attention flinched away, voice shrill. "Nobody b-b-but the Bank Manager can open it! Please don't kill – "

Torch Guard interrupted her, brows furrowed and flame licking his outstretched finger. "So tell the Bank Manager to open it."

"Y-y-you just k-k-killed him!" The teller lifted a shaking hand, pointing at the blackened lump in the center of the lobby.

"You have got to be kidding me." His face twisted and the flames from his fingers intensified, but Windy's voice broke in.

"There's plenty in the tills, Candle Of My Heart. Let's just take this and go."

Please do that, whispered Sophie's heart, and she had to force herself not to say it aloud. The villains stepped through the ruined glass and into the main lobby. *Just go. Take the money and don't hurt anyone else.*

"Never fear, citizens! Black Frog is here!" The ebony-suited figure leaped through the front doors, his squat figure anything but heroic.

Black who? A fragment of a recent news story floated to the surface of Sophie's memory, sparking a flicker of hope. *The newest superhero.*

Frog opened his mouth, releasing a fat blob of his signature super-sticky bile. The black lump arced through the air toward Windy, who was unable to completely dodge. The goo hit her left arm with enough force to jolt her back, cementing her to the wall.

Torch pointed his fingers at the superhero and released a jet of fire just as Frog spat out another bile bomb. The two powers met in a stunning explosion.

Sophie flinched as a fragment of flaming tar shot into the cluster of hostages. A woman stood, shrieking and flapping a flaming arm in the air. A blue-suited bank guard helped the woman remove her jacket and fling it away.

Horror numbed Sophie's limbs. *Frog's spit is incendiary?*

Outside, sirens wailed as the police arrived, likely blockading the building. *What idiot spits flammable material at a firestarter?* Sophie's heart pounded.

They were trapped. Everyone in the building was trapped, and now the villains didn't have a quick escape route. They were cornered, and a cornered enemy was a truly dangerous thing.

Fragments of nightly news stories floated up through Sophie's foggy memory.

"Dozens dead."

"Civilian casualties."

The tingling she so often suppressed began again, pinpricks of anticipation and power sparking the pads of her fingers.

This time, she let the sensation build. *I refuse to be "collateral damage."* Paper fluttered against her chin and she looked down, surprised to find her business plan still clutched in nerveless fingers.

Beside her, the loan officer's eyes widened and she sat up in alarm.

Sophie looked up just in time to see a ball of flaming tar about the size of a basketball headed straight for them. Unthinking, Sophie lifted a warding hand. The tingling in her fingers shifted, spilling over her hands and up her forearms. The papers shot from her grasp, layering upon themselves to form one continuous overlapping sheet.

The tar ball collided with that thin barrier and exploded.

The paper disintegrated immediately, but it had served its purpose. The flaming mess of sticky shrapnel described a blast pattern that would have spelled massive injury or even death for anyone in its path.

Sophie looked down to find a dozen wide eyes staring at her. A child, face red and tear-streaked, pulled his thumb from his mouth long enough to ask, "Are you a super-hero?"

Sophie opened her mouth to deny it, but an explosion from the central lobby silenced her. She turned just as green dollar bills began to rain upon them.

Through the monetary shrapnel, Sophie saw that Windy had freed herself from Frog's bile and joined the fight. The bagful of money she'd been carrying must have been hit; the air was thick with cash.

Sophie's arms tingled again, spreading over her shoulders to cup her scalp and suddenly she *felt* every dollar in the room. Part paper and part cloth, something about them felt more right than any sheet of paper she'd ever practiced with.

Windy rose into the air, arms lifted, and the money, some of it already on fire, swirled around her. Small items lifted from desks to join the expensive cyclone.

Neither villain nor hero seemed to be paying any attention to the hostages, so Sophie sprang into action. "Go, all of you, now. There are cops outside."

Nobody moved, everyone fixated on the growing battle in the center of the room.

"NOW!" Sophie shouted. Some people visibly started.

"We'll be killed," the loan officer whispered.

"I'll protect you," Sophie said, and forcibly lifted the woman and pushed her toward the door.

Another person stood, and a softball-sized missile of Frog's goo shot towards the group. Sophie reacted, lifting her hand. A few bills obeyed her silent command and split from Windy's cyclone to wrap the bile and deflect its course harmlessly to the side.

"GO!" Sophie shouted.

Remarkably, they went.

With every parried projectile from the battle, Sophie's tingling spread. By the time the last hostage escaped through the front doors, Sophie brimmed with fizzy, sparkling power. She had never tried to control so much. Had never allowed herself to try.

She paused at the door, torn between leaving the super-idiots to their battle, and staying to … to do what?

Hand on the ornate brass handle, she turned.

The hero was losing.

Windy whisked away his spit before it could do any harm, and even if Frog was immune to his own sticky emanations, he was certainly not immune to fire or to being bombarded by random items caught up in Windy's cyclone.

Paperweights, staplers, photo frames … all these became weapons against the superhero, and Torch never let up his gouts of flame. Black tar and incendiary dollar bills filled the air.

Frog looked exhausted.

There are two types of people in this world.

Sophie released the handle and really looked at the building for the first time. She needed to somehow negate at least one of the supervillains. From news stories, she knew that Windy couldn't control multiple objects at once. Her cyclone was clearly out of her control, and maintaining the winds to keep it spinning was all she could manage.

Every power had a weakness.

Torch had been captured once before. A firefighting team had subdued him long enough for a superhero to arrive. They'd done it with …

Sophie cast her eyes upward and spotted familiar silver fixtures on the ceiling.

She lifted a hand, and a spiral of smoldering bills escaped Windy's cyclone. Sophie almost laughed at how easy it was. Just a flick of the wrist and the money folded itself into enkindled bats.

Her creations plastered themselves against the sensors. Almost immediately, the system activated, showering the room with a fine spray of water.

Torch screamed and began clawing at his skin instead of attacking Frog.

"Nooooo!" shrieked Windy, and her cyclone weakened.

Sophie took advantage of the lapse and reached out. She made a fist and *pulled*.

Every shred of paper in Windy's cyclone zoomed inward to envelop the villain, wrapping her in a wet, sticky cocoon.

Sophie opened the door and left. If Frog couldn't take advantage of that opening, he didn't deserve to win.

The rush of scintillating power drained away, leaving an empty Sophie shell behind.

"I'm the last of them," she said to whoever would listen. "Only supers are left."

She accepted the aid of an EMT and everything got a little fuzzy. She found herself seated on the back of an ambulance, a heavy blanket wrapped around her shoulders and a growing cloud of reality smothering her soul.

Now, what? Just… go home and say goodbye to my bookstore?

"Miss Rivera?"

Sophie looked up to see the bank loan officer standing awkwardly in front of her.

They stared at each other for a moment, and Sophie wondered if the other woman would turn her in to the police for unlicensed power use.

"Come by tomorrow. The bank has reconsidered your loan," the loan officer said.

Dazed, Sophie shook her outstretched hand.

Maybe there were three kinds of people in the world.

Those who controlled their fear, those who let fear control themselves ... and those who refused to let fear control anyone else, either.

The End

Thank you for reading this anthology. If you liked the stories, please leave a review on Amazon, Goodreads or any other platform. Thank you in advance.

Biographies

Russell Adams is an American writer who has written short stories, novels, and plays, speculative and otherwise, most of his life. Russell is presently retired and treating writing as a full-time challenge. Follow him on Facebook: http://www.facebook.com/russell.adams.5688

Ted Atchley lives in beautiful Charleston, SC with his wife and two children. He writes computer code by day and words by night. When not writing, he enjoys reading, volunteering, and the NFL. Find out more on his website: http://www.tedthethird.com

Ms. Blackburn shares her home with two boisterous children and three large flatulent dogs. Scented candles bring a lot of joy to her life.

Faith Boughan is an unabashed bibliophile with a penchant for good coffee, Star Trek: TNG, and fuzzy creatures. And judging by the equal parts of self-loathing and narcissism, she also must be a writer...

J. P. Brindley is a writer, geek, typography lover, Whovian and avid reader. He also pretends to Twitter. Find out more on his website: http://www.jpbrindley.com

Piia Bredenberg is a writer, painter, sculptor, knitter and a practical witch. She has stroked the tail of a snow leopard, had her hand in a lion cub's mouth and been bitten by an Emperor Tamarin monkey, although not at home. Piia lives in Finland, in the everlasting winter.

Zoe Cannon writes about the things that fascinate her: outsiders, societies no sane person would want to live in, questions with no easy answers, and the inner workings of the mind. If she couldn't be a writer, she would probably be a psychologist, a penniless philosopher, or a hermit in a cave somewhere. She lives in New Hampshire with her husband and a giant teddy bear of a dog, and spends entirely too much time on the internet. Find out more on her website: http://www.zoecannon.com

Connie Cockrell lives in Payson Arizona with her husband and daughter and Phoebe the Chihuahua. A retired Air Force Master Sergeant, she volunteers as a Director in the Phoenix Project Management Chapter and the Northern Gila County Fair Board. She loves hiking in the Arizona countryside and plays Bunko once a month. Visit her website: http://conniesrandomthoughts.wordpress.com

Sally Jane Driscoll is from New York, Baltimore, San Jose and now the Texas Hill Country. She's a long-time editor and lifelong writer. Her short stories have appeared in Daily Science Fiction, Asimov's, Ellery Queen's Mystery Magazine and Interzone, but she's still learning – and working on her fifth (seventh? ninth? lost count!) novel. Find out more on her website: http://sjdriscoll.com

Molly Felder took How To Think Sideways in 2012 to make writing fiction as consuming as teaching English Comp. Between classes, she's completing a YA novel and developing flash fiction for her first collection of short-short stories.

Rabia Gale breaks fairy tales and fuses fantasy and science fiction. A native of Pakistan, she now lives in Northern Virginia where she reads, writes, eats chocolate, avoids housework, and homeschools her three children. Visit her online at http://www.rabiagale.com

Born and raised German with a good helping of Scottish adoptive heritage, **Katharina Gerlach** has been writing stories in the realms of fantasy and historical fiction for many years. She managed to convince a German agent, but the search for a fitting publisher took too long. So she began to self-publish her novels in German and English. Visit her website: http://www.katharinagerlach.com

Melinda Hagenson knew before she was ten that she would one day be a writer. Although her work was accepted for publication in campus creative writing magazines in both high school and college, it was not until 2006 that she finally sat down to write the composite novel that had been growing inside her for fifteen years. This story, a brand-new addition to Melinda's *Eighteen Crossroads* collection, is the product of Melinda's engagement with Holly's methods. Visit her website: http://www.melindahagenson.com/

Jessi Hammond is an Australian author of teen/adult speculative fiction, with a few 'normal' stories thrown in. She has three teenage children (sympathy accepted gratefully), is almost blind and also writes children's and YA books under her real name of Michelle Tatam. Find out more on her website: http://www.jessihammond.com

Jenn Johnson works in the publishing industry, and writes young adult fantasy novels in her spare time. This short story was inspired by her current project, which she hopes to publish in serial form within the next few months. Visit her website: http://asinglebell.inspiredbyausten.com

A. E. Kalquist writes speculative fiction that asks compelling questions. She lives in Florida with a preschool-aged ballerina and a husband who spends his days ordering 0s and 1s around. Find out more about her on her website: http://www.aekalquist.com

Kate Lansky is a freelance editor currently living in Chicago with her husband, son, dog, and three cats. She is also an avid reader, writer, researcher, and doodler. The cats help to keep her from procrastinating too much by acting as constant lap weights and, as such, she owes her writing prowess to them. Find out more about her on her website: http://www.katelansky.com/

Taven Moore is the pseudonym for the married writing team of Tami and Steven Moore. Although the word-smithing is done by Tami, the planning and building and creating and dreaming is done as a team. We've been constructing worlds and crafting stories together for as long as we've known each other, with no end in sight. Find out more on her website: http://tavenmoore.com

Debbie Mumford specializes in fantasy and paranormal romance, with the occasional contemporary story thrown in for good measure. She loves mythology and is especially fond of Celtic and Native American lore. Debbie writes about faeries, dragons and other fantasy creatures for adults as herself, and for tweens and young adults as Deb Logan. Visit her website: http://debbiemumford.com/

Jimena Novaro was born in Argentine Patagonia and grew up speaking Spanish and English. Ever since she could hold a pencil she's been writing stories, and has always had a passion for creating all sorts of things, from imaginary worlds to toys, clothes, and games. Her stories can be found at http://www.JimenaNovaro.com, where she also blogs weekly.

L.M. Orbison is a 31-year-old author with DiGeorge Syndrome. She lives at home with her husband and four cats. She loves dragons and Dr. Pepper.

Amy Padgett is involved in a wide variety of creative endeavors including music, photography, desktop publicshing, art and, of course, writing. While she sometimes tends towards the analytical, she is always drawn back into creativity, and that is where she finds her deepest satisfaction. She is a staff member at her church, acting as webmaster, blogger, desktop publisher, and general tech interpreter. Amy lives in North Texas with one husband, two grown children, and a pair of neurotic dogs.

Liz Schröder is a mom, a student, a radio operator, and she's editing her first fantasy novel. She lives in Wisconsin, USA, where she wages a repetitive 6-month war against snow. Visit her website: http://www.danzierlea.com

Vanna Smythe is the author of Protector (Anniversary of the Veil, Book 1) and Decision Maker (Anniversary of the Veil, Book 2). She has been writing creatively since her early teens, though one could say her creative writing efforts started long before that. While still in kindergarten, she once tore up a library book to make alphabet soup, and has been fascinated with what words can do, the pictures and worlds they can create, ever since. Book 3 of the Anniversary of the Veil series will be available in Summer, 2013. Visit her website: www.vannasmythe.com

Laura Thurston loves creation in many forms, whether it's writing, performing on stage, or painting 25mm miniatures. She is one of the translators of (and has acted in) A Klingon Christmas Carol, the only play ever performed in professional theater in the Klingon language. Her first short story, "The Buddy System," was published in Marion Zimmer Bradley's Sword and Sorceress VII anthology.

Amanda Tompkins is an animal lover and bibliophile who resides in Ontario, Canada. She holds an Honours BSc in Biology, and loves to travel.

Thea van Diepen hails from the snowy land of Canada and that fairest of cities, Edmonton, Alberta. She is, of course, completely unbiased (being a psychology student) and is also obsessed with Doctor Who, Madeleine L'Engle, and the workings of the subconscious mind. If she ever grows up, Thea wants to be boring so that she can serve as a warning to younger generations as to why growing up is a terrible career choice. Find out more on her website: http://www.expectedaberrations.com

Martha Verlander lives in Missouri, USA, where she earned a 5th-degree black belt in RyuTe Karate--a big advantage when writing fight scenes! She's "retired," which means busier than ever with her writing, and her household contains her, her adult daughter, and four dogs--all rescues. Visit her website: http://www.MarthaGilstrap.com

In this case, **Tom Vetter** writes as Lieutenant Commander Tom Vetter, US Navy (retired)

Vanessa Wells lives deep in an enchanted forest (in Texas) where she is currently editing her début novel *Seventeen Stones* and writing the sequel, *Night of the Bandersnatch*. She battles infestations of plot bunnies…and dust bunnies, but that's another matter entirely. Find out more on her website: http://officiallyvanessawells.com

Debbie Zubrick lives in Northern California with her husband and two teenage children. She likes to swim, read and eat Italian food. She does not like to clean house.

Michele Zugnoni is a graduate student and instructor of college-level composition at CSU Stanislaus. She has written two NA paranormal romances and is hard at work on the third. Her second novel, Starfire, won a finalist position in the prestigious "Smooch" contest held by the Yosemite RWA.
Her Facebook page: www.facebook.com/michelenzugnoni

Why We Took Holly's Courses
Collected experiences:

I waffle less. I can put the ingredients of a story together faster, and I can identify my blunders sooner so I can fix them. The Sweet Spot Map alone is a wonder. *Piia Bredenberg*

In HTTS I discovered a process for completing a manuscript and how to deal with the various complications that arise during the process; which allowed me to complete my first novel after six failed previous attempts over the last forty years. Through HTRYN I learned a systematic approach to taking the written first draft and turning it into the book that I really wanted to write, not the shadow of the story that I had written during first draft. *Peter Cruikshank*

I've become much more prolific. Back when I used to write stories from the seats of my pants, it took ages to finish a story. Now, I outline my stories the way taught in HTTS, and find that I can finish two to three novels every year (or very many short stories). *Katharina Gerlach*

More than any other source of information on the writing life - from business to musing to planning, and everything in between - Holly's course, "How to Think Sideways," has pushed me more towards allowing myself to become the writer I was meant to be. The course is very real, very raw - pure fuel. It's the only source material I go back to over and over again. *J. P. Brindley*

Holly's courses had a deeply positive effect on my writing, due to the impact they had on me as a person. Her course encouraged me to confront fear and weakness in all facets of my life, not just writing. In addition to teaching me the workings of good storytelling, she gave me the tools I needed to overcome lifelong vices such as procrastination. Now I actually finish things and let people see them. *E.L. Blackburn*

Holly Lisle is a gifted teacher. She gives her students her best advice while leaving them free to modify those tips and techniques to fit their own process. Holly's HTTS course gave me courage and confidence and taught me to trust my muse. I'd recommend her courses to anyone interested in furthering their writing career. *Debbie Mumford*

There's a reason why I have all of Holly's courses: They're easy to grasp, full of concrete and specific advice useful for any genre. It's changed how I think about my stories and much has spilled over into other aspects of my life. *Laura Thurston*

Holly's courses have helped my writing immensely; they've helped me organize my thoughts and get them out on the screen instead of staring at a blinking cursor all day. How to Think Sideways also helped me to tame my muse, and get the creative bit of my brain working on my own terms, and not when it felt like it. I go back and brush up on each lesson every once in a while, to help me when I get stuck. *Amanda Tompkins*

Among the myriad of helpful tips standing out from the course are the promises I must make to my reader. Before the course, I wrote only for myself. The course has taught me how to write for others. *Branka Valcic*

Holly Lisle's course and its additions have changed the style of my writing in so many different ways it's hard to choose just one or two. The first biggest impact that the course had was the "The Four Thinking Barriers to Success." Without that lesson I would never had the courage or insight to compete in a writing contest! The second most important impact on my writing would be the dot and line application. It provided my muse with a way to plan a story and NOT kill the inspiration. *Holly MacKendrick*

I found Holly Lisle's How To Think Sideways course at a very low time in my life. Since working through HTTS and How to Revise Your Novel I have completed new stories and revised old ones, and have regained the joy in writing that I used to have as a kid – with a lot more skills. Thank you so much, Holly, for your willingness to share. *Jessi Hammond*

I'm freer now, because Holly's process allows for so much flexibility from the initial idea down to the last bit of revision. Holly has given us techniques for rooting out many kinds of internal resistance, from destructive patterns of thinking to "goals" that are not goals at all, but merely wishes. *Texanne*

Holly Lisle has a unique, creative and easy-to-follow teaching style. Every lesson contains real life illustrative examples and comprehensive workbooks for homework. This was like a breath of fresh air and it rekindled the fire in me to start serious writing again, after a lapse of five years. *Neil Campbell*

Sideways has taught me organization and the ability to write succinctly. The Wow factor that helped immensely is The Sentence. *Jane P. Welch*

My favorite of Holly's courses so far is 'How to Revise Your Novel', which was a major factor in publication of my first book as 2012 rolled into 2013! *Martha Verlander*

I brought a hopelessly broken, reeking mess of a novel to Holly Lisle's 'How to Revise Your Novel' course. Holly broke the daunting revision process into manageable steps and gave me all the tools I needed to accomplish them. By the time I came out of the wringer, I had a novel that was in every way stronger and better. *Rabia Gale*

Holly taught me to look at writing in a different way? as a process helped along by tools and techniques that can be used to construct a work that comes alive thanks to your passion. She made me realize the reasons why I write, and the things that make my writing matter to me. The courses grounded writing itself as a job just like any other (albeit ridiculously fun) as opposed to some magic stroke of genius that only comes to some lucky few. *Jimena Novaro*

Two of Holly's Lisle's concepts and courses have had a profound effect on this piece of fiction. The concept of 'The Sentence' from 'Holly's How to Think Sideways' Course has helped me find the subtle but critical conflicts in this story, while the revision process in the Seven-Day Crash Revision Course provided an excellent framework for finding the story amidst the wanderings of the first draft. I look forward to learning from Holly as I grow in this craft. *Debbie Zubrick*

In just one year, HTTS gave me the tools and encouragement to write a 500-page anthology, plot and write historical fiction and tackle non-fiction as well. *Tom Vetter*

Since taking the 'How to Revise Your Novel' course in 2010, I have written, revised and published two novels. I am certain that I would still be on my first draft of my first novel right now, had I not enrolled in HTRYN. I am now following the How to Think Sideways course to write my third novel, and I've already learned enough to make this one the best so far! If you're serious about pursuing a writing career, then I can't recommend Holly's courses heartily enough. *Vanna Smythe*

HTRYN showed me that almost any mistake I made drafting a novel could be identified and fixed using well-defined techniques. It changed my writing by easing concerns about creating a first draft so flawed as to be unfixable and also by sharpening my awareness of such elements as promises and scene structure that resulted in fewer first draft problems. *Russell Adams*

Holly's courses have done more to move my writing career forward than everything else I've read combined. Holly's course "Mugging the Muse" forced me to look at myself as a writer and justify what I was doing. It helped me understand that writing wasn't something I just wanted to do. It was something I *needed*. Her Plot Clinic took me from having a nebulous book idea, to formulating my story, creating the plot and actually getting words on paper. Since taking Holly's courses, I've gone from being a guy who writes to being a writer. What a shift! Thank you, Holly, for your time and energy. *Ken Dickson-Self*

Holly's insights, questions, and straight talk about her writing career have helped me to think critically about why I want to write and what I'm willing to do to follow this dream—and have dispelled a couple of crippling illusions. I've learned that I need to pursue my writing dream, and do the work to create stories, books, and a career that I can be proud of. Now I know that when I submit my books, they'll be the best books I can write. *Liz Schröder*

I have only just started this course (I'm on lesson 1), but I did her free plot clinic too and I think she's given me a way to rescue a book I loved but which had fundamental flaws I was unable to see past by myself - I will always be grateful for that. *Jackie Kowalczyk*

Before Holly's courses, my writing was a mess, filled with info dumps and characters sitting around thinking (yawn!). Taking her courses has brought both structure and additional creativity to my work; every lesson I feel less like a novice and more like a budding professional. *Isabel Sterling*

Holly teaches that having joy in your work is essential. She has encouraged me to lose the self-doubt and the excuses, and to seek the passion instead. *Prospero*

I've taken several of Holly's courses, and they've affected my writing to such an extent that it's hard for me to imagine what I did without them. With Holly's courses, especially How to Revise Your Novel, I learned how to take apart fiction to see what it's made of, and how to build every piece of a story deliberately. I use her techniques in everything I write. *Zoe Cannon*

Dramatic improvement is the only way to describe what the courses have done for my writing. I was a newborn writer with a draft from NaNoWriMo on my hands and no idea what to do with it. The HTRYN course helped me polish that draft into something a person would actually want to read. The HTRYN course helped me write my second novel, which I'm in the process of revising with, you guessed it, HTRYN. *Connie Cockrell*

I have learned that my job as a writer is to create characters that will matter to my readers and not to waste their valuable time. In order to make characters that people will care about, I sometimes have to look at unpleasant personal experiences. Writing has taught me to think about my disabilities differently. This process has helped me learn that my disabilities can be great assets to my fiction and to see that using them in my work will make my characters unique. *L.M. Orbison*

Most importantly of all, I learned to write what I truly love. I constantly keep recognizing and overcoming my own psychological barriers. Holly has taught me that writing is always a challenge, and she has taught me to enjoy this challenge and have fun with it. *Ieva Melgalve*

Holly's courses have given me structure to develop my writing ability. She has shown me how to approach my writing and how to wake my muse up so I'll always be full of inspiration. *Felicia Fredlund*

Thanks to Holly, I identified my weakness (Perfect Never Finishes), and I have been able to embrace what I have, harness what I think, organize my ideas, and work through my projects. I'm so grateful for the "game plan" that is HTTS and HWAS--I'm well on my way to FINISHING a great story that I'm proud of. *K. C. Wise*

When I first started writing 'Breath of Life', I had a grand story in mind, with all the right epic parts in all the right mind-blowing places, but the world was flat. It was empty and basic, while the characters spoke and acted a lot like me and my friends. Not good. Holly helped with that. Her 'Create a Culture Clinic' has helped me to shape my world into a unique, living, breathing culture—two, in fact. It is tremendous work and I appreciate all that I have learned from her. *Devin Milliron*

Taking Holly's courses is like going from being afraid of the dark, clutching a flashlight and huddling under a thin blanket ... to unloading a round of rock salt buckshot into the belly of the thing hiding in your closet. Her classes are grueling, unapologetic, and easily the best investment I could possibly have made as a writer. Period. *Taven Moore*

I have taken the 'Mini Plot Outline' course and the 'Create a Character Clinic.' I found it invaluable in helping develop characters by asking just enough questions to propel a plot along new avenues that I'd probably never have otherwise traveled. *Angela Apps*

What a gift the Sentence is—and the Sentence Lite for scenes. My writing is tighter and I'm constantly reminded to write about things that deeply matter to me, because my Sweet Spot Map is always nearby. *Molly Felder*

It's the strangest thing: One day I just sat down, started writing and didn't stop. Well, I had to work and eat and sleep and stuff, but whenever I had a spare moment, I wrote. Little did I know I was writing my first book. One hundred thousand words later, give or take, I realized that if I wanted this manuscript to be more than a lark, I needed help of the literary kind! Enter 'How to Revise Your Novel'. Scenes, subplots, character arcs, settings, conflicts, time lines, themes, and everything in between are the best thing that ever happened to my novel--and to my stories. Because I still haven't stopped writing! *Kirsten Bolda*

How to internalize structure to the point where it becomes automatic. How to trust my subconscious. How to let go. That's what I've learned from Holly Lisle. I am the story, the story is me. *Sally Jane Driscoll*

'How to Think Sideways' and 'How to Revise Your Novel' refined my writing style, bolstered my confidence, and gave me the tools I needed to make a living doing what I love. Years after completing the courses, I still pull out my worksheets whenever I hit writer's block and use the tips and tools every single day when I sit down to at my computer. There is no way I can ever thank Holly for the real-life experience she generously shared in these courses...the information is priceless. *Vanessa Wells*

After six years of writing, my manuscript still was not completed. Frustrated and mired in a cycle of eternal revisions and producing no new material, I was on the verge of giving up when I stumbled onto Holly Lisle's website in the wee hours of an especially bad night. From the very first lesson, Holly's 'How to Think Sideways Ultra' course provided useful and creative invention tools and confidence-building support. Thank you, Holly. *Melinda Hagenson*

'How To Think Sideways' increased my confidence in my own abilities like crazy. Before taking it, I'd had a really hard time writing a story that was for me and not for school, but the lessons on listening to my Muse allowed me to realize that I could come up with tons of ideas on my own, and that a lot of them were really good, too! *Thea van Diepen*

Thanks to 'How to Think Sideways', my writing has improved because of the Sentence and Sentence Lite. I'm able to figure out if something is worth writing or a waste of time before even writing it, and the Sentence Lite makes it so much easier to write because it gives each scene a sense of direction. This technique has saved me time, effort, and hours of frustration from writing terrible scenes. *Jennifer Johnson*

One of my biggest problems with writing has been completing projects. With 'How To Think Sideways' I learned how to break past the fear of a blank page and work with the muse. *Eliza K. Gilham*

The course didn't just change my writing; it changed my life. Holly's lessons have taught me to trust my instincts, to trust myself, and to look for the strength I have inside. In so doing, they have caused my writing to rise to a level I never imagined possible. *Michele Zugnoni*

Using 'How To Revise Your Novel,' I turned my 205,000 word story into two novels of 93,000 and 65,000 words, deleting over a fifth of what I'd written (47,000 words.) The result was a tighter story and a commercially viable product with a completed query letter ready to go. I completed my next novel in only a few months, due to further skills I learnt in HTTS, and HTWAS. Holly provides structured frameworks in which my creativity can flow. Holly Lisle has inspired me to put my dreams on paper, to dream big and write tight, and have fun with a great community of writers that encourage each other on the way. It's been a fabulous journey. *Eileen Mueller*

This short story came to me the first time I used the mind maps I made while working through HTTS. Holly's mind maps have completely changed the way I get new ideas for stories. *A. E. Kalquist*

Holly's teaching has taken me from wishing I could be a writer to actually being one. 'How To Think Sideways' taught me how to finish the projects I start with better results than I thought possible. I am hoping to complete my first full-length manuscript in 2013, with the intention of self-publishing. *Amy Padgett*

Holly's courses have been a godsend. Over the years I have found an abundance of ideas without the skills to put them into a completed a story. With Holly's courses I have learned not only how hear and understand the ideas that I have but also how to transform those ideas into words on the page. *Nycole Crow*

I've taken two classes with Holly – HTTS and HTRYN. Both have been invaluable in my writing, teaching me how to keep my stories focused and fun, to help me absolutely love the ideas I put down on paper – as well as figure out what's keeping me from doing just that. *Kate Lansky*

Holly's courses gave me the confidence and courage I needed to push past my self-doubt, perfectionist tendencies, and equally crippling fear of failure. Not that these things are gone for good, no -- but HTTS and HTRYN taught me that I can write, will write, and need to write in spite of these things (and how to do it). So, now I do! *Faith Boughan*

HTTS changed my understanding of my writing. Holly masterfully points out all the hurdles, trials, and challenges a writer faces, and gives you the tools to overcome them. *Ted Atchley*

I have discovered much more joy in writing with Holly's unique idea-generating and problem-solving techniques in Pro-Plot Outline, Character Clinic, and Plot Clinic. HTRYN has replaced my endless piddling around revision with an organized, in-depth method of bringing out the best of everything I want while making it publishable. *Elaine Milner*

www.ingramcontent.com/pod-product-compliance
Lightning Source LLC
Chambersburg PA
CBHW071602180626
46819CB00002B/99

* 9 7 8 3 9 5 6 8 1 0 0 0 8 *